Praise for the Haunted Bookshop Mysteries

"Full of riveting twists!"   —*First for Women*

"Utterly charming. . . . An entirely absorbing mystery."
                                              —*Mystery Scene*

"A magnificent cold case mystery!"
                                 —Fresh Fiction (fresh pick)

"Jack and Pen are a terrific duo who prove that love can transcend anything."   —The Mystery Reader

"I highly recommend the complete series."
                                 —*Spinetingler Magazine*

"A charming, funny, and quirky mystery starring a suppressed widow and a stimulating ghost."   —*Midwest Book Review*

"The plot is marvelous, the writing is top-notch."
                                              —Cozy Library

Berkley Prime Crime titles by Cleo Coyle

Haunted Bookshop Mysteries

THE GHOST AND MRS. McCLURE
THE GHOST AND THE DEAD DEB
THE GHOST AND THE DEAD MAN'S LIBRARY
THE GHOST AND THE FEMME FATALE
THE GHOST AND THE HAUNTED MANSION
THE GHOST AND THE BOGUS BESTSELLER
THE GHOST AND THE HAUNTED PORTRAIT
THE GHOST AND THE STOLEN TEARS

Coffeehouse Mysteries

ON WHAT GROUNDS
THROUGH THE GRINDER
LATTE TROUBLE
MURDER MOST FROTHY
DECAFFEINATED CORPSE
FRENCH PRESSED
ESPRESSO SHOT
HOLIDAY GRIND
ROAST MORTEM
MURDER BY MOCHA
A BREW TO A KILL
HOLIDAY BUZZ
BILLIONAIRE BLEND
ONCE UPON A GRIND
DEAD TO THE LAST DROP
DEAD COLD BREW
SHOT IN THE DARK
BREWED AWAKENING
HONEY ROASTED

The Ghost

AND THE

Stolen Tears

CLEO COYLE

BERKLEY PRIME CRIME
New York

BERKLEY PRIME CRIME
Published by Berkley
An imprint of Penguin Random House LLC
penguinrandomhouse.com

Copyright © 2022 by Alice Alfonsi and Marc Cerasini
Penguin Random House supports copyright. Copyright fuels creativity, encourages
diverse voices, promotes free speech, and creates a vibrant culture. Thank you for
buying an authorized edition of this book and for complying with copyright laws by not
reproducing, scanning, or distributing any part of it in any form without permission.
You are supporting writers and allowing Penguin Random House to continue to
publish books for every reader.

BERKLEY is a registered trademark and BERKLEY PRIME CRIME and
the B colophon are trademarks of Penguin Random House LLC.
A HAUNTED BOOKSHOP MYSTERY is a registered trademark of
Penguin Random House LLC.

ISBN: 9780425255483

First Edition: October 2022

Printed in the United States of America
1 3 5 7 9 10 8 6 4 2

This one is for the late C. J. Henderson—novelist and friend.

FOREWORD

The Ghost and the Stolen Tears marks the eighth entry in our Haunted Bookshop series, though our hardboiled ghost began haunting the cozy streets of Quindicott, Rhode Island, all the way back in 2004.

We sincerely thank our publisher for allowing the series to continue, not only with this entry, but with *The Ghost and the Bogus Bestseller* and *The Ghost and the Haunted Portrait*, both of which we wrote after taking a decade-long hiatus from the series. A grateful tip of the fedora goes to our new editor, Tracy Bernstein, along with everyone on the Berkley production team, who guided this entry into publication.

The seed of inspiration for *The Ghost and the Stolen Tears* came from the masterful short story "The Heavy Sugar" by Cornell Woolrich. Though the plight of its protagonist—trapped between criminals and the law—was first published in the January 1937 issue of *Pocket Detective*, the story still resonates today, and we thank the late great Mr. Woolrich for the priceless gem of his literary legacy.

We also wish to thank our longtime agent, John Talbot, and the many loyal readers of our Haunted Bookshop series for your faith in us and our characters. Your love of Jack and Pen kept them alive during our long break, and we look forward to sharing many more of their adventures with you.

As for our other works and worlds, you can learn more about them (and us) by visiting coffeehousemystery .com and cleocoyle.com.

—*Alice Alfonsi and Marc Cerasini*
aka Cleo Coyle, New York City

CONTENTS

Prologue   1

1. Happy to Be Haunted   5

2. A Walk in the Woods   8

3. Judging a Book   13

4. Diamonds Aren't Forever   18

5. The Searchers   22

6. Let's Roll the Tape   28

7. À la Cart   33

8. Two for the Road   39

9. Where the Heart Is   43

10. Like a Bat Out of Hell   47

11. Finders Keepers   52

12. Back to the Present   59

13. The Purloined Post-it   62

14.	Pillow Talk	65
15.	No Business Like Jack's Business	69
16.	Silent Sobs	75
17.	Vagabond Ways	84
18.	Fingering a Suspect	89
19.	Next of Kin	94
20.	The Chase	99
21.	Third Degree	103
22.	A Free Ride	109
23.	On Hold	112
24.	Tearful Homecoming	116
25.	A Mere Quibble	121
26.	A House of Fashion	130
27.	Fashionably Late	135
28.	The Little Church on the Corner	142
29.	Taken for a Ride	148
30.	Juvenile Delinquent	154
31.	Dancing Queen	160
32.	Let's Face the Music and Dance	167
33.	Danse Macabre	174
34.	To the Principal's Office	178
35.	Unblinded by Science	182

36.	Off the Beaten Path	186
37.	The Little Trailer on the Creek	191
38.	We're Going to Kritzerland!	196
39.	Mashed Couch Potato	203
40.	Hanging On	208
41.	A Novel Experience	212
42.	Campfire Tales	216
43.	Hot on the Trail	220
44.	Phyllis on Ice	226
45.	Delivering the Goods	231
46.	As the Crow Flies	238
47.	The Varnished Truth	241
48.	Untitled Manuscript	246
49.	A Way Out	251
50.	Stumble Bums	255
	Epilogue	263

Only now, in the solitude from social activity . . . was she coming to the realization that there were other ways of living that might be better suited to herself.

—*The Ghost and Mrs. Muir* by R.A. Dick
(aka Josephine Aimee Campbell Leslie)

PROLOGUE

I needed a drink. I needed a lot of life insurance. I needed a vacation. I needed a home in the country. What I had was a coat, a hat and a gun.

—Raymond Chandler, *Farewell, My Lovely*, 1940

Broadway
New York City
November 1947

"I TOLD YOU before. The name's Jack Shepard. Miss Syble Zane is expecting me."

The balding man at the stage door chewed on his worn stogie while he gave Jack Shepard the fisheye. "A lotta joes say that about Miss Zane."

"I'm not a lotta joes. I'm Jack. Jack Shepard, private detective." Jack flashed his license.

With sluggish deliberation, the doorman at the Martin Beck Theater stared down his nose at a handwritten list on the wall, grunting when he came to Shepard's name. He slid the metal door wider and jerked his thumb over his shoulder.

"You can wait for Miss Zane in front of her dressing

room. Take the stairs. When you hit bottom, make a left. You can't miss it. Her name is on the door."

"Okey-doke, Saint Peter. And where is Miss Zane now?"

"Still onstage." The man rolled the door closed and threw the bolt. "She won't be long. They just brought out the snakes."

"Snakes?" Jack blinked. "Real snakes?"

The doorman nodded and suddenly Jack was sorry he'd missed the show's climax. He wasn't an admirer of the Bard—frankly, he needed a translator for all the *thys* and *thous* and *forsooth what-ho yonders*. But he was familiar enough with the story of Antony and Cleopatra to follow the plot.

Only Jack reminded himself that he wasn't here for amusement. He was here on business—good-paying business, the private eye hoped. For tonight's meeting he sported the navy suit he reserved for court dates and had dug out his favorite tie—a broad swath of silk as red as spilled blood and dotted with little blue clocks. His fedora was tucked at a jaunty angle, and the fresh shave of his rugged face showed off his square-john jaw, though it failed to hide the dagger-shaped scar on his anvil chin.

In truth, Jack was feeling pretty chipper for a guy who hadn't earned two nickels in as many weeks. Until he bumped into this mug.

He always got a kick out of show business jobs. The pay was good, they were easy, they didn't involve fists or knives, and no one ever flashed a gun. Plus, he always met a few interesting characters—like the ventriloquist who accused his partner of talking out of the wrong side of his mouth. He'd claimed the man stole his prop dummy along with his act. Jack recovered the dummy okay, but he couldn't do much about the act. In the end, he convinced the two men to reconcile. They got a new comedy routine and nowadays seemed as happy together as Martin and Lewis at the 500 Club.

Then there was the case of the magician who vanished—a neat alimony dodge, or so he thought. Nor did the seasoned PI forget the embezzling escape artist who didn't manage to escape an extended stay at Sing Sing, courtesy of Jack's bloodhound act.

As he reached the stairs, thunderous applause erupted in the theater with the players taking their final bows. When he hit bottom, Jack hung a left, entering a corridor that seemed longer than a Tom Mix serial.

Finally, he located Miss Zane's dressing room, nestled between doors marked ANTHONY RANDALL and CHARLTON HESTON.

Jack was about to knock when a whiff of perfume teased his nostrils, and a sultry, breathless voice blew warm air into his ear.

"The door is unlocked, Mr. Shepard. Go on, open it."

He felt the heat of her presence behind him, and when he turned, Jack couldn't help but blink in surprise. The striking brunette standing close wore full Egyptian regalia, from her sandaled feet to her scarab necklace.

"I wasn't aware you were the star, Miss Zane."

"Don't be droll, Mr. Shepard. My part is small. If I were a man I'd be carrying a spear."

"Yet your name is on a door?"

"Making the right friends comes with fringe benefits."

As they entered the cramped dressing room, Syble Zane yanked the dark wig from her head and tossed it onto the makeup table.

"For this production, the benefits are pathetic," she said as she unpinned her blond mane and shook it out with irritation. "In my sad little role, I deliver the asp to the Queen of the Nile. It's a real snake, but not poisonous, unfortunately."

"A real snake. Imagine that."

"You see, Mr. Shepard, our director insists on realism, but our poor, pathetic Cleopatra is terrified of snakes."

The woman curled her red lips into a cruel grin. "Thrusting a live reptile at our star six nights a week is the only jolly I get from this lousy job."

"I'm sure you didn't ask me here to complain about your gig," Jack replied.

Syble Zane turned away from her reflection in the lighted mirror. Her gaze fixed on Jack, hitting the detective like a loaded .38.

"I want you to find someone, Mr. Shepard. He's a truly horrible man. A thief, a liar, a two-timer, and a criminal."

"I hate to let you in on this, Miss Zane, but the cops iced Dillinger thirteen years ago."

"Very funny," she replied, like it wasn't. "I want you to find Harry Amsterdam."

"The Broadway producer? What did Amsterdam do to you that he hasn't done to any other wide-eyed ingenue in this burg?"

"He stole something that belonged to me, and he gave it to somebody else."

Jack sniffed. "Like I said—"

"Oh, I know what you're thinking, Mr. Shepard, but it's not a role in a play or a Hollywood picture. It's more important than any part."

"He stole money?"

Her head moved slowly from side to side as if her eyes were following a hypnotist's watch. When Syble Zane spoke again, her voice was cold as a slab in the city morgue.

"*Tears*, Mr. Shepard. That man stole my tears."

CHAPTER 1

Happy to Be Haunted

The imagination feeds on phantoms.

—Cornell Woolrich, "Mind over Murder,"
Dime Detective magazine, 1943

**Quindicott, Rhode Island
Present day**

A PENNY FOR your thoughts.

"You don't have a penny, Jack. You haven't had a penny in decades."

I beg to differ, doll. You still carry around my Buffalo nickel, don't you?

"Yes."

So I got at least five cents in my Penny bank.

The ghost was right. Ever since I pocketed that ancient nickel of his, the one that spilled out of his dusty PI files, I'd made a mobile connection to a gumshoe spirit I couldn't control (or always comprehend) yet kept talking to anyway.

But then life was like that, wasn't it? Driven by phantoms we didn't always understand.

My name is Penelope Thornton-McClure. I'm a widow in my thirties who moved myself and my young son back to my hometown in recent years to help save my aunt Sadie's bookshop.

Using my late husband's life insurance money and my New York publishing connections, I revived the family's dying business, overhauling the stale inventory, restoring the crumbling façade, polishing up the wood-plank floor, and replacing the ancient, rickety decor with beautiful oak bookshelves, standing lamps, and overstuffed armchairs fit for a cozy New England library.

I put us online for global sales and expanded us into the neighboring storefront, adding an event space for author appearances, reading groups, and community gatherings. It was the noise of that expansion that appeared to have roused Jack Shepard from decades of supernatural slumber.

Why exactly the gallant gumshoe was gunned down on our premises, I don't know, but the question felt fitting, given our shop's specialty. We sell all kinds of books, you see, but we specialize in crime and mystery fiction. Not that everyone *likes* a mystery—literary or otherwise.

If a doorway opened to a darkened room, would you walk through it? Or swiftly pass it by? If a disembodied voice started giving you advice, would you listen? Or plug your ears and cover your eyes?

Cornell Woolrich once wrote "the imagination feeds on phantoms," but I never considered myself especially imaginative—or brave. What I am is incurably curious, intellectually itchy. *That's* why I couldn't stop talking to the ghost. Or asking questions about Norma. She was a curiosity. A puzzle of a person with so many pieces missing that I couldn't see her big picture.

True, few people in our lives are totally open books. Nearly everyone we know conceals personal secrets. But if someone you knew (and liked) was accused of a major crime, wouldn't you be shocked enough to ask a few questions?

In Norma's case, those questions began on a cool autumn afternoon. I'd been working all day in the shop and back office and felt the need for some fresh air and exercise, which is why I ventured out on foot, taking the back, wooded trail that led to the Finch Inn, a lovingly restored Queen Anne Victorian bed-and-breakfast run by my good friends Fiona and Barney Finch.

I usually enjoyed this walk, but today's trek felt ominous. The dry leaves around me rustled with a kind of death rattle. The shortened days and drop in temperature had choked off their green vibrance and bright fall colors for last-breath pigments of tired yellow and dried-blood brown. Tree branches swished menacingly with every salty gust from the nearby Atlantic, and the air felt raw. I could smell the rain coming. As gathering clouds began to smother the sunlight, even the birds went eerily silent.

Alone on this path, I pulled my jacket closer around me, trying not to shiver, when suddenly I wasn't alone anymore.

How many times do I have to tell you, baby? There are wolves in this big, bad world. What are you doing wandering through this forest all alone, like a Little Red-headed Riding Hood?

My ghost was back.

CHAPTER 2

A Walk in the Woods

Keep close to Nature's heart . . . and break clear away,
once in a while . . . spend a week in the woods. Wash
your spirit clean.

—John Muir

"HELLO, JACK. NICE to hear from you again. And this is
hardly a forest. It's a scenic nature trail and quite popular
with the town's joggers and bikers. I'm only out here alone
because it's an overcast Monday. On the weekends this trail
is nearly as busy as Cranberry Street. The after-church
crowd takes it to their Sunday brunches at Chez Finch."

*That a fact? So you're puttin' us on the path of the righ-
teous?*

"A road you know well, I'm sure."

Me? The ghost laughed, a sure, masculine chuckle. *Don't
get me confused with some dull-as-dust do-right rube. I
strayed off the path of virtue long before you were even born.*

"I don't buy it, Jack, now that I've gotten to know you. If
you still had a body, there wouldn't be a bad bone in it.
You're just too embarrassed to admit that down deep you're
a knight of the streets—and a sweetheart—and you always
were."

Don't try to perfume my past, baby. Night was when I operated. No K in front of it, unless it was a KO. And I been called a lotta things back when my ticker tocked, but nobody ever called me "sweetheart"—nobody who meant it, anyway.

"Saint or sinner, I'm glad you're here. I missed you . . ." And I had to admit, "Right now, I appreciate the company."

Because you're scared?

"Me? Don't be silly!"

Jack's warning about "wolves" was ridiculous. There were no such things in our safe little town. And I knew these woods well enough, though the gloom and chill were far from cheery, and the wind gusts were becoming sharper and stronger. As dead leaves began raining down, I did begin to worry a heavy branch might follow—then suddenly I was smacked in the nose!

"Ahhhh!"

As I jumped back—waving my arms like a madwoman at the ossified bird's nest that had struck me—dark purple clouds eclipsed the last sliver of afternoon sun and thunder rolled over the treetops.

Geez, Jack cracked. *I can see why your panties are bunched.*

"My panties are just fine! Not that my unmentionables are any of your business."

Okay then, if it's not these creepy trees that have you rattled, what is it? You got ants in your pants about something.

"Stop talking about my underthings."

The ghost did. Then he stopped talking altogether.

With resignation, I sighed and admitted the truth. "All right, Jack, you're not wrong. I mean, I am—for lack of a better word—antsy."

What's the headache?

"I hate doing things I don't want to do, and right now I have to ask someone to do me a huge favor."

Okey-doke. Who do you want sprawled on a cold marble slab and how do you want it done?

"Stop teasing. Nobody's getting whacked. I'm heading to the Finch Inn to offer a woman a job, that's all."

And she's doing you a "huge favor" by accepting? The world sure has flipped its wig. In my day, a job offer was followed by a tip of the fedora and a hearty thank-you.

"Under normal circumstances that would be true, but not in this case."

What makes this dame so special?

"She's not a dame. She's a nomad."

A what?

"Norma has no permanent address. She lives in a van and travels around the country for most of the year."

She's a hobo, then? A bum?

"We don't use those words anymore. Norma is a vaga-bond. They call it living the van life. It's a cultural trend. They've even got a hashtag for it."

Hash what? Oh, you mean they're hopheads? Hooked on hashish?

"No, not hashish! *Hashtag.* It's a social media category, a trend so popular, thousands use its label to brand their life-style. Norma lives the #vanlife."

I don't follow.

"I'll break it down for you. Norma moves around the country, taking different jobs during different seasons. For the last two years, she's spent her autumns in New England, doing housekeeping work at the Finch Inn. In exchange for her help from Labor Day to the New Year, Fiona pays Norma a weekly wage and provides a room for her, too."

So, you're trying to snatch her away from the competition?

"Not at all. Norma works part-time at a few places, includ-ing Buy the Book. Aunt Sadie hired her six weeks ago to work in the store on Sundays, so I could spend more time with my son—and help him with his big science fair project."

You mean the one that's got your little tyke fingerprint-ing everyone in sight and leaving ink stains in the sink?

"Yes. Spencer has decided to be a forensic investigator when he grows up. Of course, in a few months he'll likely change his mind, but I'll always encourage his interests, and one day he'll find his true calling. Anyway, that's not the point."

Then what is?

"The numbers. I added them up, and there is no disputing them."

I never played the numbers. That's penny ante stuff. I bet the house on the nags, though, hundreds of times.

"I'm not talking about gambling, Jack. The numbers that concern me are the unit sales in my ledger. You see, not long ago, Sadie and I debated whether to close Buy the Book on Sundays because business slowed considerably that day. But since Norma started working, sales have increased, week over week. This past Sunday we made double what we grossed on that same weekend a year ago, and it's all because of Norma."

She must be a natural pusher, then, a real huckster—

"No, Norma doesn't hard sell anyone."

Horse pellets. Trust me, Penny. Good hustlers are so slick at the fast hand, you never see that three-card monte swindle coming.

"Goodness, Jack, this is Quindicott, Rhode Island, not the New York Bowery! And Norma isn't a hustler."

Call me skeptical.

"You shouldn't be. You inhabit my shop, don't you? Haven't you noticed what's been going on there?"

Piles of paper, small-town small talk, and the dull daily comings and goings of mortals don't interest me, baby. You do. And you haven't needed me lately—till now. Which makes sense. I can see you're in trouble. You been taken in by a lady hobo running some kind of confidence game.

"You're way off the mark."

Really? Convince me, then. Tell me why I shouldn't scare your Norma into next week.

"Don't you dare. I like her. And the store needs her."

I'll be the judge of that.

"Look, the best way to explain Norma's selling ability is . . . well, she's got a special kind of empathy. She's brilliant at understanding customers. She reads them like a book page. Aunt Sadie calls her 'the Book Whisperer.'"

Whispering to books? Sounds like a looney tune.

"And what do you think the general public would call me for talking to you?"

Hmm. Point taken.

"I'll put it another way. Norma loves books and takes great joy in connecting every customer with just the right author or title. She seems able to sense which souls are especially sad or lonely or troubled. She'll go right up to them, even in a crowd, and draw them out. I've seen it with my own eyes. It's like . . . book medicine and she's the doctor."

I need more, doll. Gimme a concrete-as-brick example.

"All right. Then listen to what happened one Sunday after Norma came to work for us. I was about to drive Spencer to Newport to get him registered for the regional science fair. I went downstairs to grab my jacket from behind the counter when I heard a raucous uproar coming from the main floor."

A drunken brawl?

"In a family bookshop? No, Jack, the uproar came from a group of women laughing—"

Like cackling hens?

"Don't embellish. Just listen . . ."

CHAPTER 3

Judging a Book

They who dream by day are cognizant of many things
which escape those who dream only by night.

—Edgar Allan Poe, "Eleonora"

"WHAT'S GOING ON?" I asked my aunt. Laughter continued to rise up, little noise balloons bursting from the rows of bookshelves.

"It's Norma." Sadie smiled as she rang up a customer and cocked her head toward the stacks. "She's holding court."

Folding my jacket over my arm, I approached the cackling aisle—Au to Do (Jane Austen through Arthur Conan Doyle)—and peeked around the corner.

Three smartly dressed women, one of whom I recognized as a well-heeled resident of Larchmont Avenue, Quindicott's poshest neighborhood, were in a lively conversation with our new part-time employee, Norma.

"Don't be coy, sisters. You know what I'm saying is true." Norma swept a hand through her cinnamon-brown pixie cut.

"Men are work. We all know that. They're messy and difficult. They're noisy. They snore, and they do the things we ask them to do in their own time or not at all."

"Mostly not at all," said Hazel Kraft, the bank president's wife. The other women tittered.

"You see what I mean, then," Norma went on. "I'm telling you this store is full of alternatives, because a book boyfriend is the better bet. He can sweep you off your feet, protect you like a Pinkerton, battle like a knight-errant, or be as deliciously daring as a pirate. He can take you on vacation, on an adventure, on an impossible quest. Why, a book boyfriend can even make sweet love to you."

The women laughed as Norma lowered her voice conspiratorially.

"Best of all, you don't have to cook for them, clean up after them, do their laundry, or even pay attention to them when you want alone time—which for me is *the* most important time of *my* day."

Hazel Kraft frowned. "Sometimes I miss them when I've closed the book for the last time."

"You can never really close the book, dear, because the warm feeling remains," Norma insisted. "That's because you've made a new friend—two of them really. The character you love, and the author, who likely has many more adventures for you to go on together."

As Norma described potential "book boyfriends" as diverse as Sherlock Holmes, Walt Longmire, Jack Reacher, Philip Marlowe, Jamie Fraser, and Hercule Poirot, the ladies began chatting among themselves about their own favorites.

As they talked and laughed, Norma stepped back long enough to notice a boy, maybe fourteen, lurking nearby. She moved away from the group, and it looked to me like she was about to engage the youth. I quietly moved down a parallel book aisle so I could overhear that conversation—and peek between shelves to spy on them.

"You look like you're lost," Norma said to the youth, who simply shrugged.

"Don't you like our young adult book selection?"

He made a face. "It's a lot of girl stuff with romance and unhappy endings. Or adventure stories with girls as the heroes, while the guys just stand around, so who cares?"

I bit my tongue hearing that. I could have rattled off dozens of books we carried with boy protagonists. Or tried to persuade him to give a girl-led series a try. But Norma didn't argue. Instead, she gently asked—

"What kind of books do *you* like, then?"

"Except for school assignments, I don't really read books . . . much."

"What's your name?"

"Teddy Kraft."

"Hazel's your mom?"

"My stepmother. My real mom died when I was a kid."

Norma nodded. "If you don't read much, why did Hazel bring you?"

He shrugged again. "I don't have anywhere else to go. My dad is out of town on business—again—and my best friend moved away last week. His mom got a good job in Boston."

Norma nodded sympathetically. "That can be lonely, losing a buddy. Sounds like you need a new friend, someone who understands what you're going through."

Teddy didn't reply.

"So, tell me, Teddy. Did you go to the movies with your friend? Watch TV?"

"Sure. All the time. Spooky stuff, mostly."

"You like spooky stories, then?"

"Sure. They're the best."

"How about a whole book full of spooky stories, all of them written by an author who lost his mother when he was a baby? In fact, this author lost pretty much everything he ever loved. His home, his family, his friends and schoolmates. He even lost his young wife to tuberculosis. And do you know what he did?"

The boy shook his head.

"He put all the pain, all the loneliness, fear, and uncertainty he felt into his stories. And they are excellent stories. Some of the spookiest ever written. Poems, too. But along with the scary stuff you'll find wisdom."

As if by sleight of hand, a copy of *The Portable Edgar*

Allan Poe appeared in Norma's hand. She handed it to Teddy, who quickly leafed through the pages to the table of contents. Suddenly his sulking face lit up.

"'The Fall of the House of Usher.' 'The Premature Burial.' 'The Pit and the Pendulum,'" he cried. "I saw these movies on TV. This Poe guy must have written them, right?"

"Something like that," Norma replied, laughing. "You'll find that the stories are a little bit different from the movies, but they are plenty spooky in their own way. There are a lot of big words, but this edition has notes to help you with those. So, are you interested?"

Teddy smiled and nodded.

"Your stepmother already has a full basket. Let's slip this book in there with the rest of them, shall we?"

OKAY, JACK CONCEDED when I finished my story, *you convinced me that Norma is as sweet as a hot cross bun on Easter Sunday. But I still don't trust her.*

"That's no surprise," I told the ghost. "Given your disposition, you'd suspect Mother Teresa of ulterior motives."

Heaven's got halos, baby, not the dirty earth. In my experience, everyone has a self-serving motive. And I'm suspicious of anyone livin' on the lam when they don't have to.

"There are plenty of people, perfectly respectable people, who choose to live off the grid."

Off the griddle?

"The grid, Jack. Back in Aunt Sadie's day they called it 'dropping out,' but it means the same thing. I'm sure Norma has her reasons for remaining a nomad."

Yeah, but what are they? According to you, she's some kind of book saint. So why hasn't some Alvin stuck a ring on her pinkie?

"For goodness' sake, Jack, why do you think she gave that book boyfriend speech? It's not the 1940s anymore. Since your time, women have taken a giant leap forward. We have our own careers now, own our own businesses, forge our own futures. I'm living proof!"

Then why doesn't Norma get a career? Or own a business, instead of traipsing around the country like a hobo?

I paused. "Maybe she's trying to find herself."

Or maybe she's on the run, which is why you shouldn't trust her, either.

Jack's declaration was followed by another rumble of thunder. Just ahead I spied the first sign of my destination. The highest turret of the Finch Inn was peeking over the trees.

"We're almost there," I announced. "And you've failed to dissuade me. Despite your suspicions about Norma, I'm still offering her a job. I just hope she accepts."

And I hope the broad's not some escapee from a padded cell with a split personality and violent tendencies.

I would have laughed if it hadn't been for the horrified shriek. A woman's bloodcurdling cry blasted through the autumn air. I froze for a moment until I realized—it came from the direction of the Finch Inn!

CHAPTER 4

Diamonds Aren't Forever

A good many dramatic situations begin with screaming.

—*Barbarella*, 1969

WITH ALL SPEED, I ran across the manicured lawn, up the porch steps, and through the antique glass doors. Stopping dead in the middle of the foyer, I saw I wasn't the only one to hear the woman's shriek.

The genteel tranquility of Quindicott's renowned bed-and-breakfast had been completely shattered. Guests who'd been enjoying high tea in the common room peered through the door in tense alarm.

Behind the carved mahogany front desk, fifty-something Fiona Finch had been so startled she'd dropped a host of travel brochures across the gleaming polished floor. Like her surname, Mrs. Finch was small and slight in stature with a bird-like manic energy and focused work ethic that had helped transform her husband's broken-down family home and tangled estate into one of the most popular getaways in New England, complete with a newly constructed (and highly rated) French restaurant, Chez Finch.

The single scream had set her eyes so wide they seemed to raise the level of her wren-brown hair. Even the ruby cardinal brooch, pinned to the collar of her sea-green dress, appeared rattled enough to take flight.

"Where did it come from?" I gasped.

"The Peacock Room on the third floor," Fiona said, gazed fixed on the ceiling. "It's the only room currently occupied."

"Who's staying there?"

"Her name is Peyton Pemberton," Fiona whispered. "She arrived yesterday with a friend, a handsome young—"

A second howl echoed through the great house, this one in anger and frustration.

Fiona, still in shock, appeared riveted in place. Not surprising. Outside of high school football games, Quindicott seldom heard screaming. Even though our bookshop sold hair-raising thrillers, we were a quiet concern. The same could be said about the Cooper Family Bakery, Koh's Market, and Colleen's House of Beauty.

The Finch Inn was especially serene. Situated outside town on a picturesque pond (really an inlet) near the shores of the Atlantic, the stately Victorian and the manicured grounds surrounding it were ringed by verdant woodlands with hiking trails that led to a pristine beach, all part of the package that made Quindicott's only B and B a jewel-in-the-crown destination for our region and an economic engine for our main street businesses.

Now, as the echo of that second scream faded, Fiona and I made a beeline to the polished staircase. We nearly collided with each other in our rush.

We needn't have bothered. Hurried footsteps came pounding down the carpeted stairs. The feet belonged to a petite young woman in pink spandex pants, matching midriff-baring top, and fluorescent yellow sneakers. Her luminous blue eyes were wide, her long blond hair tied so tightly behind her head that her features appeared pinched. The woman's attractive face was without makeup and flushed beet red. Despite her workout gear, her breathless agitation was not a result of rigorous exercise.

"They're gone!" she cried when she saw Fiona.

To avoid the curious stares from the teatime crowd, Fiona gently ushered the distraught young woman into the deserted library. At Fiona's nod I followed and closed the door behind us. Together we faced the agitated guest.

"Now, Miss Pemberton, *what* is gone exactly?" Fiona's tone was soothing, a futile attempt to calm the young woman. "Tell me what's missing."

"My antique gold-and-diamond necklace, that's what!" she screeched. "Along with two teardrop-diamond earrings! They were clearly *stolen* while I took my afternoon run. They're irreplaceable, one of a kind!"

Like a deflating blowup doll, Peyton Pemberton sank onto a chair and buried her face in her small, perfectly manicured hands. "Great Aunt Cora's legacy," she sobbed. "My great-aunt was once an acclaimed stage actress. Cora even ran her own theater company. Those jewels are the only thing I have left to remember her by, and now they're gone!"

"Are you *certain* they're gone?" Fiona prodded. "Because I don't see how it's possible. You were only out for an hour or so. No stranger entered the premises, or I would have seen them. Could your jewels have been misplaced, perhaps?"

"No! They're gone, I tell you. I looked everywhere. I just wore them Saturday night at the Met Costume Ball in New York. They were in my luggage when I got up this morning. The jewels were obviously stolen while I was out."

I had no reason to doubt Peyton Pemberton's account, but Fiona stubbornly resisted the very notion that such a thing could happen in *her* establishment.

"Perhaps we should take a second look," Fiona suggested. "We'll search for your jewels together. I'm sure they'll turn up."

Miss Pemberton jumped out of her chair. "How do I know *you're* not the one who stole them, or that you're not in on it in some way?"

Fiona bristled. "Why, that's, that's—"

"I don't know you people," Peyton Pemberton ranted, throwing a paranoid glance my way. "Why should I trust anyone here?"

Fiona stood still as an ice sculpture, mouth agape. Nothing like this had ever happened before—not at her beloved inn. Barney, her husband and business partner, appeared to be absent at the moment, and she clearly didn't know what to do.

The ghost did.

Don't involve the cops if you don't have to, he warned in my head. *Get the house detective.*

Jack, we're not in New York, I silently reminded him. *And the Finch Inn isn't some three-hundred-room luxury hotel. They don't employ a house detective!*

Why not? he argued. *If they got the kind of clientele who wear priceless diamond necklaces, they should have put up the coin for a plainclothes dick.*

Well, they didn't. And they don't—I mean they don't usually have the kind of guests who wear priceless jewelry.

As Jack and I debated, Peyton Pemberton ran out of patience.

"Don't just stand there like a cow," she shouted at Fiona. "Call the police right now. I demand you call them, or I will!"

Fiona winced, then flushed red. I knew she was fighting mad. I also knew she was trying *not* to involve the local authorities.

Jack? What should we—

Call the coppers, Penny. If you don't, Blondie here will assume you and Bird Lady are tryin' to cover up the crime.

As Fiona began to sputter, readying an angry retort, I touched her arm.

"Call the police," I advised her. "Let them handle it."

CHAPTER 5

The Searchers

I'm not against the police; I'm just afraid of them.

—Alfred Hitchcock

IN THE END, I was the one who called the police because Fiona refused to.

"Not until I speak with Barney," she insisted and explained that her husband was at a local garage picking up his just repaired Lincoln.

So, while Peyton Pemberton fumed—and Fiona phoned Barney about the theft—I called in the law.

By "law" I mean the Quindicott Police Department, a tiny force headed by Chief Ciders, a bad-tempered bureaucrat who should have put in his retirement papers a decade ago. I dreaded dealing with the man, who had only gotten more cantankerous with age. And if the chief didn't show, the person who answered my call would likely be one of his officers—and Ciders was not prone to hire the best. Nepotism was the rule at the QPD.

A carnival of Keystone Cops, Jack muttered, having witnessed them in action—and inaction.

So, you can understand the relief I felt when the sole shining light of the QPD knocked on the library door. Deputy Chief

Eddie Franzetti wasn't just the finest local law enforcement could offer; he was a devoted family man, as well as my late older brother's best friend, and now a trusted friend of mine.

The deputy chief noticed me as soon as he entered the wood-lined library but suppressed his usual affable smile, wisely maintaining a demeanor that better reflected the gravity of the situation.

Though the young woman was still incensed, the darkly handsome officer managed to disarm the excitable Peyton Pemberton with a few flattering and—to me, at least—surprising words.

"It's a thrill to meet you, Ms. Pemberton. My thirteen-year-old daughter is a big fan. She follows you on TikTok, or maybe it's Instagram. I'm not really sure."

"Probably both," Peyton Pemberton replied, waving a manicured hand.

For the next few minutes, the innkeeper and I stood silently by while the deputy chief listened to Miss Pemberton's account of the theft. He stopped her periodically to ask questions. What time did she go out running? How long was she away? Did she see anyone lurking around when she left for her run?

Finally, Eddie suggested that Miss Pemberton accompany him upstairs to the Peacock Room, where together they could determine whether her valuables were in fact missing—or simply misplaced.

As soon as the pair headed upstairs, I grabbed Fiona.

"Quick, tell me. *Why* is Peyton Pemberton famous?"

"She's what they call an Internet 'influencer.' Apparently she's very big with girls—preteen through college age. She earns a fortune Instagram modeling and promoting products for companies."

"How do you know all this?"

"Are you kidding?" Fiona lowered her voice. "I look up all my guests on the Internet. After I found out about Miss Pemberton, I *was* hoping she'd mention her stay at the Finch Inn and post a few selfies on our grounds—but not so much now."

"Can you show me her activity online?" I asked.

"Come on!" Fiona pulled me to the computer behind her registration desk.

"You know we have an Instagram account now," Fiona mentioned proudly as she brought up the Finch Inn's page. "I just posted pictures of the fall foliage. And when we decorate for Christmas, I'll be posting pictures of our tree and lights."

"How nice."

Fiona moved her cursor to the search bar and entered Peyton Pemberton's name. Rows and columns of photographs appeared.

"Who's the hunk?" I asked.

"He is a dish, isn't he?" Fiona arched an eyebrow. "His name is Hollis West."

"He's a preppie?"

Fiona shrugged. "He gave a Newport address and I noticed tennis and yachting photos. Miss Pemberton calls him Hal."

"You talked to Peyton about him?"

"Oh no. I just overheard them talking. He and Miss Pemberton arrived together yesterday afternoon. They asked for our largest room." She cleared her throat disapprovingly. "Without a reservation, I might add."

Jack laughed. *Entitled much?*

Ignoring the ghost, I pointed out, "You were able to accommodate them."

"Because they checked in on a Sunday afternoon—and since most of our guests check out on Sunday, it worked out for us all."

"And where is Mr. Hollis West now?"

Once again, Fiona shrugged. "I have no idea. Mr. West used his Sapphire Reserve Card to pay for the room, but he only stayed a few hours—long enough for him to dine with Miss Pemberton at Chez Finch. Then he kissed Miss Pemberton good-bye and drove off in his BMW. He hasn't been back since."

"So Peyton Pemberton was alone in her room last night and all day today? You didn't see Hal return?"

"No, I would have recognized his car." Fiona scrolled

down to find more photos of the young Hal, shirtless in a Speedo on a white-sand, azure-skyed beach. Beside him, Peyton Pemberton wore a string-thin azure bikini with matching cobalt-tinted sunglasses.

"Goodness," the innkeeper said. "They're hardly wearing any clothing at all."

It's called cheesecake, Jack declared in my head. *At least that's what they called it in my day.*

Cheesecake? I silently replied. *Are you talking about the Instagram picture of Peyton and Hal?*

I'm talking about photos designed to titillate. They're not informative like a mug shot or pretty like a portrait. Cheesecake is designed for salivating over. Frankly, I'm surprised.

About what?

After all your lectures on how things have changed since my day, I'm surprised that provocative pictures of pampered playthings are still around.

I glanced at the bathing suit photos again and frowned. *This isn't cheesecake, Jack. Peyton Pemberton and her boyfriend posted these pictures themselves. They're what you call influencers . . . Internet influencers.*

The ghost laughed. *You can fancy up the name all you like and sell it on some re-hatched version of a mini movie screen, but any dame who earns money by taking off her clothes and posing for pictures, well . . . Different century, same racket.*

Maybe there's some truth in what you say, but it's not a racket.

I call 'em as I see 'em, Penny. And if this is the "career" path your young women of today are takin', I wouldn't exactly call it a giant leap forward.

"Look at this," Fiona said, pointing at the screen. "There are pictures posted from that charity ball that Peyton said she attended in New York the other night."

"I thought the Met Gala was held in May."

"It is. This is the Met Costume Ball, their new Halloween-season fundraiser. Look, I think Peyton Pemberton is wearing the jewels she's crying over now."

When I glanced at the necklace, Jack also saw the jewelry—through my eyes—and a bone-chilling sweep of frigid air suddenly filled the reception area.

Jack, what's wrong?

Dead silence followed, so I went back to studying the photos on Peyton's Instagram page. The next image showed Hollis West costumed as a desert sheik. Long white robes flowed around his athletic body. A kaffiyeh covered his dark hair, and an absurdly curved plastic sword dangled from a hempen belt around his trim waist.

Beside him, hardly dressed at all in filmy, see-through pink "harem girl" attire, Peyton Pemberton showed off an elaborate gold necklace—the one apparently missing. It was a beautiful piece. The heavy-looking setting was large, almost like a collar.

"That faux-Egyptian pattern is telling," Fiona remarked. "I'll bet it was made during the Art Deco design craze of the 1920s."

A second photo showed a close-up of the collar, its vintage gold embedded with teardrop-shaped diamonds. Matching teardrop diamonds dangled from Miss Pemberton's coral-pink ears, while she and Hollis spoke with a singer named Nicki Minaj. The caption identified "Hal" West as "The Sheik."

Apparently the jewels had an identity as well.

"The Tears of Valentino," Fiona read breathlessly. "I wonder if this remarkable necklace has some connection to the silent movie star."

"You mean Rudolph Valentino?" I asked. "Does anyone even remember who he was anymore?"

"The first male sex symbol? Of course they do," Fiona insisted. "Someone obviously knows that Valentino starred in a movie called *The Sheik*. As for Peyton's see-through number . . . she certainly has the figure to pull it off."

I ignored the cheesecake—and the beefcake—to study the jewels. I counted at least a dozen diamonds on that elaborate setting around Peyton Pemberton's swanlike neck.

"The Tears of Valentino sounds rather poetic," I murmured aloud. "I wonder what it means . . ."

Fiona had no answer. But the ghost did.

I know what it means, doll, and there's no poetry involved.

My heart began to pound. *Then you've seen these jewels before?*

Oh yeah. And you better heed my warning.

Warning? About a piece of jewelry?

Plenty of real tears and a lot of blood have been spilled over those rocks. I got a feeling more of both are about to be shed now that those hard-luck stones have surfaced again.

Before I could ask Jack what he meant by his ominous remark, I heard footsteps descending the stairs. Fiona quickly pressed a key on her computer and the on-screen Instagram photos were instantly replaced by the inn's staff schedule.

We shifted nervously, waiting for Deputy Chief Franzetti and Peyton Pemberton to reach the bottom of the steps. When they did, I was sorry to see that Eddie's expression was grim.

As Peyton hung back, an I told-you-so smirk marring her pretty face, Eddie approached Fiona and spoke.

"You have cameras upstairs."

It was not a question.

CHAPTER 6

Let's Roll the Tape

Like burglars . . . we leave our fingerprints on broken
locks, our voiceprints in the bugged rooms, our footprints in the wet concrete.

—Ross Macdonald

"I HAVE ONE camera on each floor and one on the stairs,"
Fiona informed Eddie. "We're not the Hilton. That's as
much security as we can afford."

"I need to see the footage from the third-floor camera."

Fiona blinked, lips tight. "Then you didn't find the jewels?"

Eddie shook his head. "Her valuables are not in that room.
I tore the place apart and found nothing."

In the corner, Peyton Pemberton now decided to ignore
us, as if she wasn't the least bit involved in the current drama.
Seemingly bored, she turned her back on the reception desk,
checked her phone, and made a call.

Fiona sat back down in front of her desktop computer. A
moment later a shot of the third-floor hallway appeared on
the monitor. I knew it was live when I spied the tiny digital
day and date counter on the lower right corner of the screen,
displaying the current time.

Eddie leaned close and spoke softly. "Miss Pemberton

tells me the jewels were in her room before she left for her run and gone when she returned. She said it was the only time she left her room today."

Fiona nodded. "Shall we start with that?"

"Yes, please roll the recording back to the time Miss Pemberton said she went for her run."

Fiona nodded again. The picture dissolved into blurry shapes and fuzzy lines as the clock on the corner of the screen ticked backward.

"Stop," Eddie commanded.

The recording froze on the image of Peyton Pemberton leaving her room wearing her pink spandex workout clothes and canary-yellow sneakers. She carefully locked her door before stepping out of camera range.

"Okay," Eddie said. "Now let me see the footage from the camera on the stairs."

Fiona called it up and we watched Peyton Pemberton descend the staircase in the same outfit, draping a hand towel around her neck as she bounded down the steps.

"All right, she's clearly gone," Eddie said. "Now let's look at everything that happened after that."

The third-floor camera showed an empty hall until twenty minutes after Miss Pemberton departed. That's when a lanky, forty-something woman unlocked the Peacock Room door. She wore a dour gray shift and a hairnet which covered her cinnamon-brown pixie, but I recognized her instantly.

Fiona fast forwarded fifteen minutes, until the maid reemerged, locked the door behind her, then rolled a small cleaning cart on to the next room.

"That's Norma," Fiona said. "She works afternoons as a maid."

"I know Norma," Eddie replied. "It can't be her. Let's keep searching."

We did, but after reviewing the tape twice, it was obvious that only Norma had entered Peyton Pemberton's room during that crucial time period.

Eddie took a slow, deep breath. "Where is Norma now?"

"Like I said, she gave Barney a ride down to the garage.

They went off in that big white van of hers. He needed to pick up his car and—"

The deputy chief cut her off with a wave. "When will Norma be back?"

"Not until tomorrow afternoon. Usually, she stays in her room downstairs, but tonight she's going to visit her sister in Millstone. I have the address here somewhere."

"Can you call Norma?"

"She doesn't have a phone." Fiona shrugged. "You know Norma."

"Is she still with Barney, do you think?"

"Maybe," Fiona said. "Norma was still with him when I called a few minutes ago—"

"And that's when you told Barney about the theft?"

Fiona nodded and Eddie frowned.

Busted flush, the ghost cracked in my head.

What are you talking about, Jack?

If the maid is guilty, the bird-lady innkeeper already tipped the woman off that the caper's blown. You won't see that dame again until the police lineup, if your Keystone Cops can catch her, that is.

I know Norma, Jack. She's a lovely woman with a wise spirit and kind heart. She's no jewel thief.

Oh, you know that? Jack replied. *Well, maybe you don't. After viewing that third-floor picture show, I'm sure your pal Eddie has doubts.*

It's his job to have doubts, I pointed out.

It's also his job to question the accused.

Jack was right, which is why Eddie instructed Fiona to contact her husband.

"Fiona, I want you to call Barney right now. If Norma is still with him, tell them both to get back here, pronto. If Norma's gone, find out exactly *when* she left and *where* she was headed."

Fiona reached for the phone.

"One more thing," he added. "Where is that housekeeping cart Norma was pushing around?"

"It should be in the third-floor utility closet. That's the unmarked door right next to the third-floor landing."

"I didn't see that door on your security camera footage."

"Need I remind you we only have one camera on each floor?" Fiona chided. "We don't have a camera pointed at that door because nobody is going to rob the linen closet."

"Where is that door again?"

"It's on the right as you reach the top of the stairs. The very first door. Farther down the hall is the Peacock Room, the door opposite is the Robin's Roost. At the end of the hall you'll find the Osprey's Den and Sparrow's Suite.

"Are any of the rooms occupied?"

Fiona shook her head. "Everyone on that floor checked out early this morning. Everyone but Miss Pemberton."

"May I have the key to the maid's closet?"

"You don't need one, Eddie. It's never locked. We leave it open so our guests can grab soap, shampoo, or towels if they need them."

"What's on that maid's cart?"

"Cleaning products. Extra washcloths and towels. More of those little bottles of shampoo and bars of soap. There's a bin on the bottom for used bedclothes and towels."

Eddie rubbed his chin. "Is that where I'd find Miss Pemberton's sheets from last night?"

"Actually, yes. By now that bin would have been emptied in the laundry room, but Barney needed a ride to the garage to pick up his Lincoln, so he asked Norma to knock off early and drive him. He promised to take care of it when he got back."

"Then I'm going to check that bin," Eddie said. "Those jewels might have ended up tangled in the dirty sheets."

"You think that's likely?" Fiona asked.

Eddie shrugged. "I admit I'm groping. This has got to be some sort of misunderstanding, or an accident. There's no way Norma stole those jewels."

I agreed with Eddie, though I wondered what convinced him she was innocent. Did he know something about Norma that I didn't?

While Fiona dialed up her husband, Miss Pemberton continued talking on her mobile phone.

With her insurance company, no doubt, Jack cracked.

As Eddie headed for the stairs, the ghost goosed me with an icy draft.

What are you waiting for, doll?!

Huh?

Go on upstairs with your copper friend.

Why? I replied. *Eddie doesn't need help.*

But you do! It's clear as crystal your Book Whisperer is in a peck of trouble. If she was desperate or greedy or stupid enough to swipe that necklace, then she's also in a pile of danger. Believe me, I know.

What do you know? I demanded. *What kind of danger?*

This ain't the time for a long story. It's time for you to make short work of those stairs. Now, get us up there, pronto!

Considering Jack's words (and chilly kick in the pants), I didn't waste any more time arguing. The deputy chief was all the way up the first flight of stairs when I called out—

"Wait, Eddie! I'm going with you."

CHAPTER 7

À la Cart

The first time we met I told you I was a detective. Get
it through your lovely head. I work at it, lady. I don't
play at it.

—Raymond Chandler, *The Big Sleep*

DEPUTY CHIEF FRANZETTI was clearly annoyed by my
presence, but he didn't stop me from following him up the
stairs.

The Victorian's rich carpeting muted our footsteps. On
the third floor, circular windows on either end of the hallway
allowed the late afternoon sun—now breaking through the
overcast sky—to stream through. Fiona had hung intricately
cut crystals in front of the glass, fracturing the light into
multicolored sunbeams that danced along the walls and sent
solar sparkles rippling across the uneven landscape of the
embossed tin ceiling.

There were only four rooms on this floor, all of them un-
occupied. Peyton Pemberton was now downstairs, and (according to Fiona) the other guests had long since checked out.

No surprise, Peyton's guest room door was closed.

That's a tough break, the ghost groused. *Who knows
what that cornpone flatfoot might have missed? If this were*

my case, the first thing I'd do is shake down that ditzy doll's room myself. Check behind the pictures on the wall, rifle her pockets, even her girdle and garters.

News flash, Jack, young women don't wear girdles and garters anymore.

Jack grunted. *Guess that's for the best. Makes things easier on the joes. Less armor to unscrew before you get—*

I cut off that conversation quick. *Anyway, I agree with you. I wish we could search that room, too, but Eddie will never allow it. He isn't aware that you and I are also on the case, and it's not like I can tell him.* I paused. *Of course, that doesn't mean I can't try for it.*

With a deep breath, I walked quickly and quietly over to the Peacock Room, but as I reached for the knob—

"Wrong door, Pen," Eddie called. "Linen closet's over here."

The jig's up, baby, Jack said with a barely suppressed chuckle.

I clenched my teeth. *I suppose you would have done it better?*

I wouldn't have done it right in front of him. Nice try anyway. Now go join your friend the flatfoot.

I did. As promised, the linen closet was unlocked, and the light sprang on as soon as the door opened. The walk-in space was long and narrow and the shelves were stacked with fluffy towels, perfumed soaps, and tiny bottles of shampoo.

The maid's cart was shoved all the way back, at the far end of the narrow space. Eddie wheeled it out into the sun-sparkling hallway and pulled the plastic bin off the bottom shelf. It was full to brimming with soiled linen, which he promptly dumped on the carpeted floor. For the next five minutes Eddie went through two bedsheets, six pillowcases, two damp bath towels, a washcloth, and six hand towels. Despite the thorough search, all he found was a wrapper from the maple candy Fiona had placed on everyone's pillow.

We quickly found out we'd been looking in the wrong place.

When Eddie refilled the bin and shoved it back into place,

the whole cart shuddered. A box of rubber cleaning gloves on the top shifted position, and I spied a glint of burnished metal.

"Eddie, look . . ."

Eddie saw it, too. While I stood back and watched, he gently slid the box aside to expose a single teardrop-shaped diamond earring in a setting of glistening antique gold.

"Don't touch it," Eddie cautioned, "there might be fingerprints."

Without touching anything else, Eddie gingerly wrapped the single earring in a cotton washcloth and tucked it into his jacket. Then he thoroughly searched the rest of the cart with his eyes alone. Finally, he returned to the linen closet and searched among the clean towels, bars of soap, and tiny bottles of shampoo. But after long minutes of patient hunting, he found nothing.

Moments later, he closed the linen closet door behind us.

"What are you thinking, Eddie?"

"It *appears* that Norma removed the jewels from Peyton Pemberton's room and hid them on her maid's cart. In her haste to flee the inn, she left one earring behind—probably because it got covered by the box of gloves."

"So it *appears.*"

Eddie's shoulders sank. "Let's face it, Pen. I don't like believing it, either, but that's probably what happened, according to the evidence."

"Do you really think she's guilty?"

"It doesn't look good, but I am withholding judgment. I'd like to hear Norma's side of the story before I declare this grand theft and have anyone charged. Of course, if she doesn't return to answer my questions, then . . ."

His voice trailed off, but I got his meaning.

I checked my phone, surprised that Eddie and I had been upstairs for nearly half an hour. We returned to the lobby just as Barney Finch came through the antique doors. Tall and lean, the spry seventy-year-old tucked car keys into the pocket of his flannel shirt before he shook hands with the deputy chief.

"Sorry to see you here, Officer Franzetti. Bad business, this, and bad for business, too."

"Did you get your car back?" Eddie asked.

"Yep. Cost me six hundred dollars. Why, the oil change alone—"

"So where's Norma?" Eddie curtly interrupted.

Barney shuffled his feet and stared at the rug. "I told her you wanted to talk to her, and when I left the garage, Norma was following right behind me in her van. We got separated at the railroad crossing by one of those long freight trains. She should be along any minute."

Yeah, Jack cracked. *She'll be along—along the shortest route out of town.*

Quiet, Jack. Norma will show up, you'll see.

I was never so sure. And never so wrong.

Another thirty minutes went by without any sign of Norma. In that time Deputy Chief Franzetti interrupted Peyton Pemberton's phone conversation long enough to show her the earring, which she positively identified as part of the missing set.

"Where's the rest of my jewels?" she demanded.

"I'm working on that," Eddie said.

Peyton ended her phone call, and after a huddled conversation with my friend, she proceeded to pitch a hissy fit worthy of our cat Bookmark, just because Eddie wouldn't return her diamond.

"It's my property, Officer. I insist you give it back!"

"I'm sorry, Miss Pemberton, but now that you've filed a police report—"

"I did that for insurance purposes," she stated. "On the advice of my lawyer."

"But *because* you filed that report I had to contact the state police, which makes this an official police investigation. Believe me, that's the way the insurance company wants it, too. This earring is evidence. You'll get it back after we run a few tests—"

"Tests?!" Peyton cried. "What sort of tests?"

"The state police will want to check for fingerprints."

Eddie explained. "And they'll verify the authenticity of the diamond—*for insurance purposes*, of course."

"Oh," she said, mollified. "If that's all you're doing, then I guess it will be okay. That precious necklace and earring set is my only connection to my dear aunt, who's gone now. It's an heirloom, and I do not want it damaged."

Soon after that confrontation, Miss Pemberton complained of an oncoming migraine and asked to return to her room.

"Sorry," Eddie told her. "The state police will want to take a look at that room, too. Fiona will find you another place to rest. It's just for a few hours."

"But what about my clothes, my luggage?"

"They will need to be checked, too, I'm afraid. You'll get it all back after the state police have done their investigation."

"I'll be pleased to help you, Miss Pemberton," Barney said. "Perhaps you'll enjoy one of the turret rooms. They have a grand view. You'll be able to see the ocean—"

After Barney led his dissatisfied guest away, Fiona urged Eddie to make himself comfortable. He accepted a cup of Earl Grey and took a spot in the reception area, where he sat in silence, turning his head to face the door every time someone went in or out. Finally, after long minutes passed, he checked his watch, slapped his knee, and rose.

"That's it, then," he announced.

"What are you going to do, Eddie?" Fiona asked anxiously.

"I have no choice. I'm calling in the state police."

"I thought you already did that," Fiona said, surprised.

"I held off, despite what I told Miss Pemberton. I was hoping Norma would show with some kind of explanation—" Eddie shook his head. "Ah, forget it! I'm notifying the state police, so expect more visitors real soon, Fiona."

The innkeeper looked so distraught that my heart went out to her.

"I'll also issue alerts to departments in Providence, Newport, and across the state line in Massachusetts," Eddie continued. "Maybe as far as Maine and Connecticut, because I'm sure Norma's nomadic ways have taught her how to travel light and fast."

Eddie took a breath and glanced away. "I'm sorry, but you should be aware. As soon as the state police take over, an arrest warrant will be issued."

"Oh no. No!" Fiona looked ready to burst into tears.

I swallowed hard, trying not to be angry with Eddie.

He's just doing his job, said the ghost.

Jack, this is awful. Norma's gone from a person of interest to a fugitive from justice. But why? Why would she run? She can't be guilty . . . can she?

Sorry, doll, I don't like saying so, but—

I know, I know! You told me so.

CHAPTER 8

Two for the Road

Faithless is he that says farewell when the road darkens.

—J.R.R. Tolkien, *The Fellowship of the Ring*

THE DRAMA AT the Finch Inn was over (for now), and I had a bookshop to run. So while the sun sunk and clouds returned to smother the sky, I hiked back to my store, this time using the paved streets and concrete sidewalks that ran through the center of Quindicott's business district.

Civilized routes have fewer surprises, but they're easier to navigate. And given what I'd just experienced, I wasn't up for flying bird's nests or uneven terrain. Every step of the way, the road was firm underfoot. It should have reassured me, yet I felt unsteady, and my PI spirit continued to haunt me.

Honestly, with darkness descending, I was glad to have Jack's company, but there was a price to pay, because despite the ghost's claim that he didn't like saying "I told you so," he certainly found enough ways to say it!

You know your "sweet lady" is in a peck of trouble.

"Yes, Jack. I'm also aware that police all over Rhode Island and Massachusetts will be looking for Norma. It doesn't help that Fiona can't find the address of her sister in Millstone. Boy, was Eddie steamed about that."

Yeah, the canny innkeeper said she'd "misplaced" the paper it was written on, but I wonder if it wasn't just that bird-crazy dame's way of crying foul—or should I say fowl? As in F-O-W-L. Get it?

"A foul pun, considering the circumstances. So enough with the fine-feathered jokes."

I'm only making them because Norma flew the coop.

"I hope you're not expecting a snare drum rim shot, because vaudeville is deader than you are."

Low blow, baby.

"Hey, what did you say earlier? I call 'em as I see 'em."

At least you're listening to what I tell you.

"Do I have a choice?"

Sure, pluck that old Buffalo nickel of mine out of your pretty pink brassiere, throw it into a slot machine, and leave me in peace back at your bookstore.

"That would be fine, except there are no slot machines in Quindicott, and you're never at peace for long. When you get bored in my bookstore, you haunt the customers. I can't have that if I *want* customers. And would you please stop talking about my underthings?"

As soon as you stop whining and face the music.

"I can't face the music if I don't know where it's coming from."

That's what detectives are for.

"Eddie's already on the case," I pointed out. "And while you might be right about Fiona—and her being less than truthful with Officer Franzetti—I doubt it's because she's playing him. I think she's honestly discombobulated by all this. I know I am."

Da scum Bob who?

"Nobody is Bob in this scenario. Nobody's scum, either, for that matter. The word I used was *discombobulated*. It means Fiona is befuddled. Bewildered. She's in denial, Jack."

Well, she can't deny grand larceny and you can't, either. Your pal is in it, right up to her earlobes—with or without diamond teardrops dangling from them. And with no ad-

dress to track her down, your flatfoot friend had no choice but to issue an all-points bulletin or whatever they call it nowadays.

"Eddie called it a BOLO—"

"A cow puncher's tie?"

"No, not a bolo tie. BOLO is an acronym that stands for *be on the lookout*. And I think it's appalling that he had to issue it for Norma."

Don't sweat the small stuff, doll. The cops are the least of Norma's problems.

"What do you mean?

You like listening to me, listen to this. The longer Norma keeps her grip on those fancy rocks, the shorter her life span is going to be.

"What's that supposed to mean? Are you suggesting the cops are going to shoot to kill?"

No. But someone else will.

"Why would you say that?"

Because back in my day, the theft of those jewels led to an awful big sleep.

"Murder?"

That's right.

"Listen, just because something happened once—"

Thrice. That's fancy Shakespeare talk for three times. I heard the word working that very case.

"Okay, three times, but that still doesn't mean it will happen again."

You know I'm not the superstitious type, Penny. But I am talking from experience—bitter experience. When it comes to priceless ice, there's always somebody willing to give somebody else the big chill.

"The big chill? That's cold, Jack. But I shouldn't be surprised. When it comes to cold spots, you've become somewhat of an expert, haven't you?"

Funny. Looks like vaudeville's not dead—it just moved into your head.

"Whatever happened with you occurred a long time ago, Jack. Few people today even remember who Valentino is—I mean *was*—so how much can that necklace really be worth?"

Norma's life, for starters.

Jack clammed up after that, and I confess I finally appreciated the silence.

CHAPTER 9

Where the Heart Is

A home without books is like a body without a soul.

—Marcus Tullius Cicero (attributed)

THE SUN HAD set by now and the temperature was dropping. As I walked along Cranberry Street, the evening shadows deepened. The thick storm clouds made the twilight sky darken faster than usual. But amid the gathering gloom, the faux-Victorian gas lamps sprang to gleaming life, turning the concrete sidewalks into molten gold. As I approached our shop, bright light poured through our big display window, and the sight of it warmed my heart.

"Home at last," I whispered with a sigh. "No more drama."

I welcomed the calming routine of getting back to my book business—a warm cup of freshly brewed tea, talking with customers, and time with my aunt Sadie.

Everything seemed deceptively calm as I strolled through the doorway. The restored plank floor glistened and the polished wooden shelves were well stocked with titles new and old. The standing lamps and mismatched but oh-so-cozy chairs made the shop a homey haven for booklovers, and the quiet murmurs of my part-time help, Bonnie Franzetti (Eddie's younger sister), in conversation with a few customers in the aisles completed the peaceful picture.

Our bookstore was a gleaming gem of the community and a far cry from the rundown, bankrupt state I'd found it when I turned up on Sadie's doorstep just a few years ago. I was a shattered and confused widow with an equally baffled young son, a fugitive from the New York City publishing scene and my wealthy, contentious in-laws, who never approved of me—an opinion that only grew stronger after my young husband's death.

My aunt became an unwavering source of strength and a fount of wisdom. She never judged. She only loved and accepted.

I was more than happy to partner with her, invest in remodeling the shop, and rebuild the business. My years in publishing had paid off with connections in the trade. Our little independent bookstore was now a popular regional stop for author tours, and we took great pride in our new, improved, and profitable store.

Even more miraculous, our turnaround inspired shopkeepers around us to invest in their own businesses, which led to the complete revitalization of Cranberry—the main street (and heartbeat) of Quindicott. Working together, our commercial district finally arrested the town's economic decline and raised the dying spirit of our little hamlet. We were a prosperous place once more.

Reminding myself of that happy bit of personal history always encouraged me when I was feeling defeated. I had produced something good in life (other than my son, Spencer), even though I felt powerless to help Fiona and Norma now.

As I tucked my handbag away and hung my jacket behind the register, Aunt Sadie emerged from our storeroom. Her gray-streaked auburn hair was in disarray and her glasses dangled from a beaded chain around her neck.

In one arm she cradled a stack of slim paperbacks with bright, glossy covers. In her other hand, our marmalade cat, Bookmark, hung like a rag doll, purring loud enough to be heard under Sadie's greeting.

"Oh, Pen, I heard the door and I thought you were Seymour."

"Isn't it a little late for a delivery?"

It was a logical question since Seymour Tarnish was both our local mailman and a childhood friend. A big, somewhat ungainly guy with a mind like a sponge and tremendous enthusiasm about nearly everything (especially vintage pop culture), Seymour was also the owner of the sole ice cream truck in Quindicott, a vehicle he'd purchased with his winnings as a *Jeopardy!* champion—and that was the thing about Seymour. He was a unique personality. Despite his lack of formal degrees, he was one of the smartest men I'd ever known. Sure, his unvarnished opinions led others to see him as somewhat overbearing (okay, rude), but I knew he had a good heart.

"Seymour came by after work to pick up these *G-8 and His Battle Aces* reprints I special ordered for him," Sadie explained. "But as soon as he arrived he turned around and left."

"Without his precious reprints? Why?"

Sadie shrugged and set the cat on the floor. Still purring loudly, Bookmark immediately curled her furry, orange-striped form around my legs.

"Seymour got an urgent call from Professor Parker. That's all I know . . ."

J. Brainert Parker, professor of American literature at St. Francis University, was another childhood friend. Thin and somewhat frail but with a high-strung sort of manic energy, he claimed Rhode Island's great horror writer, H.P. Lovecraft, as a distant relative, and there was indeed a family resemblance. But the similarities were more than superficial. Like that renowned writer, Brainert lived his life through books.

My old friend had become an erudite scholar, esteemed in his field and celebrated among the nation's top ivory tower academics—a fact that sometimes made it difficult for me to believe that years ago, Seymour, Brainert, and I were joined together like the Three Musketeers—a trio of curious, inseparable misfits who would much rather tell ghost stories around a campfire than attend the Friday night football games.

"An urgent call from Brainert?" I pressed.

Sadie nodded. "Yes, the young man was in trouble."

I frowned with curiosity, though not alarm; Brainert's relationship with Seymour was occasionally antagonistic, and he wasn't above pulling Seymour's chain.

"What *kind* of trouble is Brainert in, do you know?"

"I believe the young professor crashed his car in Prescott Woods."

Okay, now I was alarmed! "Back up, please, Aunt Sadie, and tell me *everything* you know."

"Like I said, Brainert called Seymour while he was in our shop. Seymour put him on speakerphone. Seymour and I both thought Professor Parker sounded dazed, so Seymour advised him to call an ambulance. Then he raced out of here to find him."

Now I was *really* alarmed. "When did this happen?"

"Seymour left over an hour ago. He said he'd come back to pick up his books as soon as he helped Brainert, but he hasn't turned up or phoned."

"Then I'm going to call Brainert and find out if he's okay."

But just as I reached for my mobile, our shop's front door flew open and two bickering men strode in. Their booming voices startled Bookmark, who immediately detached herself from my (now orange-fur-covered) pant legs and scurried to the back of the store.

Sadie and I were startled, too, but in a good way. Before we even saw Brainert and Seymour, the familiar sound of the pair arguing was calming music to our worried minds.

At least *this* music I was glad to face!

CHAPTER 10

Like a Bat Out of Hell

I just met the swellest dame . . . She smacked me in the kisser.

—*The Glass Key*, 1942, adapted from the novel by Dashiell Hammett

"BRAINERT'S FINE," ANNOUNCED Seymour, still wearing his postal service uniform. "I can't say the same for his Acura. But he wouldn't have wrapped his car around a tree if Brainpan wasn't as drunk as a skunk."

"Rubbish," huffed the professor, his three-piece suit uncharacteristically rumpled.

"That's why you didn't call the cops," Seymour continued. "You were worried about the results of a Breathalyzer test. If the insurance company got wind that you were drunk, that Aussie gecko would definitely raise your rates."

"Drunk!" sputtered the indignant professor. "I'll have you know I had one drink. A *single* glass of sparkling rosé at the faculty gathering."

"One glass that you *remember*," Seymour scoffed. "But everyone knows winos are susceptible to blackouts."

If you were meeting them for the first time, you'd never guess that Seymour and Brainert were lifelong friends. The way they verbally sparred, "frenemies" seemed like a more accurate description. But despite their differences in educational background and career choices, they were two peas in a pod, and I knew from long experience they would do anything to help each other—and me and Sadie.

"Thank goodness you're okay," I cried, hurrying out from behind the counter. "Sadie and I were worried."

Brainert endured my hug, followed by Sadie's.

Don't squeeze him too hard," Jack cracked. *Your pal looks like he's gone ten rounds, then got knocked out of the ring.*

The ghost was right. Brainert's suit jacket had been twisted by the seat belt shoulder strap and torn at the seam of his left arm. The top button was missing from his vest and the poor man's tie was deconstructing before my eyes.

There were injuries as well. An angry bruise peeked out from under his mouse-colored bangs, and scuff marks marred both cheeks, making them hot to the touch and ruddy red.

"It's from that bloody airbag," he groused, shaking off my attempt to clean the head wound with a tissue.

"My goodness, what happened?" Sadie asked.

"Simple," Seymour said. "Brainert was crocked, and he cracked up."

"I was not 'crocked,'" Brainert insisted with air quotes around the offending adjective. "One glass of wine at a faculty meeting wouldn't *inebriate* anyone. One glass!"

I was surprised that Brainert—who was practically a teetotaler—was drinking at all, and I said so.

"I don't particularly enjoy imbibing, Pen. But our new dean of the arts . . . well, she's something of a wine connoisseur. She brings in specially selected bottles—tells us all about their goûts de terroirs—and acts quite miffed when any of the staff refuses a glass."

"Since when do you care if you offend anyone?" Seymour demanded. "You offend *me* all the time."

"The dean is quite a find for the university. Rhodes Scholar, Educator of the Year, the President's Committee on the Arts and the Humanities, for pity's sake. All those accolades make her a force to be reckoned with."

Brainert sighed. "Dr. Irwin, the head of the campus chapter of Alcoholics Anonymous, politely refused wine at the last meeting with a gentle suggestion that alcohol not be served at future gatherings. Suddenly, all of his classes are scheduled for *eight A.M.* next semester."

"But not you." Seymour shook his head. "You caved for an extra hour of sleep. Was it worth wrapping your brand-new car around a defenseless oak in Prescott Woods?"

"Be specific," Brainert countered. "I *hit* a tree. The car is hardly wrapped around it. And that tree happened to be an ash, not an oak—and it appeared to be dead already, so no harm done, excepting to my vehicle. Anyway, I only had the accident because I was driven off the road by a careless maniac who sideswiped my car."

"Well, I was at the accident scene and I didn't see any maniac," Seymour replied. "Just you and your car and the dead ash tree."

"That's because the woman who ran me off the road kept on going!" Brainert was hopping mad now. "Why, she didn't even stop to see if I was injured. The driver simply continued on her reckless, merry way—"

"Like a bat out of hell?" Seymour eyed his friend skeptically.

"An albino bat."

We all stared at him.

"Fine, don't laugh." Brainert waved his hand. "My poor attempt at humor."

Seymour scratched his head. "I don't get it, Brainpan. What's funny about a white bat?"

"Not a real bat, Mailman. Don't you see? It's a metaphor. The *van* was white."

My breath caught. "You were hit by a white van? Driven by a woman?"

"A big van, definitely white. You can see its paint on my car where she hit me. And I am fairly sure it was a woman behind the wheel."

"And the license plate? Was it from out of state?"

Brainert shrugged, then winced and rubbed his shoulder. "It all happened so fast I didn't get a look at the plate."

He eyed me suspiciously. "Why all the questions, Pen?"

I didn't tell him that I suspected the van that hit his car was Norma's. Jack Shepard was already convinced.

I told you, Penny. Norma breezed, now she's just a memory.

"Can you describe the driver?" I pressed, ignoring Jack.

"Slender, middle-aged, with short brown hair—I *think*," Brainert replied before explaining, "I didn't get a good look at the hair, since she was wearing a baseball cap. The driver was looking into the rearview mirror instead of the road. I suspect that's why the vehicle drifted into my lane and came at me."

Brainert shot Seymour an icy look. "So, as you can see, the accident had nothing to do with my meager imbibing of the sparkling grape."

"Where did this happen, exactly?" I asked.

"Near the junction with the fenced-in firefighting tower, right where the woods begin to get thick."

"That's the junction to Millstone."

"It's a lousy way to go to Millstone," Seymour noted, drawing on his mailman expertise. "Those twisting and turning back roads will get you there, eventually. But the highway zips you to Old Mill in half the time and a third of the mileage."

"That's true," I replied. "But the police aren't as likely to patrol those back roads looking for a white van."

That's when I broke the news about the theft at the Finch Inn. I explained how Norma had become a suspect, which was why I thought the van that struck Brainert's car might have been driven by Norma in flight to her sister's place.

A curious introduction, since Brainert did not recall ever meeting the woman before. Seymour was passing acquainted with Norma, since he and his ice cream truck were the reason Norma had come to Quindicott in the first place.

My aunt Sadie knew Norma better than any of us, and she was as stunned as Fiona. I wasn't surprised that my aunt took the same stubborn stance about Norma's innocence as the proprietor of the Finch Inn.

"Eddie Franzetti is completely off track," Sadie insisted. "Norma is such a sweet woman. Crusty, sure. Saucy, too.

But she knew about books—and the kind of people who love them."

"Wait a minute," Brainert said, surprised. "Are you saying she worked here?"

Sadie hesitated before answering. "One day a week Norma . . . helped us out."

Brainert frowned at my aunt's careful choice of words. "What do you mean by that exactly? She was employed, right? You paid her, didn't you?"

"In a way," Sadie said sheepishly. "You see, she already had two other jobs in town, but Norma had heard from Fiona that Buy the Book was short of help on Sunday—"

"My day to spend with Spencer," I explained.

"So, I had Norma fill out the standard application. When she was done I looked it over and hired her on the spot." Sadie shook her head at the memory. "But then that woman surprised me. When I told her what she would be paid, Norma told me she didn't like the salary."

"What did she want for part-time work?" Seymour cracked. "A 401(k) and a pension?"

"No," Sadie replied. "Norma wanted to be paid in books."

CHAPTER 11

Finders Keepers

A good traveler has no fixed plans and is not intent on arriving.

—Lao Tzu

SEYMOUR LAUGHED. "PAID in books, huh? That's a unique tax dodge."

I spoke up. "Norma also bought a lot of books. Right off the shelves, and special orders, too."

"Maybe we should check the titles of those purchases," Seymour said.

Brainert threw up his hands. "Now, why would we do that, for goodness' sake?"

"Because . . . if she bought *An Idiot's Guide to Burglary*, or *How to Fence Stolen Goods*, or even a book by Bill Mason, then I think we may have found our culprit."

"Bill Mason?" Brainert cried. "I read *Confessions of a Master Jewel Thief* myself. Does that make me a suspect?"

Seymour smirked. "Nope. You have the perfect alibi. You were drunk as a skunk."

Brainert sneered but said nothing. Seymour swung around to face me.

"What's Norma's last name, anyway?"

"You're the one who brought her to town," Brainert huffed. "Don't you know?"

"Hey, give me a break, Brainpan. Norma lives the van life. I don't know her last name because the United States Postal Service doesn't deliver mail to transients—only their PO boxes, when they have them. I'm sure Pen knows her name, though."

Seymour and Brainert both faced me, and I drew a blank. I only knew her by what some folks around town called her, though I was too polite to refer to the woman as "Norma the Nomad."

"*Stanton*," Aunt Sadie said with a decisive nod. "I remember now. Her name is Norma Stanton."

"Miss or missus," Seymour pressed. "Single, divorced, or widowed?"

This time Sadie and I both drew a blank, and I suddenly realized how few facts we actually knew about the history of Norma Stanton.

My aunt must have drawn the same conclusion, because she began to reminisce aloud.

"I remember the day she came two years ago. Norma's van was following Seymour's ice cream truck down Cranberry Street, towing that funny-looking teardrop trailer."

I remembered that day, too.

Norma arrived the same day as the crows. It was late October—almost Halloween—when the townsfolk woke to find that thousands of those ebony-feathered birds had taken over our quaint little town.

"MOM!" MY SON cried. "The bus driver said they canceled school!"

I was kneeling on the plank floor of my bookshop, assembling a display for the new John Grisham hardcover, when Spencer burst through the front door. My aunt followed him inside a moment later. Each time the door opened, the raucous *caw-caw-caws* of a thousand crows drowned out all other sound.

"Since school's closed, I'm going upstairs to play video games."

Spencer dashed past me and was on the stairs to the second-floor apartment before I could question him. That left it to Sadie to fill me in.

"The driver told me Principal McConnell sent him around to inform everyone school has been canceled because of the crows—"

"Because of the crows?"

"The woman said the playground is covered with birds. The crows took over the swing sets, the climbing bars, the sliding board, the bullpen, and all the benches around the Little League's baseball diamond."

"But they're just our fine feathered friends," I replied as I stuck Mr. Grisham's head onto the tube cloaked behind his standee body. "I'll bet the administration would be just as frightened by a horde of toddlers converging on the place as they are of the crows—"

Hah, I know I would, cracked Jack. *Be scared, that is. Kids carry disease.*

"Or maybe the principal watched Alfred Hitchcock's *The Birds* once too often," I continued, ignoring the voice in my head.

"I don't think the principal is wrong," Sadie replied with a barely suppressed shiver. "I just walked along Cranberry Street on my way back from Bud Napp's hardware store. You would not believe what I saw. Those birds are everywhere, squawking so loud you can't hear yourself think.

"They're crowded together on sagging telephone wires. Crows are on roofs, store signs, and streetlights. In the town square the birds took over the benches, the chess tables—even the gazebo. And yes, they're perched on our brand-new sign, too."

Sadie went quiet for a moment, her eyes focused on the street outside. Suddenly she pointed. "Will you look at that."

Peering through the display window I saw Seymour pulling up to Buy the Book in his ice cream truck. Parking right behind him was a white van towing a teardrop-shaped trailer.

As we watched, a lanky, middle-aged woman in a flannel shirt, denim overalls, and a baseball cap exited the van holding a half-eaten chocolate-covered ice cream bar.

When Seymour spied us through the window and waved, Sadie and I went outside to greet him and his new friend. We had to speak loudly to be heard over the bird cries.

"Can you believe these crows?" Seymour shouted. "All we need is Tippi Hedren, and we've got Hitch's sequel!"

"What are they looking for in Quindicott?" Sadie replied. "Don't crows eat dead things, just like vultures?"

"They're carrion birds, for sure," said Seymour.

Sadie hugged herself. "It's creepy."

Seymour's new friend didn't think so. "The fact that they commune with the dead is what makes crows and ravens so special," she said with the excited enthusiasm of a motivated teacher. "The Vikings believed these birds were envoys sent by Odin himself to bestow some great wisdom to the human race. In Celtic mythology, crows and ravens are interchangeable, and both are believed to carry messages between the realms of the living and the dead."

"But what's their message?" Seymour asked.

The woman smiled, green eyes twinkling beneath her baseball cap. "Sometimes you just have to watch them, listen to them, and maybe you'll understand."

I didn't know quite what to say to that. Thankfully Seymour stepped in.

"This is Norma," he announced. "She saved my skin just now, out on the old rural route from Waverly."

"Come inside," Sadie said. "It's quieter in the bookstore."

Norma was immediately taken with Buy the Book. Her eyes wandered across the parade of covers and spines almost as soon as she entered. After some small talk, Norma excused herself to use the restroom at the back of the store, and Seymour told Sadie and me how they met.

"I was driving my truck back from Waverly, where I picked up a huge consignment of frozen treats. I took the back roads to avoid the highway since my truck doesn't exactly move at the speed of a Formula One race car.

"So, I'm out in the middle of nowhere when suddenly the engine cuts out. I could not figure out what was wrong, but I did know two things: I was stuck, and the freezer had stopped working along with the engine."

Seymour frowned. "You would not believe how hard it is to find a tow truck big enough to tow another truck. I was calling everywhere and getting nowhere. Meanwhile hundreds of dollars of frozen goodies were ready to melt.

"I was cursing myself for getting into the ice cream business when Norma pulls over and asks if I need help. Before you know it, she'd unloaded a gas-powered generator from that teardrop trailer she's pulling. Like some expert, she hooked it up to my electrical system and restarted the freezers."

Seymour sighed. "It took over an hour for the tow truck to arrive, but Norma stuck with me the whole time. When the tow truck driver finally showed up, he glommed onto the problem—it was just an electrical cord that came loose. Anyway, he fixed the truck on the spot without towing it, and here we are."

Norma returned with a sunny smile. She'd removed the baseball cap to expose a brown pixie cut. Though her hair was lightly streaked with strands of gray, she had few wrinkles and wore no makeup. Her face looked fresh with glowing skin and cherub-like cheeks, and when she spoke her animated expressions and bright green eyes appeared to tap into a flowing stream of positive energy living inside her.

"This is a charming place you have here, almost magical," Norma gushed. "I can feel the good vibes. And that is some space attached to the store. Do reading groups meet there?"

"A lot of them," Sadie replied with a note of pride. "There's two or three groups who meet almost every week."

"Where are you from?" I asked Norma.

The woman shrugged. "I travel everywhere and nowhere."

"I mean where do you live," I pressed.

"In my van," Norma replied, as if it were the most common thing in the world. "There's 'nowhere to go but everywhere.' So I just 'keep rolling under the stars.'"

"That sounds familiar," Sadie said. "Is that from—"

"Jack Kerouac, *On the Road*—the *original* scroll."

Sadie nodded and returned her sly smile.

Norma turned back to me. "Wherever the road takes me, that's where I call home—and that's *my own* quote!" She winked.

"I respect your free-spirit spirit," I said, "and your love of Kerouac, but where are you rolling *at the moment*?"

"I'm heading for Maine. I heard from a road buddy about a warehouse hiring seasonal workers. Most nomads head south or west for the winter, but I actually like cold and snow. It's what I grew up with. Anyway, jobs for folks like me are plentiful around the holidays, and the Evergreens Campground in Solon offers year-round accommodations with water and electricity hookups."

Seymour jumped in.

"Because she helped me, poor Norma is behind schedule and will never make it to Maine tonight. I suggested she stay around here, but she needs a place to park her van and trailer. Trenchers' Campground up near Picket's Farm should work for her, don't you think?"

Sadie shook her head. "It's closed for the season. Annie Trencher was in here yesterday. She told me she and her husband already moved with their kids back to their place in town."

"Rats, what rotten luck," Seymour said.

Norma touched his big shoulder. "Don't worry. I'll find a place. There are plenty of roads out there and a lot of woods, too. I'll find a spot."

"I won't have you shivering in the wilderness," Sadie insisted. "Not when we can help. Let me make a quick phone call . . ."

And that's exactly what she did. Sadie called our pastor, Reverend Waterman, who agreed to her idea of letting Norma stash her van and trailer in the church parking lot.

He even allowed her to use the restroom and shower in the church basement.

Norma was grateful for the help.

Problem solved—with a little ecclesiastic charity and auntie ingenuity.

CHAPTER 12

Back to the Present

Birds are indicators of the environment. If they are in trouble, we know we'll soon be in trouble.

—Roger Tory Peterson, Environmentalist

"ALL I REMEMBER about that day are those crows taking over the entire campus," Brainert said. "They flew away in a day or so, but the mess they left in their wake was appalling—"

"They crapped all over your ivory towers, eh?" Seymour said.

"Yes, they did," Brainert said, not amused. "Along with the chapel, the Hall of Literature, and the statue of Saint Francis himself, those fiends."

"We got a raw deal, all right," Seymour agreed. "All those birds and no Tippi Hedren."

Brainert huffed. "Hitchcock may have been the master of suspense, but even he didn't dare show the aftermath of an actual bird infestation."

"We're lucky the crows didn't make a winter roost here," Seymour added. "Not long ago, when they stayed in New Haven instead of flying south, they caused thousands of dollars in damage and a major public health crisis."

"My goodness, I didn't know that," Sadie replied, impressed. She smiled at Seymour the way she used to when he was thirteen and offering to help her carry home her groceries. "But then our local *Jeopardy!* champ has always been a fount of knowledge."

As Seymour preened, Brainert sniffed.

"You call that knowledge? More like trivia. And he wouldn't have earned any points for it, either, since he failed to put it in the form of a question."

"Here's a question for you, Brainpan. How would you like a trip to the moon, Ralph Kramden–style?"

While the professor and the postal worker played verbal badminton, Jack began pumping me for information.

Give me the skinny, doll. The crows flew south but the vagabond stuck around. What's the why and how of that?

Norma changed her plans and wintered in Quindicott, that's all. Maybe she did it because her sister lives nearby. All I know is that she chose to do it two winters in a row, so she must like our town.

Okay, but that still doesn't tell me how your bird—who flew the coop with a Halloween sack full of gems—ended up working at the Finch Inn.

That happened right before Thanksgiving the first year she was here, I explained. *Fiona's full-time maid suddenly quit, and Fiona was desperate to find a suitable replacement. Norma did competent work at some small repair jobs Barney hired her to do around the property, so Fiona offered Norma the maid position. The job came complete with free meals and a room at the inn.*

Working at a busy inn is an odd job for a woman who lives a life of solitude, Jack pointed out. *Or maybe she just liked Fiona's grub—*

Now that you mention it, Jack, there must be a better reason than room and board.

Not necessarily. Three square meals on a round plate and a warm place to bunk can feel like a touch of heaven for someone living on the road. Which makes me wonder . . .

What?

Why Norma would throw away Fiona's sweet deal and the cinch job she had at your bookstore for a bunch of jewels she can't pawn without getting made. Those rocks have a history, and it's likely that everyone in the jewelry trade knows it.

"Earth to Pen."

I blinked and realized Seymour was looming over me.

"I was just saying good night, but you zoned out," Seymour said.

"Sorry, Seymour. Hectic day."

"Sure, I get it. You've got a lot on your mind. Anyway, I'm driving Professor Knucklehead to his place before he gets into more trouble. It's starting to drizzle, and I want to beat the storm home."

"Don't forget your books," Sadie said, handing Seymour a tote bag.

The departure of Seymour and Brainert was followed by a flurry of customers. The rush lasted about an hour, until the storm intensified to a point where no one wanted to venture out. Sadie took over, saying she would close the shop herself.

I was glad to be relieved of further duties, so I could check on my son. But before I went upstairs, I pulled out my mobile phone.

I needed to check on someone else.

CHAPTER 13

The Purloined Post-it

I made the reexamination . . . but it was all labor lost, as I knew it would be.

—Edgar Allan Poe, "The Purloined Letter"

THE "SOMEONE" I needed to check on was Fiona Finch. I wanted to know how she was doing, given the shocking events of today, and I secretly hoped for good news about Norma. Had she finally turned up with a logical explanation? Or had more jewels been discovered—somewhere other than the maid's cart?

I didn't think my innocent phone call would trigger tribulation. I was wrong. I barely got out my first question before Fiona began to wail—

"Oh, Pen, Norma is still missing! And I have no idea where she went. I *really* don't! I wasn't lying to Eddie, and I wasn't trying to mislead the state police, even though they don't believe me, either."

"Fiona, slow down. What are you talking about?"

"The Post-it note with the address written on it. The address of Norma's sister. I told Eddie I couldn't find it, and I still can't. It just . . . *vanished.*"

"Please calm down. Take a breath," I said, in a tone I

hoped would soothe her frazzled nerves. She sounded near hysterical. "So Norma still hasn't shown up or called?"

"No such luck. The state police searched her room for some clue about her sister's identity or address or another place she may have gone, but I don't think they found anything."

"Sounds like they were trying to be thorough."

"You don't know the half of it, Pen. They grilled me mercilessly, as if I were the accused. First they gave me a hard time because I didn't do a background check on Norma when I first hired her. Then they kept hammering me about the address until I felt like a fool." Fiona sighed heavily. "I couldn't even remember Norma's sister's name, never mind the address. I only recalled that the woman lived in Millstone."

"And you're sure you had it written down on a Post-it note?"

"A yellow one," Fiona replied. "It was stuck to the side of the computer monitor forever. Now when I finally need it, the thing is gone. The state police made me clear the whole reservation desk and empty all the drawers. They even looked under the throw rug and through the trash, but it was a complete waste of time. The note had vanished into thin air, like a nasty trickster ghost!"

Nasty ghost! Jack took offense. *Mother Machree, all this fuss over a lost letter?*

Not a letter, Jack, a Post-it note.

A postal note IS a letter!

I gritted my teeth. *Who's on first?*

Back to vaudeville, are we?

Quiet, Jack!

While the ghost and I silently debated the difference between a trademarked sticky note and a postal letter, Fiona continued fretting in my ear about the state police visit, and I felt for her. Her tone carried so much anxiety, I worried she'd have a stroke. Then, after a pause, she seemed to recover. Lowering her voice, she confided something strange.

"I haven't said a word about this to anyone, Pen, certainly

not to the police—but the note disappearing like that . . .
Well, it makes me wonder."

"Wonder what, exactly?"

Fiona's voice dropped again, nearly to a whisper. "For
half an hour this morning, Norma worked the front desk."

"Does she usually do that?"

"No, never. But the gas man came to inspect the inn's
heating system and Barney was in the basement. I had to go
to Chez Finch because of a problem with a delivery. So, before Norma went off to clean the rooms, I asked her to sit at
the desk and cover the phones."

"Then you think . . ."

My voice trailed off and the conversation died for a moment. Finally, Fiona herself broke the silence.

"I think Norma took that note with her."

CHAPTER 14

Pillow Talk

A ruffled mind makes a restless pillow.

—Charlotte Brontë

AS VEXING AS this situation had become, it was dinner-time, and I had a son to feed.

Upstairs in our little kitchen, I ladled the slow-cooker stew of beef and fall vegetables into bowls (it smelled heavenly). After slicing up the French baguette that Sadie had bought that morning at Cooper Family Bakery, I called Spencer to the table.

He claimed he was too excited about his forensic project to have much of an appetite, but when that aroma of hearty beef broth hit him, he ate like a starving pup.

After dinner, Spencer bounded downstairs to help Sadie lock up. Then we all collapsed on the sofa and watched a rerun of an old *Shield of Justice* episode on the Intrigue Channel (Spencer's choice since he'd become a devoted fan).

The show was based on the bestselling *Jack Shield* hard-boiled detective novels, which in turn were based on the real case files of private investigator Jack Shepard. How that happened is another story, but it remained a sore point for my ghost, who never could stand the author of the *Shield* books, a yellow journalist from his time.

Still, I noticed Jack always stuck around when we watched the reruns. Jack's body may have died, but his ego lived on, and it was quite opinionated. Few things the TV dick did (from how he questioned a suspect to how he held a gun) met with the dead PI's approval.

I did my best to ignore the ongoing cracks about the "baloney" the show was slinging. But I noticed the ghost couldn't fault the curves on the "tomatoes" the show continually cast as "dames in distress."

By ten thirty, I had tucked Spencer into bed, Jack had disappeared, and Sadie was sipping tea, engrossed in an advance copy of Amanda Pilgrim's new novel.

"How is it?" I asked.

"Brilliant, as usual," she pronounced, unwilling to tear her eyes from the page. "Customers will be lining up for this one."

"Good news, Aunt Sadie, and—good night."

"Good night, Pen."

After taking a long, hot shower, I pulled on my nightgown and considered doing some reading myself. But the day had exhausted me. My thoughts were still twisted over Norma, and my nerves were shot. I hoped a night's sleep would put some of the raw emotion behind me, and I was more than ready for the shut-eye. Yet, as soon as I closed the bedroom door, my detective spirit woke up.

So, you're still willing to bet Norma is as innocent as the day is long?

"Hello again, Jack—and, yes, I am."

Even after your bird-lady innkeeper friend has no explanation for a note that vanished right under her nose—a note that happened to be the only record of Norma's next of kin.

I crawled under the covers. "Talking about a mystery won't solve it."

But it's an important twist, don't you think?

"Maybe it is, Jack. Or maybe it isn't. Either way, I'm not mentioning it to Eddie."

You're withholding evidence from your cop friend?

"I'm withholding judgment. And it's up to Fiona to tell him. It's her account of what happened, not mine."

Stifling a yawn, I pulled the sheets up to my chin. Outside, I could hear the rain starting back up against my windows, a slow pitter-patter that grew into an unsettling pounding.

Sorry, honey, I'm not letting you off that easy.

"Why am I not surprised?"

The vanishing note suggests a theory.

"Okay, I'll bite. What theory?"

When Norma took her wrong turn, she had a road map.

"English please."

If your book-whispering housekeeper made light fingers with that note, it shows intent. It proves Vagabond Velma was planning the heist before she pulled it off.

"I still don't believe it," I replied, though with far less conviction.

Like it or not, that's the conclusion the coppers will come to.

I punched my feather pillow like a light heavyweight, then sank back into it. "I just don't get it, Jack. Norma had a job here—two jobs. She had friends, a place in the community. Why would she throw it all away?"

Maybe that stuff means nuts to someone living out of a tin can on wheels. Maybe she didn't want a job, friends, a community. Maybe down deep she's a Greta Garbo and wants to be left alone—and maybe that's the motive you're looking for.

"What do you mean?"

Maybe Norma saw those rocks as a ticket to a future where she never needed a job again, never needed people, where she could just drive and drive and never stop.

"You think Norma was trying to buy freedom?"

Isn't everyone?

"No. Not if it means leaving a community of friends and risking prison. But in Norma's case . . . I have to admit, I don't know . . ."

Another yawn came over me. This time I didn't stifle it. Then Jack fell silent, and I considered those jewels again.

The vintage diamond set was stunning—and its attachment to that legendary film sex symbol Rudolph Valentino made them especially valuable. Did Norma know that when Peyton Pemberton checked in? Or did she simply spy the diamonds in the young woman's room? I cringed at my own questions. I was already convicting Norma of the crime. And if she *was* guilty, didn't the ghost say something about her being in danger?

"Jack?" I yawned again. "Are you still there?"

Never left, baby.

"Earlier today you told me those jewels had a sketchy history."

To put it mildly.

"What do you know? Will you tell me the story?"

Tell you? I'd be talking all night. Better I show you.

"In the book business, they do say showing is better than telling."

Then close your eyes, Penny, and I'll start the show.

CHAPTER 15

No Business Like Jack's Business

Look on every exit being an entrance somewhere else.

—Tom Stoppard

**The Martin Beck Theater
New York City
November 1947**

I WAS LYING in bed, eyes closed, ears listening to the rain, when, clear as the bell on my morning alarm, I heard a woman's refined theatrical voice announcing—

"*Tears*, Mr. Shepard. That man stole my tears."

Opening my eyes, I found myself standing in a basement corridor lined with dressing room doors. I knew they were dressing rooms because each door had a named painted on it, right beneath a gold star.

My nightgown was gone, and I was now costumed in vintage garb, including a below-the-knee dress, girdle, stockings, and snow-white gloves. The murmur of a large crowd filtered down from the floors above, while beneath me, the black floorboards had been painted with a stain so glossy they reflected the harsh light from the big naked bulbs, which appeared to be screwed directly into the celling.

Suddenly, a dressing room door swung open right beside me.

"Excuse me, miss."

The regal voice, deep and godlike, shook me out of my paralysis.

"Sorry, my bad," I muttered, allowing the athletically built man to pass. His electric blue eyes met mine for a brief moment, and I experienced a second wave of shock. This handsome actor was a legend, one I'd seen many times in Hollywood epics—but never this young!

"Hey, Hes," another voice, more relaxed and friendly but just as familiar, called from the next doorway. I recognized the slender, smiling man immediately, though he was also younger than I remembered.

"What can I help you with, Tony?"

"The gang is heading over to Sardi's for a drink. Care to join?"

"Sorry, I have a previous engagement."

"Ta-ta, then. See you tomorrow."

"Tomorrow, Mr. Randall," the blue-eyed man said with a loose salute.

Then I gawked in awe as Ben-Hur and Felix Unger headed down opposite ends of the hallway. That's when I heard another man talking from behind a third dressing room door, this one marked SYBLE ZANE.

"And just how am I supposed to recover stolen tears, Miss Zane? You want me to track down leads to a silk hankie?"

The door may have muffled the gruff voice, but I recognized the hard-boiled ghost's sardonic attitude in a heartbeat. It was Jack. At least, I was ninety-five percent sure it was him. The reserved five percent evaporated when Syble Zane's voice answered—

"Don't be droll, Mr. Shepard. I'm not talking about emotional tears. I'm referring to teardrop diamonds—"

Turning the knob with my gloved hand, I barely pushed the wood, and the door practically flew open. My surprise entrance stopped the woman's words mid-sentence. As she gaped at me, I mirrored her expression—for several reasons.

Inside the cramped dressing room, I spied the steel struc-
ture of a man, impressively tall and powerfully built. He
wore a navy suit and red silk tie dotted with little blue clocks.
Fedora in hand, trench coat thrown over one crooked arm, he
stood toe-to-toe with the gawking girl, a shapely young
woman with full red lips who wore Cleopatra eye makeup
and practically nothing else!

I knew we were in the basement of a New York theater,
but the skimpy faux-Egyptian regalia the ingenue sported
looked more like the brazenly scandalous product of a pre-
code Hollywood film set.

At the sound of the opening door, the big man tore his
gunmetal-gray gaze away from the near-naked woman and
our eyes met.

That's when I experienced my third hard shock in as
many minutes.

You'd think I would have gotten used to these little dream
journeys by now, and mostly I had. But experiencing Jack
"in the flesh" was always a stunner. No matter how many
times the PI spirit took me back to his mean streets, the initial surprise (and yes, thrill) of actually *seeing* Jack Shepard's rugged face with the dagger-shaped scar slashing across
his anvil chin and feeling the pulsing energy of his larger-
than-life presence never got stale.

"Ah, Penny. There you are," Jack's low voice rumbled.
"You arrived at the sound of the bell. Miss Zane is about to
leave the gate and explain how I'm supposed to track down
and recover her stolen tears."

The woman gave me a hard look. She obviously saw me
as an unwanted intruder. Her big, brown, long-lashed eyes
held enough cold contempt to freeze my blood. Feeling like
a mouse in a cobra's sights, I simply stood there, not sure
what to do or say. But Jack did, and the chilly stare-off
ended with his warm introduction—

"This is my lucky Penny, Miss Zane. She's my secretary
and right-hand gal rolled up into one cute little redheaded
ball."

I caught my reflection in the dressing room mirror and

tried not to blush at Jack's assessment. I did look rather ador-
able dressed in the height of late 1940s fashion.

A formfitting Robin Hood dress of forest green, with
gold trim and matching buttons, hugged my curves and hit
me just below the knees. Matching green heels lifted my
feet; a coat the same shade hung over my arm; and perched
on my copper hair (at a jaunty angle) was a little green Sher-
wood Forest hat sporting an absurdly long feather.

"Charmed, I'm sure," Syble Zane said, though she obviously wasn't.

In fact, her animosity was almost palpable in the close
quarters of this cramped dressing room. Immediately dis-
missing me, she laid a shamelessly flirtatious hand on Jack's
manly chest.

"I need your help, Mr. Shepard. If I don't get those Tears
back, I'm ruined. I . . . I just don't know where to turn."

Miss Zane shot me a sidelong glance and smiled thinly. I
doubt Jack noticed our exchange. His attention was . . . elsewhere.

"There, there, Miss Zane. It can't be as bad as all that,"
Jack said, his deep voice practically purring.

Syble pulled him closer. "You can't know the trouble I'm in."

I cleared my throat—loudly—which elicited another hate-
ful stare from Syble Zane.

How could I be any threat to this woman? I wondered.
She was worldly. She was lovely—surely Jack noticed, because she was undressed. Her navel was right out there for all
to see. And that perfume! The scent filled my senses until I
was dizzy—and wanted to flee the room.

Unfortunately, escape was out of the question. Jack had
taken me back here, to the memories of his life, and I'd con-
sented to the trip.

"Now that Penny's here to take notes, perhaps you'd better tell me your story, Miss Zane. Start at the beginning,"
Jack said, detaching himself from her desperate grip.

"The beginning?" Syble Zane scoffed. "If you're a woman
in this business, the beginning is always the casting couch."
She paused to glance at her reflection in the mirror. Miss

Zane obviously liked what she saw. "I was luckier than most of the hopeless girls who drift into this city. Harry Amsterdam liked me. He liked me a lot. He liked that I wasn't as naive as I looked. He liked having me around."

"I get it," Jack said. "You're likable."

"Instead of a weekend doxy I became a regular."

"Sounds like quite the honor."

Syble raised a painted eyebrow and pinched Jack's lean chin with her manicured fingers.

"Wake up, Mr. Shepard. You'd be surprised at how many women would kill their mothers to be 'Harry's girl.'"

"Even so, it doesn't sound like it ended well."

"No, it didn't end well at all. But I knew it would end, eventually. I hoped I could hold his attention long enough to get a few juicy parts, claw my way up a few more rungs before he tossed me aside."

Her eyes narrowed, and she angrily shoved the chair out of her way with a dainty sandaled foot.

"Take a look around and you can see how well that went. A nothing of a part in a holiday turkey."

"Aw, stop crying the blues," Jack returned. "You're on Broadway, in a revival of *Antony and Cleopatra*. It's Shakespeare. That's classy, ain't it? What is there to bawl to your mama about?"

"I never had a mother, and I don't bawl, Mr. Shepard. Instead, I made sure I had an exit strategy. Call it a retirement plan."

She stepped around Jack and pulled a black-and-white photograph off the mirror. She handed it to the PI, who studied the image before passing it to me.

It was a portrait photo of Syble Zane wearing the now familiar necklace and earrings called the Tears of Valentino.

"Six months ago, Harry gave me those jewels as a gift."

Jack's eyes went wide. "He did like you a lot."

"Not enough to let me keep them," she shot back. "Yesterday, while I was doing a screen test at a studio in Ithaca, Harry entered my apartment—"

"He broke in?"

"No, he had a key. He used it to steal my necklace."

"You're sure it was Harry Amsterdam?"

"I'm sure. On account of the doorman, who saw him coming and going. He had a woman with him. She was wearing my necklace when she left the building."

Jack whistled. "That's tough."

"Brazen, that's what it is. That necklace and those earrings are quite valuable. They are more than pretty baubles. They are a part of show business history."

"Fancy that," Jack said with mock surprise.

"Those jewels are all I have after nine years of *acting*."

From the way she spat out the word, I could tell the "acting" Syble Zane referred to included scenes played off stage as well as on.

"Well then," Jack said. "I guess you better tell me all about those rocks."

CHAPTER 16

Silent Sobs

One doesn't dare to cry in America. It is unmanly here.

—Rudolph Valentino, *My Private Diary*

AS JACK AND I listened, Syble Zane began her story—

"You've heard of Rudolph Valentino, Mr. Shepard?"

"Sure," Jack said, "everyone remembers Rudy and his big gimmick—the Latin Lover."

"Latin Lover?" Syble Zane rolled her eyes at the phrase. "A moniker pinned on Valentino by the same sort of show business grifter as Harry Amsterdam."

"Stick to the script, Miss Zane. We were talking about Valentino and a pound of gems with his name on them."

"Oh, very well." Syble tossed her head and covered her Egyptian bikini with a powder-blue silk robe. "But you should know, Valentino wasn't born with a silver spoon. He started out as a penniless immigrant, living on the streets of New York. With luck and labor, he became the biggest silent movie star in the world. He was the most desirable man on the planet. Women swooned. And men either emulated him or hated his guts."

"Yeah," Jack cracked. "Hollywood has two species of

male. Peacocks and roosters. Go on, where do the diamonds
fit in?"

"Soon after he arrived in Hollywood, Valentino met an
actress named Jean Acker. The two had a whirlwind court-
ship. Valentino believed he had found his true love, but Acker
only used Valentino to get out of a scandalous romantic triangle."

"Sounds like a marriage made in Hollywood," Jack said
flatly.

"It was, Mr. Shepard. Like plywood sets and camera
tricks, her 'love' for him appeared to be a fake. Or at least as
fickle as the public's favor. On their wedding night, Acker
locked her new husband out of their hotel room."

Jack's laugh was bitter. "That's a tough break for the Latin
Lover."

"He was devastated," Syble said. "For months, Valentino
wrote Acker love letters and sent her gifts, trying to win her
back. But Acker refused to even see him, and their sham of
a marriage was never consummated. As you can imagine,
the press mocked Valentino for wearing his emotions on his
sleeve. It became a public embarrassment for him. Eventually Valentino moved on and he and Acker divorced."

"And the jewels?"

"According to Harry, Valentino gave them to Acker, one
of the many gifts he sent trying to win her back."

"So how did Harry Amsterdam get hold of all that
pricey ice?"

"Jean Acker lost her fortune in the stock market crash of
'29. By then, she and Valentino were long divorced, her acting roles had dried up, and not even Harry Amsterdam
could get her decent jobs. In desperation Acker pawned the
Tears to Harry for a loan she never managed to pay back.
Harry kept the Tears locked up in a safe until he gave them
to me."

Syble Zane tossed her head and flashed perfect white
teeth with a pair of incisors worthy of Dracula.

"Those Tears are mine, Mr. Shepard. I suffered enough

to get them, and I want them back. Find Harry. Choke those jewels out of him if you have to—"

"Now, just you hold on, Miss Zane," Jack cut in. "You're not thinking clear. It wasn't Harry Amsterdam wearing those jewels that the doorman saw. It was a dame, Harry's next doxy, right?"

"That's right."

"Then she's got the rocks, not Harry. Ah . . . You wouldn't happen to know the tomato's name? Better still, her address?"

"I don't know where she lives as I never associated with the hussy. In fact, I never even laid eyes on her. All I know is that she's a peroxide blonde named Thelma Dice."

"And is Miss Dice in show business?"

Syble Zane pursed her painted lips. "If she's not, I'm sure she'd *like* to be, or she wouldn't be hanging off Harry's arm. Miss Dice has got a good start. That I know."

"Yeah?" Jack cocked his head. "Tell me more."

"It's an old story, I'm sure. Pretending to be thrilled while that sweaty so-and-so slobbers all over her proves the hussy's got acting chops. Harry will find her a role somewhere, in something."

"If she is in the biz, this Thelma Dice is probably a member of the Broadway Guild."

Miss Zane shrugged. "Maybe. So what?"

"So I can find her." Jack's expression grew thoughtful. "On the other hand, the broad could have skipped town already. If she's smart, she already did . . ."

Unexpectedly, the door opened. A petite young woman entered and halted in surprise. The girl's dull brown hair hung limply down, half covering her face. And her plain beige dress hung on her thin frame like a stage curtain.

"I'm sorry, Miss Zane, I didn't know you had guests—"

The girl's melodious voice was impressive, almost regal, but we could hardly see her face. She kept it turned away from us, barely peeking through her hanging hair.

"What do you *want*, Cora?" Syble barked.

"The golden scarab fell out of your earring again. I found it in the hall—"

Syble's hand went to her ear to confirm the girl's report. "Just put it on the dressing table."

"I could take it to the costume department, Miss Zane," Cora earnestly offered. "I know you like to wear it outside the theater, I just thought—"

"Stop thinking and leave it on the table. I'll fix it myself."

Cora nodded. She set the tiny gold beetle on the desk. Then with shoulders slumped in a near-successful attempt to make herself invisible, she crept out of the room, quietly closing the door behind her.

"Freak," Syble Zane muttered. Then she faced Jack, all business again.

"You were saying, Mr. Shepard?"

"I'll take the job, Miss Zane. Should be a cinch. My rates are—"

"I don't give a hoot about your rates," she declared with an arrogant toss of her head. "I'll give you five hundred dollars right now, and another five C-notes the moment you put the Tears of Valentino back into my hands."

Jack pursed his lips in a silent whistle, and I knew why. His typical rate was twenty dollars a day.

"Well then," he said, slipping on his fedora, "why am I wasting time flapping my gums with you?"

AS SOON AS Syble paid him, Jack hustled us out of her dressing room.

"You know, I'm surprised at you," I said as we strode down the hall.

Jack stopped in his tracks. "Come again?"

"Be honest. Syble Zane is an awful human being, but she had you wrapped around her fake Egyptian pinky, didn't she?"

"Stop slingin' baloney—"

"Did you notice how she only got modest after I arrived?" I stared square into his eyes, something I usually couldn't do. "Admit it. You didn't start thinking straight until she put on that robe."

"Are you saying that dame rewired my brain?" Jack waved his hand. "Nuts to that."

"Fine. Pretend I'm wrong. Frankly, I'm shocked you believed her sob story."

"I didn't believe her story," Jack said. "I believed her five hundred smackers."

"You and Sam Spade. Only with Sam it was two hundred."

"I don't follow."

"You would if you read *The Maltese Falcon*."

"Do I look like the kind of Alvin who reads bird manuals?"

"It's not a bird manual! *The Maltese Falcon* is a classic piece of American literature, written by Dashiell—oh, forget it! Just know this. I can tell she's trouble."

Jack pushed back his fedora, put his hands on his hips, stared at me, and shook his head. "Dames."

His exasperated response triggered a memory.

"Speaking of dames, remember back at the Finch Inn, when Peyton Pemberton was crying over her lost Tears? She mentioned she'd inherited them from her 'Great Aunt Cora,' an acclaimed stage actress who ran her own theater company. I know Cora is a fairly common name, but was that young woman we just encountered Peyton's great aunt? Did she have anything to do with those jewels? She didn't steal them, did she? Or do something even worse to get them?"

"Good questions. But answers are never easy in this game." Jack folded his arms. "You want answers, you'll have to come along for the ride."

"I'm here, aren't I?" With a hand on one hip, I met his hard gaze. "So what's next? Now that you've got a pocket fat with Syble Zane's money, where are we going?"

"To spread some of that dough around."

"Let me guess. You're going to buy me dinner at Sardi's."

"Maybe in your dreams."

"That's kind of where we are, Jack."

"Fine. When the case is closed, I'll buy you dinner at Sardi's. But right now—"

With Jack's abrupt silence, I realized his attention had strayed. Turning my head, I spied what he was staring at— or rather *who*.

"Excuse me, miss!" Jack called, moving past me.

Cora tried to hurry away, but Jack's long legs caught up fast. After introducing himself and his profession, Jack offered the girl five dollars for five minutes of her time.

With a silent nod, Cora took the money and shoved it into her dress pocket. "What do you want to know?"

"For starters, what exactly do you do here, Cora?"

"I'm a production assistant. I work backstage." The young woman clutched at the limp lock of hair veiling half her face, as if to keep it in place. Only one blue eye was visible, and it avoided the detective's gaze.

"You like your job?"

"I'm grateful to have it . . . I've always loved the theater . . ."

"And how well do you know Miss Zane?"

"Well enough. I met her at the first rehearsal," Cora said.

Jack raised an eyebrow. "And?"

Cora shrugged her small shoulders. "She's always on time. She's never missed one rehearsal or performance."

"That's not what I mean."

"Well, that's all I have to say. All right? Can I go now?"

"Just one more thing, if you don't mind . . ."

Surprising Cora (and me), Jack gently reached out to cradle the woman's chin in one hand and push her hair back with the other. A jagged red scar ran down one side of the girl's face, splitting the eyebrow and ripping through her fine-boned cheek.

Cora shook herself free and stepped back.

"Not all of us take Syble Zane's path to the stage, Mr. Shepard," she said. "Some of us pay a high price for defending our honor."

"Who did that to you?" Jack demanded, sounding as outraged as I felt. "Harry Amsterdam?"

Cora slowly nodded. "I said no to Mr. Amsterdam's advances. And I paid the price. Now I'll never walk on a Broadway stage again."

"And yet you're *grateful* to stay here? Backstage, working in the shadows?"

Cora's head came up sharply and she finally met Jack's gaze. "I may not be able to walk onstage again, Mr. Shepard, but if I leave, the man who did this to me wins. And I'll never let that happen. Like I said, I've always loved the theater and I always will. I'm *grateful* to be close to the thing I love."

With that, Cora squared her small shoulders, turned on her heel, and made her exit.

Then so did we.

FEELING TERRIBLE ABOUT what had happened to Cora, I followed Jack through the stage doors and into the alley, stumbling over my two-toned 1940s heels to keep up with his long strides.

"What was all that about?" I demanded. "Questioning that poor girl, I mean? Were you out to prove I was mistaken? Okay, I admit it. My theory about Cora was totally wrong. I don't see how that shy, damaged young woman with no money or connections could have become a great stage actress or run her own theater company. Are you happy now?"

Jack shook his head. "You got my motive all wrong. I just wanted to ask Cora some questions. It's called background, doll. You wanna be a detective? Ask questions. And follow leads. You never know where they'll take you."

"Okay then. Where are they taking us now?"

"Downtown. We're going to see a man about a tomato."

"Listen, Jack, I'm fairly sure we're not heading to a farmers' market. Can't you be a little more specific?"

"We're going to talk with a bigwig from the Broadway Guild."

"Now? It's eleven o'clock at night. Won't the offices be closed?"

"Yeah, they keep banker's hours. And union president Clark Delbert is a gentleman and a real straight shooter. As such, he won't do us a lick of good."

"But—?"

Jack adjusted his fedora. "Look, sweetie, I'm not checking Thelma Dice's union papers or her last job application. I'm looking for the dame herself. I need to find out where she works, and if we get lucky, where she flops down at night. The joe we're going to see knows the real score, and his office never closes."

Jack walked ten blocks with me in tow, still getting used to my two-toned heels while gawking at the heavy vintage cars (as long as rowboats) and the spectacle of a Times Square that hadn't existed for eighty years.

Plenty of lights still dominated this crossroads of the world, but not all of them were neon and none included digital video displays five stories high. On the other hand, many of the old Broadway theaters weren't much different in appearance than they were when I lived in New York City. The movie theaters were something else again. Their façades were elaborate, with giant marquees that went up two or three stories, their entrances plastered with images—hand-painted posters of the movie's stars, scenes from the picture, or bombastic quotes praising it in huge letters.

I passed a theater premiering *Out of the Past* with Robert Mitchum and Jane Greer. Not two blocks away, John Garfield and Lilli Palmer were starring in *Body and Soul*. The "thirty-cent matinee" featured a second film, Robert Cummings and Susan Hayward in *The Lost Moment*.

We left Broadway and cut over to Seventh Avenue. Both the theaters and the crowds began to thin out. Below Fortieth Street, the avenue became a canyon of midsize office buildings of brick and granite with storefronts on the ground floor—dress shops, cafés, liquor stores, pharmacies complete with lunch counters, barber shops, newsstands, hairdressers, and occasionally staid, solid banks with brass doors and granite walls.

It felt strange not seeing a single one of those ubiquitous

phone stores from my time. No ATMs, McDonald's, Star-bucks, or vegetarian anything. And the air was laced with smoke—not just the tobacco smoke from the cigarettes every other pedestrian we passed was puffing on, but the sharp, heavy smell of smoke from coal- and wood-burning stoves that tenants used to keep warm in cold-water flats.

Just off Seventh Avenue on Thirty-Third Street, Jack made a sudden stop. We'd arrived, apparently, and I found myself in front of the type of establishment that was all too familiar in my time as well as Jack's, and enduring tradition that was not about to die out anytime soon.

I'm talking about the all-American dive bar.

With a theatrical flourish and a sly wink, Jack opened the frosted glass door and stepped aside for me to enter.

"Welcome to the Vagabond Café, honey. Watering hole for the weary traveler and a gritty little slice of my New York . . ."

CHAPTER 17

Vagabond Ways

Times are not good here. The city . . . has been buried
under . . . taxes and frauds . . . but it is better to live
here in sackcloth and ashes than to own the whole
state of Ohio.

—Lafcadio Hearn

JACK WAS RIGHT. The place was far from cozy.

The main room was dark, narrow as a railroad car, and
filled to capacity. The air smelled of stale beer and tobacco
smoke. A bar of worn wood lined with swivel stools ran
down the left side of the room. Booths dominated the right
side. Dozens of framed photographs, many of them auto-
graphed, hung on the walls—celebrities, I presumed, though
I recognized none of them.

The clientele—almost exclusively male—seemed to
come from every walk of urban life. Off-duty factory workers in dirty overalls hunched over their beers stood shoulder
to shoulder with office men in suits, shaking off the long
hours of toil by downing shots one after the other.

"They're getting a toot on before heading home to the
ball and chain," Jack explained like an anthropology professor tutoring his student in the rituals of a foreign culture.

The noise level was high—laughter and bold banter fueled by alcohol. I spied a few women in the crowd. Personally, I make no judgments, but I had no doubt Syble Zane would have waved a theatrical hand and pronounced them all "hussies."

"Why are we here, Jack? You said we were going to some man's office. This doesn't look like any office I've ever seen."

"Johnny Palermo likes to work informal," Jack replied, as if that explained everything.

"Who's this Palermo person and what does he have to do with the Broadway Guild?"

"Johnny keeps the theater owners in line and the union dues flowing. Sometimes that takes persuasion. Johnny is good at persuasion."

I was beginning to get the picture. "Are you sure Mr. Palermo is here?"

Jack leaned close to be heard over the crowd. "I told you. Johnny keeps odd hours. He's here, all right, but I'll have to slip the bartender a fin and find out if he's accepting visitors."

Before I could ask what a "fin" was, the PI caught the attention of the man serving drinks.

The bartender's bald head barely rose over the bar itself. He was an oddly built man, short and pudgy, yet with incongruously muscled arms of a kind one doesn't usually get tending bar. I assumed this fellow worked at another career on the side—a much rougher trade.

After a short conversation mostly drowned out by the raucous crowd, I heard the bartender bark to Jack.

"Johnny is in the back room. If you're bent on going in there, I got a suggestion."

"I'm all ears," Jack replied.

The man put his hand flat on the bar top and lifted himself up with his powerful arms, until he was nose to nose with the detective.

"Keep your eyes to yourself, shamus. That goes for the frail, too. There's lacework going on back there and no one likes peepers."

Jack nodded and slipped the "fin" into the bartender's apron. (It was a five-dollar bill.)

I found out the meaning of "lacework," too, when we entered the back room. The space was separated from the rest of the bar by a dingy curtain. Beyond that, there were six round tables, each filled with men playing high-stakes cards with piles of money and open bottles scattered in front of them. Their attention was so focused on their games that none of them looked up when Jack and I entered the scene.

The room had only one booth, at the very end of the space, occupied by a single middle-aged man in a striped suit and pomaded hair. As we approached him, I realized the man was playing solitaire. Besides the cards spread out, the only other thing on the table was a half-empty glass of water.

"Hello, Johnny."

"What's on your mind, Shepard?" Johnny Palermo asked, his eyes never leaving the cards on the table.

"I'm looking for someone who's a member of your union. An actress named Thelma Dice."

Johnny Palermo's cigar twisted in his mouth. "Cute little thing? Took the bus from Cleveland with dreams of Broadway? Arrived a brunette but she's a bottle blonde now?"

"Sounds about right," Jack said.

Johnny Palermo finally looked. Locking eyes with Jack, he shook his head.

"Never heard of her."

"Don't you hold out on me," Jack warned. "You owe me one for the Baxter thing."

"So what if I do?" Palermo returned to his game. "What do you want to find some burlesque prancer for? Looks to me like you already got a dame. She's easy enough on the eyes, nice and classy, too."

"This is business, Johnny, not personal. Do you know where Thelma Dice is? Where the woman works?"

Johnny Palermo laughed, but it wasn't because of Jack's question. He'd drawn the ace of spades. Clearly pleased, the man played it and flipped another card.

"You know something, Jack?" Palermo purred. "In this town a person who asks a lot of questions can get a reputation as a person who wants to find things out."

"What can I say?" Jack replied without expression. "I'm nosy."

"You should be careful, shamus. You're liable to get that thing cut off if you poke it in the wrong place."

"Look, Johnny—"

The sudden, disturbing sound of a table overturning, and glass shattering, was followed by an outraged cry.

"You stinkin' lousy cheat—"

A man in a black suit jacket, open to display scarlet suspenders, had jumped to his feet. The move knocked his chair backward. He followed its trajectory, pushing himself between me and Jack. I stumbled, almost falling off my heels, until my bottom slammed against a table.

The already quiet room went stone-cold silent when a shiny black revolver appeared in Suspenders' hand. Then the space exploded in a flurry of motion as most of the clientele immediately fled the scene. Jack was pushed away from me by the crowd. Johnny Palermo, his game finally forgotten, remained in his booth, an angry scowl on his face.

Meanwhile I was rocked again, this time by the fleeing masses. A bottle of Irish whiskey on the table teetered, and I grabbed it before it crashed to the floor. The bottle was nearly full and heavy in my white-gloved hand.

"Don't call me a cheat, you louse—"

Suspender-man waved the gun. The accuser, a much younger man with ruddy cheeks under ginger hair, naively stood his ground, his voice filled with righteous indignation—

"I saw you draw that ace out of your sleeve, ya four-flusher!"

"Yeah, and that's the last thing you'll see!"

Standing behind the man with the gun, I watched in horror as he aimed his weapon, preparing to shoot the ginger-headed boy. I couldn't let it happen. I had to do something! Raising the whiskey bottle in my hand, I swung with all my might.

I felt the shock of the blow all the way up my arm, heard a sickening clunk instead of shattering glass. I couldn't believe that the bottle didn't break. I couldn't say the same for the man's head.

He was on the floor—not dead, just dead to the world—when the short bartender and a much bigger man with a mashed nose burst through the curtain.

Palermo rose, still scowling. "About time you knuckleheads showed up. I should hire this dame to replace the both of you!"

As I set the bottle down, Jack ran up to me.

"Smooth move, doll!"

"I don't feel so good," I replied, suddenly weak at the knees.

"Well, you *did* good," Jack replied. "That's all that counts."

He eased me into a chair as Johnny Palermo approached us.

"Where did you find *her*?" the union boss said with admiration. "I didn't know the Marines recruited dames."

"She's my lucky Penny," Jack replied.

"You can say that again, Shepard. And you better thank her, too."

"For what, Johnny?"

"Since I owe you both for saving me from bribing more cops to get clear of a shooting, I'll grant you a favor."

"Yeah?"

"Yeah. I'll get you Thelma Dice's union application. It'll tell you everything you need to know about her, right down to her mother's maiden name."

CHAPTER 18

Fingering a Suspect

Contrary to common belief, the presumption of innocence applies only inside a courtroom. It has no applicability elsewhere.

—Vincent Bugliosi

I SAT UPRIGHT in the bed so suddenly that my blanket, comforter, and throw pillows flew in every direction.

"The application!" I cried, clutching my head. "The job application!"

I was out of bed and in my robe when, seconds later, Aunt Sadie burst through the door without knocking.

"Pen! I heard you yelling all the way in the kitchen. Did you have a bad dream?"

"No, Aunt Sadie, I had a revelation."

She touched my forehead with the tips of her fingers. "Are you feeling okay?"

"I'm great. But I have to ask you about something important."

Sadie nodded.

"Yesterday you told us the story about how you hired Norma to work Sundays in our store. You said Norma filled out our standard application, the one you downloaded from Forms.com."

"That's right, she did. I think I still have it, down in the storeroom files—"

Suddenly my aunt's eyes went wide behind her spectacles as she had the same revelation. "Oh my goodness, Norma must have written down—"

"The name and address of her next of kin!" I cried. "We may have had the information the police needed all along."

"Should I call Eddie?"

I froze, wondering what Jack would advise. Unfortunately, he was still sleeping or resting or doing whatever it was he did to re-energize himself after the draining experience of conjuring a dream from the memories of his past life.

"Let's make sure we have that application first," I replied, avoiding the question for now.

"I'm going down to the shop to find it," Sadie announced.

I poured myself some tea and began to serve up the slow-cooker steel-cut oats. As I was placing the bowls on the table, my son, Spencer, appeared.

"Hi, Mom."

"Hi yourself." I gave him the once-over, a busy mom's version of a fast preflight check.

"You look good," I concluded. "Sit down. The milk is already poured, and you have time for a helping of Aunt Sadie's honey raisin oatmeal before the school bus arrives."

Spencer didn't reply. Only then did I notice the frown etched across his young face.

"What's the matter? Don't you feel well?"

Spencer slumped into his chair and stared at the Crock-Pot in the middle of the table. He took his first bite of oatmeal and chewed, a pensive expression on his face. Finally, he ran one hand through his copper bangs and spoke.

"Mom, did you ever find out something bad about a person?"

Concerned now, I sat down in the chair beside his. "Sure, Spencer. People aren't perfect."

"Did you like that person?"

I thought of Norma, then my brain took a U-turn to another time, another person.

"I know people I like who may have done something bad," I said softly. *I may even have loved someone like that once*, I thought but didn't say. Instead, I hand-combed Spencer's hair and said, "It hurts to find out people have feet of clay."

Spencer blinked. "Is that like the cement shoes on the *Shield of Justice* show?"

"No, Spence. it's just another way of saying nobody is perfect. It comes from the Book of Daniel, where a statue was described as appearing powerful and strong, made of gold, silver, and bronze, but the feet were made of clay. The base was so flimsy and weak, it was easily smashed, and the statue destroyed. In other words, everyone has flaws, even the people you admire."

Spencer frowned and spooned up another bite. I could tell by his furrowed brow that my reply didn't address his problem, so I took the direct approach.

"What's up? You know you can tell me about it."

"Well," he began, "last week I heard Miss Merrimac tell the principal that someone was stealing her juice out of the refrigerator in the teachers' lounge. She said the person drank her cranberry juice and left the empty bottle every couple of days. She told the principal she was diabetic and needed her juice, like for in an emergency or something."

"I get it."

"Anyway, later that day I snuck into the teachers' lounge and took the empty bottle out of the trash—"

The subject of my son's science project suddenly loomed large. "Oh, Spencer, you didn't—"

"I lifted fingerprints off the glass," he replied with pride. "Later that day I got Miss Merrimac's fingerprints off her desk for a comparison, just like it says to do in all the books. They call it the process of elimination."

I sighed, figuring what's done is done. "And?"

"One set of prints belonged to Miss Merrimac, for sure. But I only found out who put the other print on the juice bottle yesterday. I was testing every teacher, and the very last one I checked was a match."

"Who is it?"

Spencer's frown deepened. "Mr. Burke."

My heart sank just the way Spencer's must have when he made his discovery. There weren't many men teaching elementary school, and Alan Burke, who'd just taken the job a few months ago, had become Spencer's favorite teacher in that short time. In fact, all the boys liked him. In an irony of ironies, it was Mr. Burke who had encouraged Spencer to enter the science fair.

I met Alan Burke at the first PTA meeting of the year, and he seemed like a smart young guy and a positive role model.

"I don't get it, Mom. Miss Merrimac is diabetic. She needs her juice. How could Mr. Burke do that? It's mean."

"Maybe he didn't."

"But his fingerprints are on the bottle. I kept the bottle in a paper bag to prove it—"

"Spencer, those fingerprints are what you call *circumstantial* evidence."

"Huh?"

"All the teachers use the same refrigerator, right?"

My son nodded.

"Come on," I coaxed, "you watched Jack Shield solve crimes. There are a lot of ways his fingerprints could have ended up on that bottle. Maybe Mr. Burke moved the juice out of the way to get his own lunch out of the refrigerator."

Spencer brightened. "Or maybe someone is trying to frame him!"

"I wouldn't go that far, honey, but it is quite possible he's perfectly innocent of juice theft, which I am sure is a misdemeanor."

"Then I shouldn't tell anyone?"

"No," I said. "What if you're wrong? Then you'd only cause hard feelings. I doubt Mr. Burke would be pleased to be accused of misdemeanor juice snatching by one of his favorite students."

I paused to let that sink in. "There's a lesson here, Spencer. Don't accuse anyone of a crime unless you're absolutely sure of their guilt."

Spencer actually smiled—but it was his crafty smile, the one he got right before he pulled a prank on his pal Amy. If that didn't set off my alarm bells, what he said next certainly did.

"That's it!" he cried. "I should try to find out who's guilty and *prove it* to everyone. Maybe I can catch them in the act!"

"Spencer, I don't think you should—"

A loud horn from the street below interrupted me.

"The bus is here!" Spencer cried, jumping out of his chair and snatching his backpack from the floor. "Bye, Mom!"

"We're not done talking about this!" I called after him. "Don't do *anything* until we do!"

He either didn't hear me or pretended he didn't. Either way, he was off to school, and I was suddenly off to the races. No sooner did my son depart than my aunt entered the kitchen, triumphantly waving a piece of paper.

"What is it?" I asked.

With a grin, she told me what she'd found.

Norma the Nomad's job application.

CHAPTER 19

Next of Kin

Every strike brings me closer to the next home run.

—Babe Ruth

"WHERE DID YOU find Norma's paperwork?"

"Not where it *should* have been," Sadie said excitedly. "That's why it took me so long. But I found it!"

"Did you check for her sister's name and address?"

Sadie shook her head. "Not yet. I thought we could do it together."

"It's on the back of the application—"

"I know, I know," Sadie replied. "Let me get my reading glasses on. Norma's handwriting is like chicken scratch as it is."

I vibrated with impatience as Sadie blew lint from the spectacles hanging around her neck and slipped them carefully over her ears. Finally, she turned the application over and peered down her nose at the handwriting.

"Dorothy Jane Willard," she read. "109 Forest View Road, Millstone, Rhode Island." Sadie squinted as she deciphered the handwriting, Finally, she looked up from the paper.

"Norma left the zip code and phone number spaces blank."

"It's okay," I replied. "That should be enough."

"So should we call Deputy Chief Franzetti?"

"Not yet. I think we should find out if the address is real."

"What are you saying? That Norma made up the address?"

The anxious expression on my aunt's face rivaled Spencer's. I could tell she wanted to keep believing the best about Norma, as much as Spence wanted to believe in his favorite teacher. But in Norma's case, the circumstantial evidence was mounting to a distressing level.

"Don't worry," I told Sadie, retrieving my laptop from the bedroom, "we can easily check the address on Google Maps."

I could only hope Norma hadn't done the same, and then used some random name and address when she wrote down her "next of kin."

"It's real," I confirmed, after typing in the address. "There's even a street view."

I called up the picture of the property, which was over two years old, the last time Google had photographed that tiny hamlet. A small garden fronted a two-story white clapboard house with lace-curtained windows on both floors. Two evergreen trees stood on either side of the entrance, partially blocking the first-floor windows.

"Now we know the address is real. Next, we have to find out if Dorothy Jane Willard is also real."

"In the old days, I would just check the local phone book," Sadie said.

"There are still phone books, Aunt Sadie, they're online now. The search engines use public records."

Unfortunately, my public records search came up with a dozen Dorothy Willards across the country. Only two were listed as Dorothy J. Willard.

"I found one in Palm Beach, Florida, and one in Vermont, but none in Millstone."

"Maybe she moved to Millstone recently," my aunt speculated. "She could be living with a friend or relative—one of her children or grandchildren."

"You know what? We don't have to guess." I powered off the notebook.

"You want to call Eddie?" Sadie assumed. "He can drive over to Millstone."

"He can, but if Norma *is* there, the sight of his police uniform will spook her. I won't. That's why I'm going over there myself. I'll leave for Millstone as soon as I get dressed . . ."

As I explained to my aunt, I was about to take the same advice I'd given to Spencer. Like Mr. Burke, his favorite teacher, Norma could be the victim of circumstantial evidence. And even if she was guilty, I still wanted to help her—or at least hear her side of the story and try to convince her to turn herself in.

Sadie nodded but she didn't look happy. "I'll take care of the shop. But I would be happier if you weren't going alone."

"Why, for goodness' sake?"

"Because you don't know what you'll find."

I took Sadie by her arms and looked her in the eye. "I'm going to talk to Norma—if she's there. That's *our* Norma, remember? She wouldn't hurt a fly."

Sadie's frown only deepened. "You may be right about Norma, Pen. But what if she has an accomplice?"

IN AN EFFORT to ease Sadie's fears, I made two phone calls.

Seymour said he'd be happy to go to Millstone with me, but only in the late afternoon, when he was done with his postal worker duties. I thanked him, but time was of the essence, and I didn't want to wait. Brainert had morning and afternoon classes and an evening lecture, so he was out of the picture.

Though my aunt offered to come, I insisted she open the shop.

"There's no need to be overly dramatic. I have a mobile phone with geo-tracking and I'm completely capable of calling 911."

Of course, I couldn't tell Sadie that I wouldn't really be going out to Millstone alone. I'd have a ghost detective with me. Okay, so Jack was still silent, after the dream he gave me had exhausted him, but I was sure he'd wake up if I really needed him. (Pretty sure, anyway.)

"Call me as soon as you know something," Sadie insisted thirty minutes later, as I headed out the door with Jack's Buffalo nickel tucked into its special little pouch next to my heart.

Though the highway was faster and more convenient, I decided to take the back road to Millstone—the one that ran past the abandoned fire tower and into the woods. It was the route Norma herself took yesterday afternoon when her van sideswiped Brainert's car.

The midmorning air was damp and cool, but the driving storm of the night before left cloudless blue skies in its wake. Once out of Quindicott's town limits and on the rural route, things turned a bit rugged. Dips and valleys in the road had been transformed into muddy pools, and I was forced to drive around several fallen branches.

Once I reached the outskirts of Millstone, I followed their main street through what passed for the business district. A poor stepchild of Quindicott, the hamlet of Millstone never recovered after its primary employer, a textile mill, shut down. More than half the businesses here were closed. Some buildings were even boarded up. Unlike thriving Quindicott, there was no movie theater, no library—the state had turned it into a records depository—no sign of economic activity in sight.

I turned off Millstone's main drag onto Whippoorwill Road. After buzzing by a row of dingy federal-style buildings of faded red brick, I reached Forest View, a narrow road that circled a tall hill on the edge of town.

Forest View was aptly named. On one side of the narrow street was a sheer wooded embankment, on the other side were the houses spaced widely apart, with more woods crowding the edges of their grassy yards.

I instantly recognized the white clapboard house from the Google image. The screen door was closed, but the interior door stood open, presumably to let in the cool morning air. The twin evergreen trees looked a little taller now, and someone had planted a late autumn bloom of purple flowers around the entire house.

I kept on driving, right past the house. The property had no garage or even a driveway, so I decided to circle the neighborhood in search of Norma's van. There were only a few houses along this road, a few late-model cars parked in front of them, and I quickly concluded that if she were here, Norma had hidden her vehicle well.

Returning to my original destination, I parked in front of the clapboard house and left the car, wondering what I was going to find. The street was deserted, the only sound the chatter of birds coming from the woods.

As I climbed the concrete steps to the front door, I noticed a sunporch was attached to the right side of the house. An evergreen tree had obscured it from the street view—and the Google car cameras. Like the rest of the house, the sunporch was fringed with purple flowers. Through the porch screens, I spied a jumble of potted plants. I saw movement, too. Someone was in there.

When I reached the front door at the top of the steps, I paused for a moment, just to listen. No sound came from the interior of the house. Taking a deep breath, I pressed the doorbell.

That's when all hell broke loose!

CHAPTER 20

The Chase

Dogs chase cars. But woe to the mutt who catches one.

—Anonymous

THE ECHO OF the doorbell's *ding-dong* barely faded when I heard a sharp *pop*, like a single firecracker exploding. Then came a loud slam that shook the whole house.

Someone had crashed through a door at the side of the house!

I flew down the concrete steps, practically jumping into the purple blossoms below. I raced around to the side of the house where the sunporch stood. I pushed through some unpleasantly wet evergreen branches, frantically looking for the person fleeing, but I saw no one.

What I did see was a tall line of bushes along the yard, separating the well-kept lawn from the wild, wooded area beyond. Some of those hedges were still shaking, as if someone had just passed through—and the ornamental birdbath was so recently overturned that tiny birds still squabbled around the fast-seeping water.

If I had any doubt someone had run into the woods, it vanished when a huge flock of startled birds suddenly flew up from the trees and took off into the blue sky, squawking angrily.

"Norma!" I cried as I crashed through the hedges. "If that's you running, please stop! It's me, Penelope McClure! I only want to talk to you!"

I could hear but still couldn't see someone crashing through the tangled brush ahead of me. Though the trees were mostly bare this late in autumn, high bushes, saplings, and evergreens blocked much of my view.

The lawn had been slippery from the storm last night, and I nearly fell when I'd crossed it. The forest floor was twice as treacherous, more mud than solid ground, and I began to slip and slide.

"Norma! Stop! Please!"

The noise ahead suddenly ceased.

"That's it! Wait for me to catch up," I called, slogging forward.

Unfortunately, I was dressed for work in a bookstore, not a hike through mushy woods. The sucking mud slowed my progress and threatened to pull off my ankle boots.

"Wait, Norma, I'm coming!"

At last, I pulled free from the sludge and lurched forward—only to have three shocking things happen in lightning succession. First I heard a firecracker pop. Then a cold wind whipped around me. The invisible force blew a thick dead branch in front of me so fast that I couldn't stop myself from tripping over it. My arms flapped like the wings of those angry birds, only I didn't take to the sky.

A split second before I landed facedown on the muddy ground, I heard another firecracker *pop*, then something slapped a tree where my head had been before I fell.

Showered with wood splinters from the trunk, I realized with a shock that someone had taken two shots at me!

That's right, doll, Jack roared in my head. *Lucky for you I was here to knock you clear!*

"Jack!" I cried (fully out loud).

Are you nuts? Running through the woods after someone with a gat in their hand?

"I thought I was chasing Norma!"

Well, think again, honey.

That's when I realized there were footprints in the mud. More accurately, boot prints—and big ones, too.

That foot's the size of a U-boat. Unless Norma joined the circus and got herself some clown shoes, those aren't her prints.

Again, I heard the snap and crackle of someone moving through the woods. I wanted to stand up for a better look.

"The shooter is getting away!" I rasped.

Stay down! Jack commanded.

Splat!

Another arctic blast pushed me back onto the ground—in the nick of time, as things turned out. Another *pop* and another *slap* followed. This time the bullet dinged a tree not two feet away.

I sputtered but stayed flat on my stomach until the sound of movement in the woods finally faded. I had no choice really. The branch I tripped over was now pressing on my back, applying just enough pressure to keep me pinned to the soggy earth.

Finally, the cold press eased.

Groaning, I pushed off the branch, rolled over, and sat up. I was shivering, a combination of post-traumatic shock and the fact that my clothes were soaked—the ones that weren't covered in thick mud the consistency of wet plaster, anyway.

"Are you crazy?!" I cried.

Me? You're the one acting like you ought to be fitted for a straitjacket. So don't argue with someone who knows better than you.

"Hmm," I replied. "And just what do you know better than me?"

I know that the person with the gun wins every argument. It's the law of the jungle. So, unless you've got a .38 tucked between those two—

"I get it! I get it!"

I climbed unsteadily to my feet. "Okay, Tarzan. Let's get

out of these woods and call 911. I'll report the shooter, and if we're lucky, we'll get some answers about Norma's so-called next of kin. The local police should be able to confirm who lives here. And if we find Dorothy Jane Willard inside, maybe she'll have some answers.

I slogged my way back to the hedges and pushed through the narrow gap the shooter had created.

The backyard was still peaceful, almost serene. Purple flowers bobbed in the breeze on high stalks. The tiny birds had given up on the overturned birdbath and flown away. That's when I noticed the sunporch screen door was standing open. And when I saw the inside of the porch, and what lay there, I stopped dead in my tracks—and *dead* was the operative word.

I was speechless.

Not Jack.

If that's your Dorothy Willard, she's not giving anyone answers, not with her brains scattered all over her nice, neat potted plants.

CHAPTER 21

Third Degree

There cannot be a crisis next week. My schedule is already full.

—Henry Kissinger

I THOUGHT I couldn't be shocked more than I'd been with the discovery of the corpse on the sunporch. But when I called 911, I learned that Millstone no longer had local policing. The town was struggling financially and decided to cut their force entirely, delegate their duties, and rely on the state or other jurisdictions when necessary.

Gut your police force? Jack cracked. *Gosh, what a swell idea. Why not just give felons a key to the city?*

The dispatcher assured me that a "community volunteer" would respond to my call in a few minutes. Meanwhile, as per the town's new police-free procedure, the operator summoned a law enforcement officer from a nearby jurisdiction to handle the preliminary investigation.

The community volunteer who showed up a few minutes later was a twenty-three-year-old school crossing guard who seemed just as unsettled as I felt. Her face was ghostly pale, and she looked like she was trembling under her yellow vest.

The tender young thing peeked into the sunporch once, then moaned.

When I asked, the young crossing guard allowed me to use the backyard garden hose to clean off the mud—a relief because it was getting mighty itchy, and the stuff in my hair threatened to cake. In that sense, I was lucky. No real police officer would have permitted me to potentially wash away evidence.

I was wet and cold but moderately clean when, fifteen minutes later, the officer from "another jurisdiction" arrived. I spotted the Old Q symbol on the police car and realized the other jurisdiction was Quindicott. A state police crime scene van pulled to the curb right behind my hometown police cruiser, and four officers exited the vehicle.

I was mortified when I realized that Quindicott policeman was Deputy Chief Eddie Franzetti.

"Oh, Jack. He's going to find out I withheld information from him—"

If he doesn't know already—

"Eddie is not going to be pleased with me."

Relax, doll. It doesn't hurt to have an ally with a badge.

"I'm not sure I have an ally. Not if I'm reading Eddie's expression right."

Disappointment was evident on the deputy chief's face, and something more. Was he angry?

If so, then Eddie already deduced why I was here. He approached me with a plainclothes policeman in tow, his badge swinging from a strap around his neck.

"Look, I know what you're thinking, Eddie, and I'm sorry—"

He abruptly cut me off. "This is Detective Toland, Pen, from the state police. He's going to be taking your statement."

Uh-oh, doll. Looks like you're right. The kid gloves are off. Your ex-pal Eddie has just thrown you to the staties.

Jack wasn't wrong, though things didn't start out too badly. Detective Toland noticed I was wet and fetched me a blanket from one of the police cars. Then he led me around to the front of the house and sat me down on the steps. He asked me to describe everything that happened, starting with why I was here.

With complete honesty, I explained my motive (to find Norma or speak with her sister). Then I took him through the timeline from the moment I arrived. He stopped me once in a while to clarify some incident—and he would then summon one of the uniformed officers to verify what I told him.

That took over an hour, and when we were finished, he had me write up everything I'd said and sign it.

Jack was quiet through the whole ordeal, probably because I was handling myself pretty well and Detective Toland was friendly and reasonable.

After the interrogation was over, Detective Toland called everyone together for a confab. He didn't seem to care if I overheard them. The crux of the discussion was that the state police verified everything I'd told them. The dead woman was indeed Dorothy Willard. They found her driver's license in her purse. She was a renter who'd lived at this address for the past two years, and there were no indications anyone else had been living with her.

They also found the boot prints in the mud and my face print, too. While one state trooper took casts of the boot prints, another tried to find the spent bullets, while a third followed the shooter's prints to the other side of the woods. There the mud-splattered trail ended at sparsely populated Grant Street, where the shooter presumably got into a car and drove away.

At that point two new men pulled up in a state police SUV.

The first newcomer was stocky, middle-aged, and wore a state police uniform. The other man was leaner, taller, and appeared to be much older. He was dressed in an expensive-looking suit and long black coat. With grim faces, the pair crossed the lawn in quick, aggressive strides and joined the huddle of officers.

The discussion immediately grew more animated. Finally, Detective Toland broke from the group and proclaimed in a loud voice—

"Everything Mrs. McClure told us checks out. I've got her statement, so I think we should cut her loose."

"Not so fast, Detective Toland—" barked the older man in the suit.

The rush of relief I felt evaporated when I faced this imposing stranger. Though he stood with stooped shoulders, he was tall enough to easily loom over me in his long black coat. He had a severely receding hairline, a gravelly voice, and a cantankerous disposition. He was also very unhappy with me—easy enough to deduce since he was glaring down at my head through half-slitted hazel eyes.

The stocky state police officer stepped up to join the older man, but he remained silent and seemingly disinterested, his bloodshot blue gaze aloof.

"This is Captain Rayburn," the half-bald man told me, loud enough for everyone to hear. "The Captain works out of a specialized unit of the Rhode Island State Detective Bureau. He will be overseeing this investigation as of now."

Detective Toland frowned at that but said nothing. His uniformed officers remained stoically impassive, too. But Eddie, who was local law enforcement and not under the jurisdiction of the state police, was not intimidated. He stepped forward to stand toe-to-toe with the stooped-shouldered bully, who hung over Eddie like a hovering buzzard.

"Who are you to come in here and take over?" Eddie demanded.

Seemingly astonished by the pushback, the older man's narrowed eyes opened wide, wrinkling his high forehead all the way up to his half-bald head.

"Who's asking," he growled.

Eddie stood tall. "Deputy Chief Edward Franzetti, Quindicott Police Department."

"You have no jurisdiction here, son, and I do. My name is Max Braydon and I represent Delaware Mutual Insurance, an international institution with a financial interest in this case."

Eddie's eyes narrowed. "You're looking for that stolen necklace, aren't you?"

"You mean a stolen heirloom worth in excess of three million dollars?" Braydon countered in a cutting tone of contempt. "Of course that's what I'm looking for."

"So, why butt in on a small-town murder case?"

"Don't play the Podunk hayseed with me, Franzetti," Braydon fired back, practically spitting out the *zetti* in Eddie's last name. "We both know the theft of the Tears of Valentino and this murder are directly connected."

Max Braydon turned his head. The morning sunlight reflected off his bald pate and his beady eyes skewered me once again. "And Mrs. Penelope McClure is connected to this case, too. I have reason to believe she participated in the crime."

"What?" I cried.

"Don't play the innocent, Mrs. McClure. You came here for a reason. To speak with this mystery woman, Norma Stanton, correct? Or maybe to collect your share of the take—"

"Don't be ridiculous," I sputtered.

"Or perhaps you planned to blackmail Norma, threaten to give her hiding place away to the police if you weren't properly rewarded for your silence. Why else would you withhold the name and address of this associate of Norma's?"

Braydon paused before adding, "The *now-deceased* associate of Norma's."

"That's enough, Braydon," Eddie said. "Penelope has been a respected member of our community since she opened her business. She was born and raised in Quindicott. I've known her all my life—"

"Which is why you are completely bungling this case. That incompetence ends now." Max Braydon faced Captain Rayburn's aloof form. "Have your troopers take Mrs. McClure into custody."

The captain's disinterest disappeared, and his bloodshot eyes sharpened. "On what charge?"

Detective Toland finally spoke up. "On *no* charge, Captain. We've investigated the scene and taken her statement. Everything Mrs. McClure told us has been backed up by the physical evidence. I was about to cut her loose."

I could see Captain Rayburn was stuck between a rock and a hard place. Braydon obviously had heavy political clout—and he was trying to throw that weight around—but the law was the law. And as far as this captain was concerned, the law won.

"Mr. Braydon," he evenly countered, "we have nothing to arrest Mrs. McClure for. There's no evidence she had anything to do with this crime or any other."

Brayden's cold sneer could have killed. "Then I insist you begin to *collect* that evidence. If I can't have the woman, I'll have her car. I want that vehicle impounded—"

"What?" I cried. "How am I supposed to get home?"

"I don't care if you walk," Braydon spat.

"But . . . why?"

"That vehicle must be thoroughly searched," Braydon replied. "For all I know, you may have already stashed the jewels inside some hidden compartment."

Max Braydon lowered his voice again.

"Believe me, Mrs. McClure. We'll find where you've hidden them. Even if we have to take that vehicle apart piece by piece."

After issuing his final threat, Max Braydon brushed past me, callously crushing a cluster of lovingly planted purple blossoms.

With Captain Rayburn in tow, the insurance investigator entered the sunporch and approached the murder scene. The corpse had already been removed. Only a tape outline remained.

The two men stood talking over that grim memorial, their voices too low to be overheard. As I strained to listen anyway, someone touched my arm.

"Come on, Pen," Eddie said. "I'll take you home."

CHAPTER 22

A Free Ride

I hate the world. Everything comes into it so clean and goes out so dirty.

—Cornell Woolrich, *Cover Charge*

"GIVE ME A MINUTE, EDDIE."

With a sigh, I pulled my phone from the pocket of my slacks. I made a quick call to Sadie on her personal cell because I didn't want to tie up the store phone. My aunt was obviously busy with a customer, so I left a voice mail message that I was okay and on my way back.

Eddie opened the police car door for me. Thankfully I was riding on the passenger side, and not in the back seat.

"Look, Eddie, I'm sorry I didn't tell you I found Norma's sister's address. I didn't mean to hold out on you, I just wanted to talk to Norma—"

"Without a policeman around." It wasn't a question.

"I didn't want to frighten her off."

"Norma would never have run from me, Pen. But you couldn't have known that," Eddie insisted. "Anyway, it's water under the bridge now. You didn't find Norma. Instead, you got yourself into a peck of trouble."

"I didn't talk to anyone. Someone killed Norma's sister the moment I arrived."

"Dottie Willard is not Norma's sister," Eddie said as he started the car.

"What?" I cried over the roar of the engine.

"They're not related. Dorothy Willard is an only child. She never had children, either. In fact, she was never married. I found out when I asked Detective Toland if the next of kin had been notified."

"What's her connection to Norma, then?"

Eddie shook his head. "None that I can find."

"Did they work together?"

"I doubt it. Dorothy Willard moved to Millstone fairly recently, about two years ago. She was raised here. Prior to that she worked on the domestic staff for some wealthy family in Palm Beach, Florida."

Eddie hit the gas pedal as soon as he left the outskirts of Millstone behind.

"While the crime scene unit was working, I went around the neighborhood and asked people if they knew Dorothy Willard, or if they'd seen a white van in the vicinity."

"Any luck?"

"Nobody remembered seeing Norma or her van," Eddie answered. "Dorothy Willard's closest neighbor said she never had visitors. Meanwhile, the guy up the block said he conversed only once with Dorothy, when he came across her while fishing in the woods. He said she was friendly enough, but all they did was make small talk."

"Anything else?"

"The woman on the other end of the block said she talked to Dottie Willard several times. Two weeks ago she mentioned to Dottie that she loved the flowers around her house. The next afternoon Dottie turned up on her doorstep with a bunch of potted plants. The woman wanted to pay for the plants, but Dottie said they were free, that she collected them in the woods—"

"What kind of plants?"

Eddie shrugged. "More of those purple blossoms, I

guess. The neighbor had them planted all over her yard just like Dottie."

"Do you think maybe Dottie Willard led the van life, like Norma, part of the year anyway?"

Eddie shook his head. "There's a Buick registered to her name. That's it."

"So, who murdered poor Dottie and why?"

That question hung in the air for a minute. Then I asked—

"How did Max Braydon find out about Dottie in the first place? What exactly led him to show up at her house today?"

"I don't have answers to any of those questions, Pen. I know as little as you do."

"Okay, then what do you know about Max Braydon?"

"The same answer. Nothing."

"Well, Eddie, don't you think you should find out? I mean, he had you thrown off the case, insulted you, and then decided I was the devil incarnate."

I saw a light go on behind Eddie's eyes. A moment later, he pulled over to the side of the road.

"Back in a minute, Pen. I have to make a phone call."

CHAPTER 23

On Hold

I will not be at the mercy of the telephone!

—C. S. Lewis (attributed)

"THIS IS RIDICULOUS!"

For going on twenty minutes, I'd been watching Eddie in the side-view mirror, pacing back and forth behind his police car, mobile phone plastered to his ear.

Don't get your bloomers in a bunch, doll. You'd be cuffed and booked and sitting in stir if that insurance hustler got his way.

"Well, I don't see why Eddie couldn't make his call in front of me. If it involves me, I have a right to know, don't you think?"

What I think is your copper friend figures that "next of kin" address involved him, and he had a right to know.

"You're saying turnabout's fair play?"

I'm saying your pal holds all the cards and you're playing by his rules now. He'll tell you what he wants to tell you when he wants to tell it—

My conversation with the ghost was cut short when the driver's-side door suddenly opened, and Eddie jumped behind the wheel.

"Were you saying something just now, Pen?"

"I was . . . talking to myself. Who were you talking to?"

"First I called Ben Clayton—"

"The notary on Cranberry Street?"

"He's a notary, sure. But Ben is also the biggest insurance agent outside of Providence. He peddles Delaware Mutual, among other products."

Eddie started the engine and rolled the police car onto the traffic-free rural road.

"So?"

"Ben told me all about Max Braydon. He's one of the most successful insurance investigators in the business. They call him the Hunter. At last year's Delaware Mutual Banquet, they gave Braydon an award."

"What else did he say?"

"Nothing, so I dug a little deeper," Eddie replied. "I called Detective Toland—"

"But he's off the case."

"Sure, but he knows all about Braydon. That award they handed him was a message that Braydon should retire. In the last couple of years, he's gotten sloppy—and aggressive. There have been complaints about his tactics, even a lawsuit."

"Well, he's obviously messed up big-time if he thinks I'm in on some jewel-heist conspiracy with Norma."

Keeping his eyes on the road, Eddie shook his head. "Braydon's wrong thinking Norma is guilty, too."

"Do you have some evidence I don't know about? Another suspect, maybe?"

"No, but I know Norma. Better than most."

"You've seemed convinced of Norma's innocence from the start, Eddie. Can you tell me why?"

Eddie sighed. "I guess I can, even though I promised Norma I wouldn't tell anyone."

Eddie stopped at the junction, then made the turn toward Quindicott.

"Do you remember when Rita Mae Charles retired last Christmas, after thirty years working at Greene's?"

"I sure do."

Greene's was a big-box store up on the highway, a sort of independent Target or Walmart. "My aunt Sadie thought maybe Rita got sick, seeing how she swore many times she would never quit. Rita bragged they would have to carry her out on a stretcher."

"It wasn't really her choice to retire, Pen."

Eddie told me that a couple of days before Christmas last year, Norma came into the station and handed him a manila envelope filled with money—big bills, small bills, all paper money adding up to twenty thousand dollars and change.

"She found it on the counter at the post office," Eddie explained. "Norma took one peek inside, saw the money, and came directly to me. Inside, I found the register receipts for Greene's and called the manager."

"What happened?"

"Rita Mae stopped at the post office to mail some Christmas cards before going to the bank. She got distracted and walked away without the money. She was getting addled, apparently, because she even forgot she was supposed to make the deposit drop at the bank."

"The folks at Greene's must have offered Norma a sweet reward."

"They did. Only Norma insisted that I keep her name out of it. She said she didn't want the attention, and she didn't care about the reward. She told me to turn over any reward to Reverend Waterman's substance abuse program. Norma made me swear to keep her involvement a secret, and I did until just now."

"Unbelievable," I said.

"You can say that again. That envelope was full of unmarked bills that were untraceable. Norma could have kept that money, easy."

"But she didn't."

"No, Pen. So why, a year later, would Norma steal jewelry? Even if it is worth millions of dollars, I just don't think it's plausible."

"That's why I went to Millstone, Eddie. I'm sure Norma is innocent, too, but I wanted to hear her say it."

We rode the rest of the way to Cranberry Street in silence. But after he pulled up to my bookshop, Eddie turned
to me for a final comment.

"Braydon may have taken me off the case, but I'm not
dropping it. If you find out anything, anything at all, tell me
you'll come to me."

I wanted to say no. Or cross my fingers behind my back.
But Eddie was too good a friend to refuse—or mislead.

"I will," I said (and meant it).

CHAPTER 24

Tearful Homecoming

Then, siren shrieking, they proceeded to do their stuff.

—Perry Paul, "The Jane from Hell's Kitchen,"
Gun Molls, October 1930

AFTER GIVING EDDIE my promise, I popped the car door, and when I finally walked back into my shop, it was close to three o'clock.

I felt incredibly guilty about leaving Sadie alone so long—completely alone since today was Bonnie's day off and Spencer was still at school.

I assumed business must have been brisk because I'd phoned Sadie twice to check in during my Millstone trip, and she never picked up or returned my call. I was ready to jump into action when I pushed through the door, but to my surprise the store was deserted, and my aunt was nowhere to be seen. More surprising, my friend Professor Parker was behind the checkout counter, a strained look on his long, pale face.

"Brainert? What are you doing here?"

"I came in to pick up a book I ordered," he said. "Next thing I know I get roped into this customer service job. You're lucky I've manned the ticket booth at my Movie Town

Theater on occasion and already knew how to work the register—not that there have been many customers in the last hour."

"You've been here that long?"

"Probably longer. I did wait on several customers. One of them was my student. No doubt, the rumors will start flying around campus that I took a part-time job to make ends meet."

"Where's Sadie?"

"In your event space." He gestured to the doorway. "And she's not alone."

Without another word I walked to the back of the store. I heard voices and loud sobs before I even reached the event space, so I knew I was walking into an emotional maelstrom of some sort.

"Goodness, Pen, I'm glad you got here," Sadie said. She sat on a folding chair beside Quindicott's favorite innkeeper. Fiona's shoulders heaved and her face was buried in tissue. Our little marmalade cat, Bookmark, stood a few feet away, watching the innkeeper with a cocked head and concerned feline eyes.

When Fiona finally looked up and spotted me, she noisily blew her nose and began babbling.

"Oh, Penelope, it was awful. So awful. What a terrible way to start my day—"

"What happened, Fiona?"

"Last night, the most horrible old man barged into my bed-and-breakfast! He had a warrant, issued by a judge in Newport. He said he was from—"

"Delaware Mutual Insurance Company," I interrupted. "And he had a state trooper with him, a Captain Rayburn."

Fiona's jaw dropped. "How did you know?!"

"I just met them both."

"Where?" Fiona asked.

"At a murder scene."

With wide incredulous eyes, Fiona and Sadie listened as I recounted everything that happened in Millstone, including Dottie's murder, my meeting with Max Braydon, and the threats he made to me personally.

"And if all that wasn't bad enough," I concluded, "Max Braydon impounded my car—"

Now Sadie's jaw dropped. "Oh no."

"That awful man threatened to shut down my inn!" Fiona cried. "He was at my place for hours, harassing me, Barney, even our guests. He didn't leave until midnight. Then, at six A.M., Braydon sent a squad of state troopers to tear apart the room Peyton Pemberton stayed in, then the basement room where Norma lived."

"Braydon wasn't with them?"

"No," Fiona replied. "Only Captain Rayburn."

Fiona began to cry again, and Bookmark attempted to comfort the poor woman, rubbing against the innkeeper's legs. Fiona stroked the little cat's head, but even Bookmark's feline hug and sweet purring couldn't alleviate Fiona's misery.

"Braydon must have found that missing address *somewhere*," I declared, "because he turned up in Millstone, two hours after Dottie Willard was murdered."

"He didn't find that woman's address at my inn," Fiona said. "It was Mrs. Waterman who gave Braydon the address."

I sat back. "Mrs. Waterman? The Reverend Waterman's wife?"

Fiona nodded. "She dropped by for tea—and to help me with the planning of our annual fundraising party at Chez Finch to benefit the church's outreach programs. Mrs. Waterman saw what was happening and told the insurance investigator that her husband had the address of Norma's sister. She called the reverend on the spot, and he read it off to Max Braydon over the phone."

So, I thought, *Max Braydon had the address last night. That's curious.*

Ain't it, though, Jack said (in my head). *You'd think a gung ho guy like him would have charged right over there and shaken poor Dottie down at once.*

Well, he didn't, Jack. He got some shut-eye first and then he went to Millstone. Do you think we should speak with Reverend Waterman? I doubt he'll have much more information to offer.

Pick up every crumb you can, honey. That's the PI game. And it's why we call 'em leads. You never know where they'll take you.

I turned my attention back to Fiona. "What happened next? Did Braydon and Captain Rayburn leave after that?"

"Actually, Captain Rayburn left before Mrs. Waterman arrived. But as I said before, Mr. Braydon stayed until almost midnight. He was anxious to speak with Peyton Pemberton."

I was incredulous. "Peyton Pemberton is still staying at your inn, a day *after* her heirloom jewels were stolen?"

"She's not in the same room—not even in the main building. Miss Pemberton moved out to our lighthouse."

Fiona was referring to the old Charity Point Lighthouse, a wreck of a tower that Fiona and Barney had purchased from the town and completely transformed into an extension of their B and B business, offering a single luxury suite overlooking the Atlantic.

"Has she spoken to you about the robbery?"

Fiona shook her head. "Miss Pemberton won't let any of us near her, not even to serve her meals. She's eaten nothing but takeout from Silva's Seafood Shack, which she has delivered."

"Tell Pen what happened next," Sadie urged.

"Well, last night, after he spoke with Miss Pemberton, Mr. Braydon came back and accused *me* of being part of a conspiracy! Can you believe it? He insisted that you were in on it, too, by the way. He said he knew you were involved because the guilty party is often the person who calls the police, in an attempt to deflect blame. It was you who phoned the Quindicott police about the jewel theft."

"Great," I said, resisting the urge to roll my eyes. "I was the one who called the police about Dottie Willard's murder, too."

"I'm sorry I dragged you into all this," Fiona said tearfully.

"You didn't drag me into anything."

I hugged her slender shoulders, but the gentle gesture only

set her off again. She broke into sobs, long, deep ones that ended in a bout of hiccups. Sadie ran to get her a bottle of water, leaving me alone with an inconsolable woman and reeling from the realization that Max Braydon wasn't just misguided; the man was absolutely crazy to accuse Fiona and me of being in on some kind of conspiracy. So, of course, it was the perfect time for Jack Shepard to pop into my head.

Sounds like you've got yourself a new fire hydrant. It works swell, too.

Not funny, Jack. We're talking about murder—

Which is exactly what I warned you would happen once the Tears of Valentino entered your little cornpone community.

I sighed. *Those jewels are certainly well named. They're causing nothing but tears.*

And crying won't solve your problems, doll. What are you going to DO about it?

"Oh, Pen, what are we going to do?" Fiona moaned, eerily echoing the exact sentiments of my PI spirit.

I knew the answer. And Jack did too. It was the only answer possible, given the situation. We *had* to find Norma, and the faster the better. She was the only person who could clear up this mess up and clear our good names.

CHAPTER 25

A Mere Quibble

The world is a book and those who do not travel read only one page.

—Augustine of Hippo (attributed)

THE REST OF the afternoon was mercifully uneventful. Customers came and went. I restocked the endcaps with new releases and reviewed our upcoming orders. By six P.M. I was ready to take over the register so Sadie could go upstairs and start supper for the three of us.

Those plans were suddenly scuttled when a call came from Bud Napp, my aunt's beau and owner of Napp Hardware. Bud was calling in his capacity as president of the Quindicott Business Owners Association, a group of local merchants involved in community affairs, local governance, and "watching one another's backs," as my aunt succinctly put it.

Our members were all fairly headstrong and included such a diversity of shops, interests, and opinions that the debates and disagreements among us were practically legendary—hence our nickname, the Quibblers. In times of crisis, however, we somehow managed to form a unified front.

"Fiona has called an emergency meeting," Bud informed us on speakerphone. "We'll need your event space tonight."

"What's this all about, Bud?" Sadie asked.

"Norma."

"It's pretty short notice," I warned.

"I don't expect a huge attendance, Pen, but I sent out a text message to all our members anyway. I'll see you at seven-thirty."

A leisurely meal was out of the question now, so I ordered Spencer's favorite meatball and mozzarella sandwich from Franzetti's Pizza, and calzones for Sadie and me. While we waited to take delivery, we arranged folding chairs in a half-circle around the event space and set up a table and a single chair in the middle for Bud to hold court.

When I took Spencer's sandwich upstairs, I found my son in the dining room with no thoughts of dinner. Instead, he was working on some concoction for his science project that involved repeated trips to the kitchen and lots of running water. His focused activity reminded me how he'd single-handedly fingerprinted the entire teaching staff of his elementary school.

With a deep breath, I sighed over my son. Spencer was a good kid. And he had good intentions. Sometimes he just needed a little extra guidance to keep him on the right track.

"Enjoy your supper, then do your homework," I told him. "I still want to have that talk with you later."

THE BALL PEEN hammer banged promptly at seven thirty, as Bud called a surprisingly crowded meeting to order. Formalities like reading the minutes and taking attendance were dispensed with. Instead, Fiona kicked things off by informing everyone that a popular internet star was staying at her inn. Then she shocked the crowd with news of the jewel theft and Norma the Nomad's supposed involvement in the crime.

I took the stage next to give my account of trying to track her down in Millstone, only to be shot at by an unknown figure (in large boots) before discovering the dead body of the person Norma claimed to be her next of kin. Finally, I mentioned the insurance investigator Max Braydon, who was sure Norma was the culprit.

"That's bull," cried a gruff voice from the third row.

Leo Rollins stood, his bearlike form blocking the view of those sitting behind him. The owner of Rollins Electronics was a combat veteran and part-time biker—though I had to take a second look to make sure it really *was* Leo. His formerly wild beard had been tamed, his long hair trimmed, his ratty denims replaced by neatly pressed pants.

All smiles, Colleen—proprietor of Quindicott's House of Beauty salon—sat beside him. Leo had obviously accepted the beautician's flirtatious offer of a trim at our last emergency meeting.

"Norma's the sweetest lady I've ever met," Leo declared. "I can't believe she would steal anything."

Rollins told us how Norma brought in a vintage CB radio to his shop for repair.

"It was a 1970s Midland 40 Channel, Model 77 just like the one I grew up with. She got me to reminisce about the hours my pop and I shared with that old radio."

"Tell them what happened next," Colleen coaxed.

"Well, I ordered the parts and Norma paid for the repairs—which weren't cheap. Then Norma shocked me by handing the radio back. 'I can see this brought you happy memories, so you should have it,' she insisted."

Milner Logan, head baker and co-owner of the Cooper Family Bakery, spoke up next.

"Remember the fry bread we sold at the July Fourth Festival? That was Norma's recipe. The bread was such a success we still sell it at outdoor festivals year-round, but Norma wouldn't accept a penny in compensation."

Now Seymour stood and told them about the ice cream truck incident that brought Norma to Quindicott in the first place. Others shared similar tales. None of us believed big-hearted Norma was guilty of anything. But we also agreed that we knew next to nothing about the woman we were all praising.

Seymour faced Aunt Sadie. "You mentioned that your shop special ordered books for Norma. Do you have a list of those titles? We may find out something about Norma's intentions from her reading habits."

"Seymour may be onto something," Brainert said, changing his tune from the other night. "I do believe it's possible to learn the character of a person from the books they've read."

"You mean the *characters* they read," Seymour countered. "Jack Reacher fans have little in common with Potterheads—"

"Potterheads?" Linda Cooper-Logan cried. "I know what a pothead is, but what's a—"

"It's a Harry Potter fan," Colleen explained. A moment later she realized Leo was staring at her. "I read the Harry Potter books when I was in high school," she confessed. "So what?"

"I know Norma liked to quote authors when she worked at our shop on Sundays." Sadie said.

"What quotes?" Brainert pressed. "What authors?"

My aunt tugged her glasses off and let them dangle on the beaded necklace. "Well, there was one quote about fame, money—"

"And truth!" Brainert cried, his index finger pointed at the sky. "That would be Henry David Thoreau. 'Rather than love, than money, than fame, give me truth.'"

"Not bad for the guy who wrote a whole book about a pond," Seymour cracked. "At least that quote didn't make me want to Thoreau-up."

Leo Rollins cackled—even Milner Logan, part Native American and a lover of nature, chuckled. Brainert, however, was incensed.

"Thoreau's work is contemplative, meditative even. He was a transcendentalist, you know . . ."

"Hey, what's with the 'dentalist' part of that word?" Seymour asked. "Did old Thoreau meditate through his teeth?"

"Your humor is less mature than the kiddies you ply with

ice cream," Brainert sniffed. "And *Walden* is a master-piece."

Seymour groaned. "Then answer me this: Why do writers who romanticize the forest always write about flowers and trees, flitting butterflies, and picturesque little ponds, but never about mosquitoes, gnats, snakes, or poisonous spiders?"

"I've heard enough!" Aunt Sadie covered her ears and bolted for the front of the store. "I'll print out Norma's booklist and be right back."

While she was gone, the group got into a lively discussion about the American transcendentalists that split the room's opinion between contemplative and crazy. That's when Jack decided to make himself known.

These cracker-barrel philosophers are giving me fits, doll, and they're wasting your time.

Sadly, you're correct, Jack.

Happily, my aunt's return ended the discussion. Most of the attendees rose and clustered around Sadie as she scanned the printout.

"Any travel books on that list perchance?" Seymour asked, folding his arms. "You know, Venezuela, Cuba, Bolivia, countries that grant no extradition."

"Nothing like that," Sadie said. "The first book Norma ordered was *A Guide to the Maintenance and Repair of Manual Typewriters.*"

"Which means she probably owns one," I concluded. "What else?"

Sadie rattled off a dozen works of novel-length fiction, as well as collections of poetry and short stories. Some were new releases, others literary classics.

"Hmm," Brainert said, looking over Sadie's shoulder. "That's interesting."

"What?" I asked.

"*The Troll Garden* by Willa Cather," Brainert pointed to the title on the paper.

"What about it?" Seymour pressed.

Brainert's mind was clearly working, but he didn't share his thoughts.

"Norma also ordered a number of non-fiction titles," Sadie continued, mentioning a regional bird-watching manual and other books about the flora and fauna of Rhode Island. When she got to *Forest Bathing* by Hinata Morita, Colleen spoke up.

"What's that one about?" she asked with interest. "Getting naked in the woods?"

She threw a flirty glance at Leo Rollins who scratched his beard. "Maybe it's about that Japanese suicide forest."

"You're thinking of Aokigahara, the Sea of Trees," Seymour supplied.

Linda Cooper-Logan's eyes went wide under her blond pixie cut. "You mean people actually go to the woods to kill themselves?"

"In Japan they do," Rollins said.

Brainert turned to his mailman friend. "How do you know about Aokigahara?"

Seymour shrugged. "How do you think I won *Jeopardy!*?"

Sadie set her glasses on her nose. "It says in the book description that forest bathing is a form of immersive meditation called *shinrin-yoku* in Japan. To do it you smell the air, touch the soil, feel the breeze on your skin . . ."

Seymour shuddered. "Sounds like more Thoreau, but made in Japan."

Sadie tapped the paper. "It says here the practice boosts your immune system."

"By fighting off infections from poison ivy and bug bites, no doubt," Seymour declared.

The outside door buzzed.

"It must be a latecomer. I'll let them in." Sadie left and quickly returned with Deputy Chief Eddie Franzetti by her side. He asked everyone to take a seat.

Good, Jack said in my head. *Now maybe we can abandon the book club and get back to business.*

I only hope it's good news, Jack. If good news is even possible.

"I heard about the meeting and I can guess the subject," Eddie began. "Many of you know Norma, so I think it's right I bring you all up to speed."

"Fine," Bud Napp said. "You got the floor."

Eddie nodded. "The state police examined the earring Pen and I found at the scene."

"For fingerprints?" Bud asked.

Fiona moaned. "Please don't tell me they were Norma's."

"No prints. In fact, it's almost like the teardrop diamond and its setting were wiped clean. The lab guys think Norma used a cloth to grab the stuff—"

"But that only explains why Norma's prints weren't found," I pointed out. "Why were there no Peyton Pemberton fingerprints?"

Eddie ignored the question. "All I can tell you is without fingerprints there is no definitive proof of Norma's guilt. But even without prints, the circumstantial evidence is over-whelming, and the outlook for Norma isn't great."

"What else did they find out?" Sadie asked.

"The insurance company has determined to their satis-faction that the teardrop diamond and the gold setting are real."

"That's no surprise," Fiona said.

"I call it a disappointment," Eddie replied. "I felt there was something hinky about Miss Pemberton. I was hoping the diamond was a fake and she was trying to pull some publicity stunt to raise her Internet profile."

"I guess that's out the window," I said with a frown.

"Insurance investigator Max Braydon is convinced he's on the trail of a jewel thief. He's pushing for a grand jury and larceny charges for everyone involved. Grand lar-ceny."

My heart skipped a beat. "Are you telling me he plans to take my life apart the way he's dismantled my car?"

"Your life and maybe Fiona's," Eddie said. The inn-keeper gasped. "The man's a bulldog, Pen, he found you at Dottie Willard's crime scene the morning after Peyton Pem-berton accused you of being in cahoots with Fiona. Now

Braydon's got it in his head that your both guilty of something. He just needs to find the proof."

"What should we do?" Fiona cried.

"Lie low, and don't step out of line. I mean don't even jaywalk. Remember, I'm officially off the case. The state police are in charge, and they may be watching."

"Beware of Big Brother!" Seymour proclaimed.

"Meanwhile, if anyone here gets a lead on where Norma might be, call me. Just watch what you say over the phone. We can meet in person anytime, day or night."

A FEW HOURS later I was in my bed, my eyes heavy with sleep, when Jack paid me another visit.

So, kiddo, looks like you fit the frame nice enough. Max Braydon is painting a pretty picture for a grand jury.

"You and I both know it's all a lie, Jack."

Sure, doll. But you can't teach an old dog new tricks—

"Huh?"

That rent-a-cop Braydon. He's an old dog, get it?

"So?"

Old Maxie got this far by strong-arming people. He pushes around local authorities, using his insurance company like a crime boss uses hired muscle. He's done that for so long, that's all he can do.

"So how do I fight him, Jack?"

The fastest way out of this rat trap is simple. Find Norma before the other guy does.

"The other guy? You mean Braydon?"

Mother Machree! How short is your memory?!

"What do you mean?"

I mean the guy who killed Dottie Willard. Five will get you ten that guy wasn't looking for Dottie. He was looking for Norma.

"You think so?"

What I think is your Book Whisperer has a target on her back. You were too late to save Dottie. You don't want to be too late to save Norma, do you?

I put the pillow over my eyes, hoping to shut the world out. That I could do, but there was no shutting out Jack Shepard.

I see you've got to learn a thing or two, baby. So close your eyes, and I'll teach you. I know exactly what it means to be late out of the gate, and what it costs . . .

CHAPTER 26

A House of Fashion

Shopping is never over . . . It is merely suspended.

—Robert B. Parker, *The Widening Gyre*

New York City
November 1947

ONE MOMENT I was flat on my back with a pillow across my face. A second later someone jostled me, my eyes snapped open, and my other four senses sprang to life.

The chatter, the traffic noise, and the pervasive smell of unleaded gasoline told me I was back in Jack Shepard's New York—only this time we were in a lot nicer neighborhood than the ones where Jack usually dragged me.

This was Fifth Avenue, the Mecca of American shopping. The broad sidewalks weren't quite broad enough to contain the phalanx of prattling women—and a few glum-looking men—who crowded me right into the corner of a granite building.

Most of these people were shoppers, bearing neatly wrapped boxes or bags emblazoned with legendary names like Saks Fifth Avenue, Lord & Taylor, and Tiffany & Co.

"Shake a leg, Penny," I heard Jack call. "We have a date with a fashion plate."

As directed, I shook my leg, fully expecting to teeter on the peaks of twin high heels. Instead, I found myself on solid ground—in rather ugly brown flats—with bobby socks?

"Okay," I muttered.

As I stepped into the midday crowd I spied my reflection in a plate-glass window. My bulky wool coat and calf-length dress were the same horrid muddy-brown color as my ugly shoes. My hair was pulled back into an unflattering granny bun, and oversized horn-rimmed glasses hung over my nose.

"Penny, over here."

Jack Shepard waited in front of a pair of tall glass doors guarded by a uniformed doorman. The polished brass sign on the wall told me all I needed to know.

"This is a high-fashion house, Jack."

"Yeah?"

"So why did you dress me like a frump?"

"You're always complaining about your heels being too high, or your garters too tight. Isn't this better?"

"But you're taking me to a high-fashion house!"

Jack's mischievous smile creased the jagged scar on his chin. "Savor the irony, doll, and play off everything I say and do."

The doorman greeted Jack with a tip of his hat.

Why not? He was wrapped in his best suit—the same one he wore last night, though he'd donned a new starched white shirt. He stood taller. Even his fedora seemed to sit more squarely on his head.

The detective had dressed himself to fit in perfectly on tony Fifth Avenue. Me? Not so much—which was more than apparent from the disapproving looks I was getting from the fashionable women striding by.

Once we were inside the spacious store, Jack cornered one of the glamourous saleswomen. As usual, he had no problem attracting female attention.

"What can I help you with?" the slinky blonde purred, wrapping herself around the detective.

"I need to see Rene Bijoux, pronto."

The woman frowned. "Mr. Bijoux is very busy at—"

Jack cut in. "I'm from the Broadway Guild."

The woman's dark red lips formed a perfect O. "I see. I'll find him at once."

When the slinky saleswoman was out of earshot, I faced Jack.

"What is going on here?"

"Relax, Penny, you're going to do a little bit of modeling, that's all."

"I'm *what*?"

Jack silenced me as a tall, thin man in an elegant suit and dark, slicked-back hair approached us. He was roughly Jack's age, but his fair skin appeared as smooth and shiny as the building's polished brass sign. He looked down a nose shaped like a predatory eagle's—which contrasted oddly with his large, fawnlike eyes.

He blinked those eyes at Jack, in much the same way the saleswoman had.

"I'm Rene Bijoux. What may I help you with, Mr. . . . ?"

"Van Heusen," Jack said, flashing a fake ID. "I'm with—"

"Yes," the tall man interrupted with a frown. "The Broadway Guild."

"That's right," Jack replied. "Johnny Palermo sent us. He doesn't think you have enough dames to model in today's fashion show. Johnny thinks you could use another."

A flash of anger crossed Bijoux's face. He quickly tamped it down.

"I *suppose* you can never have enough attractive models," he said, forcing the words through gritted teeth. "Where is she?"

Jack nudged me forward. "Right here."

Rene Bijoux recoiled like Dracula facing a crucifix. "Gad, sir! Surely you jest?"

"What's wrong with her?" Jack demanded, acting all innocent.

Rene Bijoux stepped backward and lifted one manicured hand to his shiny chin.

"Excuse me for asking, young lady," he said, addressing me for the first time. "You *do* know the war is over? That the Air Corps no longer requires the copious use of silk for parachutes?"

"Uh-huh," I replied.

"And you know we no longer ration other types of materials, correct?"

I shrugged. "I guess so."

"Which means you need no longer dress like a school-marm!" He cleared his throat. "And speaking of dresses. Times have changed, Miss—"

"Penny," Jack threw in. I gave him a sidelong glance. He seemed to be enjoying the show immensely.

"Miss Penny," Rene Bijoux said with wrinkled nose. "As I said, times have changed. Johnny's come marching home. That means Rosie has riveted her last rivet, and sensibly made a beeline for hearth and home."

"And that's good?"

"It's where her heart always was." Rene threw his arms wide. "You're free to be a woman again. Free to explore your femininity. Free to find your own Johnny and settle down in your own little home."

"And just how do I do that?" This time it was me forcing words through gritted teeth.

"Well, first you must look . . . acceptable. The simple, utilitarian style of clothing you are wearing, inspired by the likes of Norman Norell and Claire McCardell . . . Well, to put it kindly, it's passé. Bulky wool is strictly for men in Arctic climates. And denim?" he scoffed. "Mark my words. No one will be caught dead wearing denim, ever again."

He shook his pomaded head. "No, my sweet little Miss Penny. Glamour is the key to the modern look. Rounded shoulders, full skirts, lush materials."

Rene Bijoux stepped back to appraise me once again. "Yes, on reflection I believe she will do," he said to Jack. "I'll have one of my best stylists get to work on her face, and a hairdresser to untangle that rattrap on her head. And we'll have to decide on the right dress. This is going to take a lot of attention . . . My attention."

"Great," Jack said.

"It was nice meeting you, Mr. Van Heusen—"

"Not so fast, Rene. I go with the girl."

"I don't approve of husbands or boyfriends in the dressing rooms."

"You're off the hook, then, Rene, because I'm neither." Jack smiled, baring white teeth. "I'm her chaperone, see?"

Rene Bijoux sighed. "Follow me, then."

The fashion designer spun like a ballet dancer and marched through the crowd of well-heeled women, who instinctively parted to let him pass.

"Why are we here, Jack?" I whispered.

"Relax, doll. Rene took up the challenge."

"Challenge?"

"Yep, and you were the bait. It's all going according to plan. Why, you're the perfect distraction."

"What's going according to plan?"

"I told you, Penny. We've got a date with a fashion plate."

"By fashion plate, you mean—?"

"Thelma Dice, the dame who has the Tears of Valentino."

"She's here?"

Jack nodded. "Johnny Palermo tells me she's one of the dames playing clotheshorse today."

"How can I help?"

"Baby, you're doing a helluva job already."

CHAPTER 27

Fashionably Late

You'd better run along home and think up things to tell
the police. You'll be hearing from them.

—Dashiell Hammett, *The Maltese Falcon*

RENE BIJOUX LED Jack and me to the rear of his luxury
shop, then through a 1930s-style oval doorway blocked by
floor-length drapes of pink satin.

Through the curtains, we found a high-ceilinged room
with white marble walls and a black marble floor. The space
was large and furnished with lush chairs and pillowed
couches—all facing a curved staircase that led up to another
oval-shaped door on the second floor.

Obviously those stairs would serve as a fashion runway.
Already, a line of elegantly attired young women were being
coached by a strident, leotard-clad dance instructor.

"You must learn the proper way to descend the stairs,"
she commanded in a Russian accent. "Chin up. Head held
high. No clutching the rail. I want right elbows bent, wrist
cocked, hand pointing at the sky!"

"I'm gonna fall right down on my kissah, I'm sure,"
groused a squeaky-voiced woman in Brooklynese.

With Rene still in the lead, we squeezed past the instructor and her pupils. At the top of the stairs, we passed through that second oval door and another set of pale pink curtains.

Suddenly, Jack stopped dead—then pushed his fedora to the back of his head.

"Holy cats! What a view."

Of course Jack found the scenery appealing, seeing as we'd just entered a room full of attractive young women in various stages of undress. Most were in slips, but some were down to their unmentionables. Others were being fitted with elegant Rene Bijoux originals.

A brunette adjusting the seams on her stockings jerked her head in Jack's direction.

"Here comes another one. It's like the Yankees bullpen in here."

Rene brushed past her to the center of the room. He clapped his hands, then began giving orders.

"We have a situation here," he said, pushing me to the center of a ring of women.

"I'll need Betsy to work on her makeup, Ellen to make her hair presentable. Shirley, I'll need you to take measurements, and I shall handle the wardrobe."

Within seconds I was shoved into a chair. One young woman—presumably Ellen—began to untangle my granny bun. Betsy barely introduced herself before she ripped the glasses from my face and smeared my skin all over with some sweet-smelling concoction. Rene reappeared with an armful of long, stylish evening dresses, seeking to find just the right color for my skin tone. Shirley reached for a red number with a full skirt and sequined top, which elicited a squeal from the fashion designer.

"Not that one!" Rene insisted. "It's much too daring. Remember, this show is for the Daughters of the American Revolution."

"Pucker your lips, please," Betsy commanded. "They're so pale I don't know where they end and your cheeks begin."

Meanwhile Shirley kept ordering me to stand up while she wrapped a tape measure around my waist. Ellen threw down her hairbrush and complained she couldn't work on my hair if I insisted on jumping up like a jack-in-the-box.

And speaking of Jack, while I was getting all the attention, he sidled up to the woman with the Betty Grable legs and the dark silk stockings to go with them.

"Hey, doll."

"Hey yourself," she replied with an unfriendly huff.

"Say, I heard you talking about this being like a bullpen. I figure you mean there's another joe here who doesn't belong?"

"What business is that of yours? You a copper or something?"

"Nah," Jack replied. "It's a small town, I might know him, that's all."

The brunette turned her back on Jack, stooped over, and smoothed the silk stockings with scarlet-nailed fingers.

"You'd only know him if you traveled in the wrong circles, bub," she muttered.

"Yeah?"

The brunette straightened up and faced Jack again. "His name is Billy Bastogne and he's visiting my friend. Thelma's the star of this show, seeing that she brought her own props—"

"Props?"

"A necklace from some Broadway producer." The brunette sneered. "Because of that, she gets her own private dressing room."

Jack perked up. "Would that be Thelma Dice?"

"What's it to you?"

"I'm from the Broadway Guild and I was looking for her. I might have a job lined up for Thelma if she plays her cards right. There might be a place in the show for a dame like you, too, as long as you belong to the guild."

"Sure, I belong. Wanna see my papers?"

Jack winked. "A sweet thing like you wouldn't steer a guy wrong."

A smile tugged at the corners of the brunette's mouth, but she remained silent, still skeptical.

"Take me to Thelma and I'll give you both the skinny," Jack coaxed.

With an exhale, the woman finally bobbed her head. "You got a deal, mister. But only if I get a job out of it, too."

"Scout's honor," Jack lied.

Now, remember, I watched the whole thing and overheard their conversation while three women and an insistent fashion designer hovered over me. I wanted nothing more than to jump up, push through the circle of fashionistas, and follow Jack and that curvy brunette through yet another set of curtains to the private dressing rooms.

While my hair was being curled and the third round of lipstick was being applied—the first two were "just so wrong," Rene insisted—I finally got my chance to break free.

It came when a woman's horrified scream echoed from behind the dressing room curtains. The howling brunette burst through the silk drapes a moment later, manicured fingers gripping her hair.

"She's dead! She's dead! Thelma has been murdered!"

Immediately the women around me, along with Rene Bijoux, screamed and bolted for the exit. Bucking the human tidal wave, I headed right for the dressing rooms. I had to shove the screaming brunette aside before I could push through the curtains. I was sorry she hit the floor, but I kept on going.

A narrow hallway led to a line of dressing room doors. Only one was open, and I could hear Jack cursing.

A second later I choked back a scream of my own.

The woman draped over the chair was certainly dead. No one could live with their neck twisted like that. Before I looked away, I saw bulging eyes, a protruding tongue, and a face flushed purple.

There were only two splotches of blood—the killer had cruelly ripped a pair of earrings from the strangled woman, tearing her earlobes.

I heard Jack curse again and that's when I spied him. He was leaning through an open window to the fire escape, straining to see if there was someone in the alley below.

Finally, Jack grunted in disgust. Still gripping the window-sill, he faced me.

"We were too late," he said. "Thelma Dice has been murdered. Her killer went out this window and is long gone—and he's taken the Tears of Valentino with him."

Jack tore himself away from the window and stared at the dead woman. After a moment, he shook his head and left the room.

In the hall, he gripped my elbow. "Did you see Phyllis?"

"Who?"

"The dame I was with."

"The brunette? She's back there, sprawled on the floor. My bad."

"I'm glad you slowed her down."

Jack released me, then bolted down the hall and through the pink curtains. I had to jump to catch up. When I did, I found the detective helping the tearful woman off the floor.

"Come on, Phyllis, stop blubbering. There's nothing anyone can do."

The brunette paled under her makeup. "Then Thelma really is . . ."

"Dead as a Christmas goose," Jack replied.

"Oh no!"

"Her neck has been snapped and we both know who did it," Jack growled. "Tell me more about this Billy Bastogne before the cops get here and you have to tell them."

Her pale face turned ghostly white. "I can't rat Billy out. He'll kill me! Kill me, I tell you! Just like he killed poor Thelma."

"Well, you better have some story for the cops. Use your imagination with them, but I want the truth."

Phyllis threatened to break down into tears again. Jack clutched her arms and ungently shook her back to reality.

"I get that you don't want to tell the cops, but you better tell me. Who is this Billy Bastogne? Spill!"

"He's a professional gambler, out of Quebec. Speaks real cultured like, with a fancy French accent."

"Where can I find him?"

"He . . . He lives with Thelma."

Jack scoffed. "He won't turn up there again. What else do you know?"

"Billy works as a taxi dancer at Moondance—"

"That classy bar for rich dames?"

"That's the one," she cried, nodding. "He's one of the star attractions."

"Anything else?" Jack demanded.

"Billy . . . He's in deep with a bookie, real deep. He was always hitting Thelma up for lettuce to bankroll his gambling—"

"What bookie?"

"His name is Bremen . . . Klaus Bremen. He runs the Germantown gang."

Jack cursed. "Could this get any worse?"

From somewhere downstairs, we all heard the shrill blast of a police whistle. Jack released Phyllis, who sagged to the floor again.

"Lie there and play dumb," Jack told her. "You fainted and you don't know nothing—and I was never here."

Theatrically, she placed the back of one hand on her forehead and played dead.

Jack grabbed my arm. "Let's get out of here, doll."

On the other side of the curtains, I stopped him. "How did you know Phyllis would be such a fount of information?"

"I didn't," Jack said as he pulled me down the hall. "Like I told you. Get background. Ask questions. You never know where your next lead will come from."

Jack took me into the dead woman's dressing room.

"Crawl through that window and climb down the fire escape," he ordered. "We're leaving the same way Billy Bastogne did."

"Slow down," I cried, while trying to find footing on the rusty iron platform. "Don't push me or I'm going to—"

THUMP!

I bounced off the carpeted floor, jarring myself awake. Dazed, I took a moment to realize I'd fallen out of bed. I checked for injuries, untangled myself from the blankets, and snatched my glasses off the nightstand.

The whole time, Jack's words echoed in my head.

You never know where your next lead will come from.

"I get it, Jack," I muttered—to myself, since Jack was nowhere to be found.

"I should have spoken with Reverend and Mrs. Waterman the moment I found out they had Dorothy Willard's address."

As if on cue, my alarm clock went off and I started my day.

CHAPTER 28

The Little Church on the Corner

In small towns people scent the wind with noses of uncommon keenness.

—Stephen King, *The Stand*

BOOKSHOP BUSINESS DELAYED my visit to the First Presbyterian Church of Quindicott until the afternoon. I hitched a ride with Bonnie Franzetti, who had finished her shift for the day.

Without a car, I figured I'd be walking back.

Both the Reverend and Mrs. Waterman were busy working inside the church, but the reverend was out of uniform, and his wife was hardly wearing her Sunday best.

"Hi, Mrs. McClure," the young reverend said, wiping his paint-stained hands on a towel. Though over thirty, you would never guess Tad Waterman's age by his round, boyish face. The sweatpants and Brown University sweatshirt only enhanced the image of youth. Lately, he'd grown a close-cropped blond beard, no doubt in an attempt to garner a bit of gravitas. Unfortunately, the fashionable facial hair only made the reverend seem younger.

"Oh, hello, Penelope," Mrs. Waterman said as she self-consciously patted the paint-dotted bandana covering her head. Nearly a decade older than her husband, Mrs. Waterman was an attractive woman with refined features and precise manners that came across as haughty to some, but I never saw her that way, and I knew she worked hard for her husband's congregation.

"Excuse the mess," Reverend Waterman said. "We're trying to brighten things up."

It was a tall order. The hundred-and-twenty-something-year-old stone church was solid and staid and had too much dark woodwork for the interior to be anything but somber. And the narrow, medieval-inspired windows would come in handy in defending the place from a Viking raid, but they didn't admit much sunlight.

"How can we help you?" Mrs. Waterman asked.

"I wanted to talk to you about Norma Stanton. I know you both heard what she's been accused of."

"Yes, we gave the police the address of Norma's sister in Millstone," Mrs. Waterman replied. "But only to help Norma clear her name."

Reverend Waterman nodded. "I'm positive it's all some sort of misunderstanding. I only hope the police caught up with Norma at her sister's place and she straightened everything out."

"It didn't exactly happen that way," I replied. "Dorothy Willard isn't Norma's sister and Norma wasn't there when the police arrived."

"Oh my. What did Dorothy Willard tell them?" the reverend asked, genuinely puzzled.

"Nothing. Someone murdered her."

Shaken, Mrs. Waterman sat down in a pew.

"May the poor woman rest in peace," the reverend said.

"How did you come to have Dorothy Willard's address, Reverend?"

"Norma worked with some of the members of our church. People with . . . emotional issues. We wanted to know the name of a next of kin in case something happened."

While I digested that, Mrs. Waterman spoke up. "Does this have anything to do with Norma and those missing diamonds we heard about?"

"I think so."

I let that sink in for a moment. "Did Norma volunteer her time to the church? Or was she employed? What exactly did Norma do?"

Mrs. Waterman and her husband exchanged glances. The woman lowered her eyes, while the reverend, who was not usually at a loss for words, suddenly was.

"What am I missing here?" I asked.

The pair remained awkwardly silent for a long moment. Finally, Mrs. Waterman spoke.

"Let's show her."

With a nod of agreement from her husband, the two set their paintbrushes aside and led me out of the old church to the rear door of the large house that served as the pastor's residence. The path between the church and the house was lined with the very same purple blossoms I'd seen all around Dorothy Willard's house and yard.

The coincidence struck me, and I was about to say so when Mrs. Waterman spoke again.

"We found out about the recordings only recently. We weren't sure who we should tell. If anyone—"

Reverend Waterman jumped in. "Norma should be informed of what's transpired. But it's not a crime, as far as we know—of course, it is strictly against the rules of confidentiality."

I was baffled by their statements but simply listened, like a good detective should (or so Jack taught me). Once through the back door, the Watermans led me down carpeted steps to a finished basement. There were stacks of folding chairs against one wall, a table with a large coffee maker against the other, and a desk with a computer in the corner, which is where we ended up.

"It started with these," Reverend Waterman said, handing me a bundle of envelopes, all addressed to the First Presbyterian Church.

"Anonymous donations, all of them. Some have notes.

Some don't. They began showing up in the mail only recently. Most of the gifts are small, but so far they add up to over five hundred dollars."

"And more come in every day," Mrs. Waterman added.

"What do these have to do with Norma?" I asked, handing them back.

The reverend set the envelopes aside, bent over the computer, and punched a few keys. On YouTube, he expanded the image to full screen and stepped aside.

"See for yourself. We learned about these videos in one of the first letters we received."

The screen showed a woman addressing a group of people circled around her; one of them was Reverend Waterman. It took a moment for me to realize that the speaker was Norma and the recording had been made in this very basement.

"You go where your habits take you," Norma said, sharing that wise smile of hers.

She paused a long moment, putting her hands in the pockets of her denim overalls, allowing everyone in the group to digest those words before continuing—

"Rosa Parks once said, 'I have learned over the years that when one's mind is made up, this diminishes fear; knowing what must be done does away with fear.'

"That's so true, isn't it? I've found it so on my journey— a long journey and a challenging one. You're all on that journey too. The journey of life. Divine life. Precious life. A priceless treasure you hold in your own hands. You see, you are rich because you have life. You are powerful because you are in command of it.

"*You* are the captain of your mind and body, nobody else. It's *your* ship to steer, and you're charting its course every hour of every day with every choice you make.

"If you don't like where you are, consider how you got there, and where your choices are leading you. Because there is no spontaneous condition. There is only cause and effect. What you do today is what effects your tomorrow."

Norma paused a final time before echoing the words she began with—

"You go where your habits take you."

"She's speaking to our Addiction and Substance Abuse Group," Reverend Waterman explained. "It's a rather large gathering. Over twenty regulars and more who attend a few times a month."

"The group meets twice a week," Mrs. Waterman explained. "Norma first came eight weeks ago and attended every meeting since."

The reverend nodded. "In that short time, Norma became something of a group therapist. Our members found her words inspiring. Attendance rose dramatically. And, as you can see, someone was moved enough to record Norma and post her remarks online."

"Her words were always hopeful and inspiring," Mrs. Waterman said.

"Norma's message always struck a powerful spiritual chord," the reverend added. "And she projected such authority."

"How long has this been going on, Reverend? The secret recordings, I mean."

"There are fourteen of them online," he replied. "They've been posted twice a week for the last seven weeks. By someone who calls himself Repentant."

Repentant about what? I wondered.

"In a recent video, Norma mentioned the name of this church," Mrs. Waterman said. "That's when the anonymous donations started coming in."

"You should read some of the notes that came with those donations," the reverend said. "Norma truly influenced lives and touched people's hearts."

"Norma wasn't aware this was happening?"

"Not unless she posted them herself, which I doubt," the reverend replied, "since she doesn't even own a phone."

"Then you don't know who was making these recordings?"

Mrs. Waterman shook her head. "Not yet. But we intend to get to the bottom of it."

We were interrupted by the doorbell. I figured I was done and followed the Watermans upstairs. We crossed their tidy living room to the front door, where Seymour Tarnish was waiting—this time in his official capacity as the local mail carrier.

"Hey, Reverend. Hello, Mrs. Waterman. I've got a big bundle for you today." Seymour handed over a rubber-banded wad of envelopes an inch thick. "And they're all from out of town, too. Are you running a televangelist operation by any chance?"

Before the reverend could reply, Seymour spotted me.

"Oh, hi, Pen. I'm surprised to see you here."

I was more surprised by the two potted plants that flanked the front door—those purple blossoms again, in brown clay pots.

"Mrs. Waterman, did you happen to get these potted plants from Norma?"

She blinked, surprised. "Why, yes. She brought them a few days ago. They're New England aster. They bloom in late autumn. You can find them yourself growing wild in the woods or near water. Norma called them Michaelmas daisies."

"Aha," Seymour cried. "So that's where they came up with that goofy name."

"What goofy name?" I asked.

Seymour frowned. "Don't you guys ever read those circulars sent out by our esteemed state senator?"

"No," the Watermans and I said in unison.

"If you did, then you'd know the last one had our senator bragging about the cleanup of Millstone Creek. It used to be so polluted from the old textile mill, remember?"

"What about it?" I replied.

"Well, the mill is long gone, and now the creek is all cleaned up, thanks to the state senator and the EPA. Anyway, the creek ends at a place called Michaelmas Pond. The senator claims it's so clean that fishing there is safe again."

CHAPTER 29

Taken for a Ride

A man should control his life. Mine is controlling me.

—Rudolph Valentino

I BID A hasty good-bye to the Reverend and Mrs. Waterman, promising I would keep them informed of any new developments. Once outside, I raced along the block until I caught up to Seymour, who was still delivering mail.

"Do you think you can find a copy of that circular you were talking about?"

"Sure," Seymour replied. "I pile them up in a drawer at home. That way I know exactly which bureaucrat to complain to when things go south."

"Could you bring it to me at the bookstore when you get off duty? I'd like to read about the reclamation of the creek and Michaelmas Pond."

Seymour made a face. "Sure, but why? It's surely not because of your passion for freshwater fishing."

"I'll tell you later. Just bring me that circular."

I didn't want to explain anything to Seymour quite yet because I couldn't put into words the jumble of facts that were coming together in my mind. I turned and began walking on automatic pilot while I tried to untangle the many threads in this twisted tale.

Those New England asters that Norma brought to the Watermans proved there was a real connection between her and Dorothy Willard. I had no clue what that connection could be, but I was now certain that "Dorothy Willard" wasn't a random name Norma simply jotted down on a job application.

I recalled the statement made by one of Dottie's neighbors to Eddie Franzetti about running into Dottie gathering flowers in the woods—while he was *fishing*! Was that neighbor fishing at the newly reclaimed Michaelmas Pond? My bet, he was, because there was not much freshwater fishing around Quindicott, not this close to the Atlantic!

And wouldn't a remote area like the forest along Millstone Creek, or the woods surrounding Michaelmas Pond, make a perfect camping ground? And where *was* Norma's familiar trailer, anyway? She'd come into town without it this year, which meant she'd stashed it somewhere.

Why not along Millstone Creek or Michaelmas Pond? Norma could easily winter there—she had years of experience "roughing it" and living off the grid. And then, of course, there were those books she ordered on local bird watching and *Forest Bathing* . . .

As this theory coalesced in my head, I headed home. It was a brisk fifteen-minute walk from First Presbyterian to Buy the Book in the center of the town's small but thriving shopping district. But as I walked I noticed a sleek, black, late-model Cadillac pacing me. When I turned my head in the car's direction, the Caddy rolled to a stop beside me, and the passenger-side window slowly descended.

"Please excuse my boldness, Mrs. McClure," said a smooth, cultured voice with a slight unidentifiable accent. "I'd like to talk to you about the Tears of Valentino."

"Let me guess. You work for the insurance investigator, Max Braydon?"

"In fact, I just spoke with Mr. Braydon."

"About my car? Am I going to get it back?"

The mellow-voiced driver climbed out of the Caddy to greet me face-to-face. He was over six feet tall, with large hands and a hawklike nose. He stood ramrod straight, and his salt-and-pepper hair was slicked back, his thin mustache upturned in a tense smile that made me feel slightly uneasy.

The man opened the passenger-side door. "My name is Enzo Santoro, and it would be my pleasure to give you a ride to your destination. It's important that we talk."

I was beginning to think this guy might not work in insurance. But late afternoon on Cranberry Street meant there were plenty of people around, so I didn't see much risk.

When I was comfortably seated, he started the powerful engine and quickly pulled into the roadway.

"You don't even know where I'm going."

"Ah, but I do, Mrs. McClure. We are going to your lovely bookshop. But please bear with me—a short detour first."

A moment later, Mr. Santoro pulled into a parking spot near the town gazebo. Though the sun was ready to set, mothers with children, and even a few couples, were all around us, so I still felt safe.

"Now," he said. "I wish to speak with you privately, if I may."

"About the Tears of Valentino? You did mention them already."

"Ah, you are as intelligent as you are attractive, Mrs. McClure."

Oh brother . . .

Wait, was that me, or Jack?

"Please, let me explain," Santoro continued. "I am from Castellaneta in Puglia, the place where Rudolph Valentino was born."

"And Valentino is your hometown hero."

"Rudolph Valentino is Castellaneta's gift to the world. A dancer. A poet. The first Hollywood sex symbol. Clark Gable, Humphrey Bogart, Tom Cruise, these men are mere peons. Pale shadows of the glorious Valentino."

Enzo spoke as much with his hands as his lips. Gesturing wildly, he banged the steering wheel more than once. "And of course, Valentino was the greatest of lovers. He taught America the language of love—"

"In silent movies?"

"Valentino once said 'an American may speak love with his lips; but the Italian must say it with his eyes.'" Enzo sighed. "Despite all of his success, Valentino's life was filled with tragedy. He once told Hollywood columnist Louella Parsons that the women he loved never loved him and all the others didn't matter."

I flashed back on my meeting with Syble Zane in Jack's time and the sad origin of those Valentino Tears.

"I do know his first wife rejected him on their wedding night," I said.

"And his second wife nearly ruined his career," Enzo noted. "'Women are not in love with me,' he once said, 'I am merely the canvas on which women paint their dreams.'"

Enzo paused. "Valentino died at the height of his fame. He was only thirty-one years old. One hundred thousand people attended his funeral in New York City. Many women—and a few men, too—committed suicide rather than face a world without the Great Valentino."

I thought the man might break out in his own tears at any moment.

"I take it you are a fan," was the only comment I could muster.

"I am from Castellaneta," he replied, as if that explained everything. "Even the fine citizens of my fair city have begun to forget the legacy of their great gift. That cannot stand. The memory of Rudolph Valentino must never be forgotten."

"I understand your admiration for the late actor, but why are you telling me all this, Mr. Santoro?"

"*Oh mio Dio!* In my excitement I forgot the reason for our little chat. I am here in America to represent a former citizen of Castellaneta, now a prominent member of Sicilian high society. I am talking about a very wealthy member of a powerful family who would like nothing better than to bring that legendary necklace to Valentino's home."

"Who is this prominent citizen?"

"I am sorry, Mrs. McClure, but I am not at liberty to disclose that information. The party I represent wishes to remain anonymous. But understand that this person is willing to pay a high price for the Tears. Also understand that this offer comes with no questions. How you or another party may have come by the jewels is not our concern. We merely want to procure the Tears of Valentino."

"Look, Mr. Santoro, I can see you believe I know the whereabouts of the Tears? I assure you I do not."

"I have a strong . . . let us call it a feeling . . . that you are on the trail of the Tears, the same as I."

There was no need to reply. Enzo already knew I was on the case.

After that, he started the car and backed into the traffic. A few moments later we were driving up Cranberry Street. Because of the many cars parked around my store, he pulled into a spot half a block away.

"One more thing before you go, Mrs. McClure. Any transfer of funds would be a private affair; no one need know about the exchange—"

"Especially not the police?"

"Or the . . . how do you say it? The IRA?"

"The Irish Republican Army?"

"No, no, the American taxman. The party I represent will pay in dollars, in euros, or in cybercurrency. The money will be instantly wired to any account, here in America, in Switzerland, or a country of your choice."

"One question," I replied. "If I were to come across the Tears, how would I contact you?"

"I shall find you."

"I'll show myself out," I said, reaching for the handle.

"It has been a pleasure, Mrs. McClure. I hope we meet again."

I climbed out of the car and closed the door. Without another word, Enzo Santoro sped off—but not before I spied a pair of mud-caked size-twelve boots dirtying up the back seat's elegant leather upholstery!

For a minute I was reeling from the realization that I might have just taken a ride with a killer, but I didn't have time to chide myself. Jack Shepard did it for me.

Toots, didn't your mama ever warn you not to get into a car with a stranger? That's a real knucklehead move you pulled.

"And by sheer dumb luck, I may have found Dottie Willard's killer."

Whoa! Slow down there, Seabiscuit. A pair of muddy boots are pretty slim evidence to pin a murder rap on a joe. The johnny law needs a little thing we in the investigative business like to call "evidence."

"They might already have the evidence," I countered. "I'm pretty sure the police took molds of those boot prints in the woods. I'm going to call Eddie."

I used Eddie's personal phone number. He picked up right away, and I told him about Santoro, his off-the-books financial offer, and the muddy boots.

"A black Caddy, you said. Did you catch his license number?"

"I did," I replied, rattling it off.

"Sounds like a rental," Eddie said.

"What should we do?"

"*We* aren't doing anything." Eddie's reply was swift, and ominous. "*I* am going to turn this information over to the state police right now. *You* are going to stay as far away from this man as possible. It's conceivable that this is the guy who killed Dottie Willard, took a shot at you, and is out to kill Norma, too, if you or the state police don't find her first."

My hands were shaky as I put away the phone

Sorry to flatten your tire, doll, but I warned you. Death clings to the Tears of Valentino like rust on a Model T.

CHAPTER 30

Juvenile Delinquent

Nobody thanks you for sticking your neck out.

—*Rebel Without a Cause*, 1955

STILL SHAKY FROM my call with Eddie, I received another jolt when I spotted the double-parked police car in front of my store. When I pushed through the front door, I found the sales counter empty, and a customer-free shop—no surprise there. Weeknights around the dinner hour were usually pretty slow. Unfortunately, customer-free didn't mean empty. Alongside a pale and fretting Aunt Sadie, I found a most unwelcome visitor.

Officer Bull McCoy—Chief Ciders' nephew and *not* one of Quindicott PD's brightest bulbs—waited to greet me. The yellow "safety-first" vest over his QPD jacket reminded me that Bull had been assigned to police the school, so the fact that he was in my shop could mean only one thing.

"Spencer!" I cried with worry. "What are you doing home? You're supposed to be working on your science fair presentation."

My son frowned and said nothing. But Bull McCoy was more than happy to speak up.

"Mrs. McClure, there won't be any science fair presentation for this young man"—he squeezed Spencer's shoulder until my son winced. "Mrs. McConnell, the principal, wanted me to inform you that your son has been suspended from school indefinitely—"

"What?"

"You'll be getting an official letter from the school board in a day or so."

"Why is this happening?"

"Spencer McClure's suspension is based on the school's zero-tolerance policy toward violence—"

"Violence!"

"—and the possible criminal charges which may be filed against your son."

"Criminal charges!" I was likely shouting by now.

Sadie was too upset to speak.

"That's ridiculous!" I argued. "I know my son. He would never hurt anyone. What possible violent crime could he have committed?"

McCoy sniffed. "Food tampering. Possibly poisoning—"

"Poisoning?" I faced Spencer. "What on earth did you do?"

"I caught the thief, Mom. The person who was stealing from Miss Merrimac. I set a trap in the teachers' lounge and the perp fell for it, hook, line, and sinker—"

His tone was defiant and instantly won Spencer one admirer.

Your kid dropped a dime on a thief, Jack said. *Who cares what the law thinks? Spencer has done just swell in my book.*

I faced Bull McCoy again. "What happened, exactly?"

McCoy shuffled his shiny-booted feet. "The school nurse, Mrs. Falstaff, went home in a highly emotional state, claiming your son poisoned her."

Spencer broke free of Officer McCoy's grip and stepped back to face him.

"I didn't *poison* anybody!" he shot back. "All I did was prove that Mrs. Falstaff is a thief—and her stealing was hurting another teacher."

I got down on one knee and gripped Spencer's arms, forcing him to meet me eye to eye.

"Did you tell Principal McConnell your side of the story? Did you tell Officer McCoy here?"

He shook his head. "I pleaded the Fifth, Mom, just like the accused do on *Shield of Justice*. Anything I say can and will be used against me in a court of law. So . . ." He shrugged. "I didn't say anything."

Then my son turned to look Bull McCoy right in the eye. "Isn't that right, Officer?"

"Heh-heh," McCoy chuckled through a rictus grin. "Looks like you got yourself a little lawyer there, Mrs. McClure."

"I just knew enough to keep my lips zippered," Spencer proclaimed with Jack Shield bravado.

"Well, *now* you're going to talk—to your mother," I informed him. "You landed yourself in a pot of trouble, Spencer, and I need to know everything."

Spencer shook his head so hard his copper bangs waved back and forth. Then he jerked his thumb in the direction of Officer McCoy.

"I'm not saying a word until he hits the road."

"Fine," I said, rising to face the policeman. "I think I can handle things from here."

"You do that, Mrs. McClure. And watch for that letter . . ."

When Officer McCoy was gone, I sat Spencer down in the stock room and got the straight story out of him.

"I filled up Miss Merrimac's old cranberry juice bottle with Kool-Aid, purple food coloring—"

"Food coloring?"

Spencer nodded. "I mixed it with Kool-Aid so the drink would smell fruity. I took it to school, waited until classes were over and Miss Merrimac was gone for the day. Then I snuck into the teachers' lounge and planted it in the refrigerator. The juice was always stolen after school—and I was working on my science project near the lounge, so I could watch. And it worked. Mrs. Falstaff had purple lips and Mr. Burke and the whole science class saw her."

"Honey, *why* did you do this? Just to catch a thief?"

"No, Mom! I thought Mr. Burke was guilty. All the evidence said it was him. But deep down I never believed it. I just knew Mr. Burke wouldn't do something like that."

"So, you wanted to clear his name?"

Spencer vigorously nodded. "Only for myself. I was the only one who knew about the fingerprint, and it bothered me so much I *had* to find out the truth."

"So, this Nurse Falstaff drank the juice?"

Spencer nodded.

"You know that was wrong. That the end doesn't justify the means. You could have hurt her. She could have been allergic to the food coloring. What she drank could have made her sick."

Spencer's expression was horrified. "But, Mom—"

"What you did was wrong, Spencer, and you're going to have to be punished. I just hope she doesn't press charges. It's going to be hard enough getting you back to school without juvenile delinquency charges hanging over your head."

Lighten up on the little tyke, Jack insisted. *You should be proud of your son. He cared enough about a stranger to stick his neck out. Caring, and trying to solve the problem, are the kid's only mistakes.*

Well, Jack, between Nurse Falstaff and Max Braydon, Spencer and I might both land in detention, indefinitely.

SEYMOUR TARNISH ARRIVED at my bookshop a few hours (and a few aspirins) later. He brought along the circular I asked for and Professor Parker, too.

"Sorry to barge in," Brainert said. "With my car in the shop, I have to hitch rides with Seymour to get anything done."

"I understand, because I'm going to need a ride from Seymour tomorrow. Do you mind?"

Seymour shrugged. "So long as you're not going to the airport."

I reminded them about my experience with insurance investigator Max Braydon, and how my car was no doubt in some police pound in Newport or Providence, and probably not in one piece.

"So, are we going to pick up your car tomorrow?" Seymour asked.

"I wish, but no. Let's look at that circular and I'll explain."

Seymour produced the mailer and spread it out on the counter.

"Who's that woman on the front there?" Brainert asked.

"That's our state senator," Seymour replied. "One of thirty-eight state senators in Rhode Island. Don't you know who your state senator is?"

"No," Brainert and I said in unison.

"Apathy." Seymour shook his head. "That's why things are going to—"

"Stick to the subject, Seymour," I insisted.

"Well, our esteemed state senator helped fund the reclamation of Millstone Creek. She printed a map of the project on the second page."

We studied the simplistic rendering for a moment. According to the scale provided, there were about five miles of creek that flowed through the once-polluted section of Millstone, culminating at Michaelmas Pond.

"That's a lot of ground to cover," I muttered.

"What are we covering ground for?" Seymour asked.

"We're looking for Norma." I explained my logic for believing Norma might still be in the area and hiding somewhere along Millstone Creek.

Seymour dug out his phone and checked the map.

"The creek roughly parallels the rural route to Millstone, which I guess is why they call it Millstone Creek." Seymour kept on scrolling. "There are a couple of places where the creek bank is less than half a mile from the road. Here's one spot Brainert might recognize—"

Seymour displayed the street-view image on his phone.

"Gad!" the professor cried. "That's the very curve where your friend Norma sideswiped my car."

"Good," I said. "Then it's as good a place as any to start searching for her."

CHAPTER 31

Dancing Queen

A dream you dream alone is only a dream. A dream
you dream together is reality.

—John Lennon quoting Yoko Ono, *All We Are Saying*

"YOU KNOW WHAT, Jack? I had a terrible realization
today."

*You finally figured out this hayseed town is dull as dust,
and it's time to go back to the bright lights of the big city?*

"Not even close . . ."

I was in my bed, staring at the ceiling. Hours ago, I'd said
goodbye to Seymour and Brainert and locked up the shop.
Now Spencer was in his own bed—sleeping, I presumed,
because he was thoroughly grounded. I took his phone and
his computer out of his room. I left him his little AM/FM
radio because it was also his clock.

Disciplining my little boy gave me no joy, and it was
nights like this—with my mind full of worries and self-
doubt—that I was happy to be haunted. The ghost always
knew when I needed to talk . . .

"Today I realized I am failing as a parent."

*That's a truckload of hooey, doll, a pound of baloney
with a banana chaser.*

"Please don't tell me 'boys will be boys,' because what happened today is more than boyish mischief. After I spent all those Sundays with Spencer, coaxing him in his science project; after we had a serious talk about his not using what he'd learned to solve adult crimes at his school, Spencer defied me. He went off and did what he believed was right, never mind what I thought. He acted silly, stupid, headstrong—"

And mighty brave.

"Brave?"

Sure. The kid was on a mission to find justice for his teacher. Despite knowing he'd be punished, and you'd be angry with him, he stuck to his goal. That's called courage.

"It may look like that from your perspective. But from mine, my son put himself in a terrible jam and left me a real mess to clean up, on top of the Norma nightmare, the Braydon threat, and the daily business of keeping our shop running."

Welcome to the circus of life, Penny. As crazy as it gets, it's still a better place than mine, and don't you forget it, even if you do feel like a clown in the center ring sometimes, juggling a few too many balls.

"They call it multi-tasking these days," I told the ghost. "And first thing tomorrow one of my tasks will be handling Spencer's principal. Too bad I'm not particularly good at *handling*. Principals or little boys."

Is that what you think?

"Yes. Sometimes I wish Spencer's father were still alive to help me with things like this."

You know what? There comes a time in every young man's life when he stops taking his marching orders from his mother, even if she means well. Of course, all that changes when a Jane corrals her Joe. Put a ring on his finger and a Joe will be taking orders from a dame all over again.

"You never did."

No, never did. But truth be told, I would have liked the chance. And if I were Spencer's father, you know what I'd do right now?

"What"

Take his mother out for a night of champagne and dancing.

I laughed. "Does that mean we're finally going to Sardi's?"

Not this time, honey, because tonight you need a little lesson in confidence. I know you can handle yourself in a tight situation. And you do too. You just need a little reminder.

I stifled a yawn. "Is that your roundabout way of saying I'm getting another PI lesson? Because I thought I was going dancing."

Close those pretty peepers, and you'll be doing both . . .

"RISE AND SHINE, Penny. We're almost there."

I heard a horn honk and traffic sounds and sniffed a miasma of French perfume. It took me a moment to realize the sweet aroma was wafting off me.

I opened my eyes and sat up in the taxi seat. Beside me, Jack smiled as he flipped a quarter, then tucked it into his pocket. He was dressed in a shiny evening suit complete with black tie. His signature trench coat and fedora were nowhere to be found.

"You should be raring to go, seeing as you just had a nap and you're all dolled up to beat the band."

Jack wasn't exaggerating. I was so "dolled up" I felt like a spoiled child's Barbie on her imaginary prom night—long white satin dress with a slit up the side, white opera gloves all the way up to my armpits, delicate gold-trimmed heels, an audacious neckline that displayed way too much, and a cinched waist that made me look so incredibly svelte I had to remind myself this was only a dream. Over it all I was wrapped in a luxurious ermine cape as soft as a bunny rabbit's tail.

And did I mention I was literally dripping in jewelry?

"Raring to go where?" I asked. "A precious gems convention? What if I get mugged?"

"Relax, doll, it's all costume stuff, but very convincing."

"What if some thug is convinced and I get mugged?"

"I'll be nearby the whole time."

I didn't like the sound of that! "Nearby? How nearby is nearby?"

"Near enough, but I can't be with you every second."

"Why is that?"

"You're going into an exclusive club called the Moondance. No men are allowed. Well, no men who aren't the entertainment or the staff, anyway."

"What are you saying?"

"You've got to go it alone."

"But—"

"The Moondance is where rich older dames go to taxi dance with handsome young men while their rich older husbands are out of town or visiting a doxy of their own."

"Taxi dance? That's like when a man pays a woman ten cents for a dance, right?"

"Yeah, Penny, and the house keeps a nickel and the dancer gets the same. Only tonight you won't be waltzing with nickel-hoppers. *Exclusive* is the word at the Moondance. A single trot around the ballroom is a cool ten-spot—"

"Ten dollars!"

"And the dames are footing the bill."

"And I'm going to the Moondance because . . . ?"

"Because Billy Bastogne is holed up there with the Tears of Valentino. Ironic, ain't it? Rudolph Valentino himself worked as a taxi dancer, at Maxim's."

"So, Billy is a taxi dancer?"

"He works the dance floor and figures he's safe from Klaus Bremen and the Germantown gang he owes money to because the joint is man-free."

"How do you know all this, Jack?"

"Remember Phyllis Harmon, the doll at the Bijoux House of Fashion?"

"The hysterical woman I knocked down?"

"That's her. Miss Harmon told a whopper to the coppers just like I suggested, only now she wants to get even with Billy Bastogne for killing her friend Thelma Dice."

"So?"

"So, Phyllis has been helping me, see? Billy doesn't know Phyllis was at the Bijoux, too. She played all innocent about knowing he was the killer. Meantime she did a lot of snooping on Billy's pals and talking with associates of Klaus Bremen and his Germantown mob. Turns out, Phyllis came up with a pair of aces."

"Aces how?"

"Phyllis learned that Billy figured out those Tears are worth more than the measly few grand he owed his bookie, Klaus Bremen. Billy wants to profit from the jewels he killed his girlfriend to get. He sent a message that he wants to negotiate with the mob."

"How did that go?"

"The Germantown gang decided to cooperate. Klaus Bremen is sending in a woman to appraise the jewels, make sure Billy isn't pulling a scam. The dame is meeting him at the Moondance tonight."

"And who is this dame?"

"Her alias is Veronika Von Vimko. She claims she's a Hungarian countess who lost everything in the war. But I know her from the old days."

"Old days?"

"Her real name is Molly Shaughnessy and she's a long-time bunko artist out of Hell's Kitchen. Molly knows diamonds because she used to con them off rich old ladies with her fortune-telling racket. Old Molly has a few priors, and up until this morning, three outstanding warrants."

"Had?"

"You caught that? I knew you were sharp." Jack shrugged his broad shoulders. "Yeah, I dropped a dime on the countess to a police lieutenant I know. Now Molly is in the slammer, an up-and-coming cop owes me a favor, and tonight you get to play Veronika Von Vimko."

Jack patted the silk-clad leg that peeked through the provocative slit in the gown. "How about that, doll? You'll be Countess for a Day."

"Oh, swell."

The taxi driver rolled to a stop and Jack hopped out and

helped me to my feet. I was wearing so much jewelry that when I moved I actually rattled.

I looked around. A clock on the corner told me it was near midnight. We were a few blocks from the New Yorker Hotel. I knew because I could see the iconic red neon sign that still existed when I lived here a few years ago—or decades from now if you want to look at the situation backward.

"That's the joint," Jack said, pointing.

The Moondance was obviously a very private club. A blue neon moon, about the size of a basketball, glowed over an ebony door. The name *Moondance* was nowhere to be found, and there were no other windows or any indication of what was beyond that nearly invisible single door. One could easily walk by this place a hundred times without noticing it was there.

"What do I do?"

"You go through that door, have a few words with the hostess, and buy a hundred bucks' worth of tickets—"

"Tickets?"

"You know what a ticket is, right?"

"Sure, I get them when I go to the movies."

"Well, think of this as movie night. A hundred bucks will get you ten tickets. Ten tickets means ten dances and all the champagne you can swill. Dance with a few of the fancy men, look like you're there to pour a little sunshine into your life."

"Anything else?"

"Yeah, don't look for Billy Bastogne. Act nonchalant. In his eyes you are holding all the cards. He's desperate to fence those rocks and he doesn't know how to. Let Billy find you. Make him sweat a little for what he did to poor Thelma Dice."

"You're sure I can handle this?" I asked doubtfully.

"Sure I'm sure. Piece o' cake. And once Billy makes contact, stay glued to him like flypaper. Don't let him shake you."

"You know, Jack, you could call that nice up-and-coming police lieutenant and give him another tip. That Billy Bastogne killed his girlfriend and stole her jewels."

"I could, but for two things. One. I have no evidence. None of us saw Billy kill Thelma, even though we both know that he did. There's nothing to even connect him with the victim. Our Mr. Bastogne has no permanent address. As far as the world knows, Thelma lived alone. Phyllis won't talk to the law, and I don't blame her, so there is nothing but scuttlebutt to link Bastogne to Thelma Dice."

"And reason number two?" I asked.

"If the cops snatch the Tears, we don't. That means Syble Zane won't pay me more than she already has. Anyway, I don't like to let a client down."

"Especially one as lovely as Miss Zane."

"Now, don't get all catty on me."

"Fine. Where do I get a hundred bucks?"

"You'll find a C-note in that purse of yours. I can afford it. It's Syble Zane's money. I've been keeping our Broadway starlet apprised of our progress on the case, not to mention my mounting expenses."

Jack smiled so wide the scar on his chin almost vanished. "In you go, sweetheart."

I swept a hand through my copper hair, loose and long enough to brush my shoulders. Then I pulled the ermine tighter around me and approached the forbidding-looking door.

Behind me, I heard Jack's call.

"Have a good time, doll. But not too good, if you know what I mean."

CHAPTER 32

Let's Face the Music and Dance

Dancing is a perpendicular expression of a horizontal
desire.

—George Bernard Shaw

"WELCOME TO THE Moondance, Countess Von Vimko."

The hostess who greeted me inside the dimly lit, black-
curtained reception area was barely above drinking age, but
her expression was hardened beyond her tender years. She
wore her tumble of platinum hair over one eye, just like Ve-
ronica Lake, but neither her hair nor her silver-sequined
gown managed to shimmer in such funereal surroundings.

"Would you like to purchase a dance, or simply enjoy the
club?"

"I think this will take care of it," I said, handing over
Jack's hundred-dollar bill.

The woman stuffed the bill in an iron box and handed me
ten blue coins with grinning, winking man-in-the-moon
faces on both sides.

"Present one to the escort of your choosing," the blonde
said as she drew velvet curtains aside to admit me. "The
ballroom is through here and the Bower of Bliss is on the

other side of the dance floor, beyond the golden curtains. And please, enjoy the champagne. It's on the house."

"Oh, I plan to," I replied, and I meant it. This place was already creeping me out and I hadn't even entered the main ballroom yet—let alone the "Bower of Bliss."

As I walked into the cavernous ballroom, a band struck up a lively swing number. The bandshell was a huge plaster-of-Paris oyster, its maw open wide enough to fit a dozen musicians and their instruments, including a Steinway piano.

Like the reception area, the ballroom was draped in black velvet, with a crystal chandelier hanging from the ceiling. Tables and plush lounge chairs circled the edges of the polished wooden dance floor. Among those tables and chairs, furtive black-tie waiters delivered trays of champagne.

Despite the sophisticated setting and the presumably exclusive clientele, the activity in this room most resembled the few high school dances I'd bothered to attend in my teen years.

Just like the dances in the school gym back in Quindicott, several couples who'd already comfortably connected spun to the music. Meanwhile, all the men—young, well-groomed, and clad in their best suits—stood on one side of the room while the women remained on the opposite side.

These women were mostly older but not exclusively. They sat, stood, or swayed solo to the music. Some silently gauged their choices while others, clustering in small groups, giggled like schoolgirls before one brave soul shyly crossed the dance floor, coin in hand.

A waiter drifted by. I snatched a glass of bubbly and downed it in a single gulp.

"Smooth," I gasped, coughing. I immediately snagged another and downed it, too—without coughing.

Hey, I'm getting good at this. Only now I had a glass in each gloved hand, and nowhere to put them down.

"Allow me," a mellow voice said. The empty glass vanished from my left hand, and a full glass replaced the empty one in my right.

I turned and, to my shock, Alan Ladd was standing in

front of me—okay, not *the* Alan Ladd (frankly, this one was a little taller), but a man with the same white-blond hair, sturdy chin, and confident, crooked grin.

Even in this faint light I knew the likeness wasn't perfect. But after a few champagnes . . .

I downed the third glass. "Would you care to dance, Mr. . . . ?"

"Beaumont," he said with a gracious nod. "Edward Beaumont. And I would love to dance, Miss—"

"Countess," I said with all the haughtiness I could muster after multiple glasses of liquid courage. "Countess Von Vimko."

I reached into my purse and handed over a coin just as a waltz ended and the band segued right into a slow rendition of "Moonlight Serenade."

Mr. Beaumont swept me into the middle of the polished floor. A superb dancer, he took complete control, moving me around the ballroom like a pawn on a chessboard. He held me close—a little too close, perhaps, but how often does a gal get to foxtrot with Alan Ladd?

As I scanned the couples trotting around us I realized that the dancers had all been hired for their resemblance to Hollywood leading men. The ladies on the dance floor were certainly enjoying themselves, living out their starstruck dreams.

Even I decided this might be fun after all.

When my dance with Alan Ladd ended, I did a turn with a Robert Mitchum imitator who was quite convincing—until he opened his mouth. Instead of the deep, almost melodious voice of the Hollywood rebel, out squeaked an Irish falsetto straight from Hell's Kitchen.

My waltz with Jimmy Stewart was sadly a bore. My coin partner was as taciturn as most of Stewart's characters, and when he did speak it was "ma'am" this and "ma'am" that—and *that* got old fast.

Happily, Cary Grant made up for it.

Most revealing, however, was my slow dance with the faux William Powell. Perfectly mimicking the star of the

Thin Man movies, he was older than the other dancers and possessed a level of suave sophistication that none of the other toe tappers could match.

As we swayed in each other's arms to "Begin the Beguine," I noticed one of the other dancers staring at me. When I returned the stare, the man looked away but resumed his inspection as soon as he thought I wasn't paying attention.

William Powell noticed, too.

"Do you know that man, my dear?" he whispered into my ear.

"No, but he certainly thinks he knows me," I replied. "Who is he?"

My dance partner laughed gently. "Surely you recognize our Cesar Romero?"

"Is that who he's supposed to be?"

"His real name is Billy Bastogne."

Just as Jack predicted, I thought, *Billy Bastogne found me. Time to make like a detective and ask some questions . . .*

"What do you know about Mr. Bastogne?" I asked.

"Well, he acts like a native New Yorker, but he speaks with an accent most believe is French. However, the trained ear of a seasoned radio actor such as I recognizes it as French-Canadian."

"Anything else?"

William Powell sighed as if the subject was beginning to bore him.

"I understand Billy pays the rent without purchasing the groceries. He could live a life of leisure, but he's here most nights wowing the ladies to feed a habit."

"Habit?"

"Yes. We all have them, don't we? Billy's is losing at the races."

"Now, that I understand. But paying the rent? Buying the groceries?" I shook my head, confused. "What do you mean, exactly?"

"Ah, I forgot. You are a countess from another land and don't understand our American lingo."

The tone William Powell used when he called me "a

countess from another land" suggested he didn't believe that whopper for a minute.

No matter, I wasn't trying to fool him.

"The phrase 'paying the rent' means Billy is living in a clandestine relationship," he explained. "Not buying the groceries indicates the young lady pays the bills. In plain terms, Billy Bastogne is a kept man."

"Do you know her?"

"I don't even know the trollop's name. Do you think I would associate with such riffraff if I wasn't forced to by dire economic necessity?"

Inspiration hit me, and I asked another question. "Do you know a Phyllis Harmon? She's a model, I think."

"A model?" He sniffed. "Only part-time. And I hear Phyllis only models in order to scout new . . . shall we say *talent* . . . for her boss."

"And her boss is . . . ?"

"Phyllis is Harry Amsterdam's gal Friday."

It took me a moment to digest that.

Phyllis worked for one of the most powerful producers on Broadway, the very man who gave Syble Zane the Tears of Valentino—and then took them back to re-gift them to Thelma Dice, now the late Miss Dice.

But if Phyllis worked for Harry, she wouldn't need Jack's connections to land an acting job. All she'd have to do is ask her boss. Yet back at the House of Fashion, she pretended she was some penniless wannabe actress in need of help.

Why was she playing Jack? And more importantly, did the great Jack Shepard know he was being played?

Phyllis also claimed she was simply Thelma Dice's friend and looking for justice. Could she be looking for something else too? Like the priceless Tears?

Now that Thelma was dead, did Harry want them back again?

At that point in my conversation with William Powell, the song ended. And as the ticket was only good for one dance, the pretend Thin Man star broke our clinch and gallantly kissed my gloved hand.

"Goodnight, Countess," he said, a dubious eyebrow raised.

When he was gone, I snagged another glass of champagne from a passing waiter, gulped it down, and returned it to the tray before the server could escape. Meanwhile, the band struck up another slow number.

"I'd be delighted to share this dance, Countess," a rough voice snarled in my ear. Suddenly, Billy Bastogne seized my elbow from behind, swung me around, and practically dragged me among the swaying bodies on the dance floor.

He pulled me close, and I nearly gagged on the smell of cheap cologne. Billy Bastogne didn't do a very good job of shaving, either. With his face against mine, I felt like I was rubbing my cheek on Bookmark's scratching post.

"You know who I am, right, Countess?" Bastogne's sneer told me he didn't buy my royal pedigree, either.

"Sure," I replied, trying to match his tough talk with my own. "You're going to show me some cut glass you're lame enough to think are diamonds."

He gave me a murderous look. "Hey, don't try to pull that stuff on me. You tell Klaus Bremen my debt gets forgiven, and I walk away with ten grand or the deal's off."

When I didn't reply I saw flop sweat blossom on his forehead.

"Bremen's got to give me that," he rasped. "I'm facing the chair if the police get wise to me. Don't you see that I got to get out of town fast?"

I didn't need to be reminded that the hands holding me tightly had choked the life out of Thelma Dice, and I suppressed a shiver.

"Fine," I said, relenting. "Let's see what you've got and maybe we can negotiate."

The song ended and we broke the clinch. "Where are the Tears?" I demanded.

"Hidden."

"Here?"

He nodded.

"Well, let's go get them."

"Oh no," Billy said. "I'm not going to let you see where I've hidden them. Meet me in the Lilac Garden in the Bower of Bliss. I'll be there in ten minutes. I'll have the rocks and you can take a gander at them. Then you'll know they're the real thing."

CHAPTER 33

Danse Macabre

I think you're a perfectly normal human being. Selfish and ruthless when you want something. Generous and kindly when you've got it.

—*Nightmare Alley, 1947*

BEFORE THE LAST note faded, Billy Bastogne gave me his back. He pushed his way through the crowded dance floor, toward the giant plaster-of-Paris oyster.

Jack instructed me never to lose sight of Mr. Bastogne, but that proved to be impossible. As I watched helplessly, Billy went to a door behind the bandshell, unlocked it and was through in an instant.

Well, Jack believed I could handle this task, so there was no use dithering. I had no choice but to visit the Bower of Bliss to meet Billy Bastogne at the Lilac Garden.

I reached for another glass of champagne, then decided against it. Better to keep my head clear.

Bastogne said to meet him in ten minutes, but despite the fact that jewelry hung from every possible bauble-wearing part of my body, I didn't have a watch. There wasn't a clock in sight, either, so I counted down a few hundred seconds, squared my shoulders, and set off to find this Bower of Bliss.

A waiter directed me to a set of gold lamé curtains. I pushed through to find myself in a large circular space with curtained alcoves around the perimeter. In the center stood a naked Venus fountain of gurgling water that flowed into a pool filled with dozens of little fish.

Some of the alcoves were presumably occupied, with curtains drawn for privacy. The ones that stood open were empty. Each had a large love seat in a color appropriate to the name painted in gold cursive above. The Rose Garden displayed red velvet upholstery, crimson walls, and a dozen red blossoms in a large vase. The Sunflower Garden had a bright yellow theme with a glowing sun ornament on the wall. The curtains were drawn across the Daffodil and Orchid alcoves, but I could hear murmurs and laughter from behind their drapes.

I found the Lilac Garden's violet curtains open. The love seat and walls were the same color purple as the New England asters in Dottie Willard's backyard. I didn't take that as a good omen. In fact, this whole Bower of Bliss thing gave me the willies. On top of that, I had the distinct feeling that I was being watched, yet whenever I looked around, I saw no one.

I almost regretted turning down that last glass of champagne, but I should have remembered that old saying: Be careful what you wish for, because suddenly Billy Bastogne was here, a bottle of champagne and two glasses in hand, a smirk on his sort-of-like Cesar Romero face. He seemed pleased to find me on the love seat and closed the curtains behind him. He remained standing, his back to the purple drapes, grinning like a cat who'd caught one of those little fishes in the fountain.

"I thought you and me might get acquainted before I show off the goods," he purred.

I felt my eyes narrow suspiciously. "You thought wrong, buster. Show me the jewels right now or I'm out of here. And I doubt the Germantown gang will like my report."

Billy patted his lapel. "Relax, Countess. I have them right here in my pocket—"

Abruptly, he stopped talking, his expression morphing into a combination of shock and confusion. He dropped his hands, bumping the table. The glasses shattered on the polished wood floor. The bottle struck heavily but didn't break.

I jumped up in horror, watching Billy's mouth gape like a dead mackerel before his body dropped facedown on the floor, an ice pick buried to its hilt in the back of his neck.

I was at his side when the curtains rustled beside my head—the killer was still on the other side of the thin material. I was about to tear aside that veil when a sucker punch slammed me, right through the curtain!

I saw stars, lots of them, and my knees gave—which turned out to be a lucky break. The second punch missed my face, to pound my shoulder instead, and that was enough to lay me flat.

I heard the curtains parting. I tried to move, to see my assailant, but the ermine cape was now tangled around me and fur covered half my face—which ultimately saved me.

The next blow was a kick to the head, and the thick ermine cushioned the worst. My attacker didn't have a clue I wasn't dead, because that vicious kick from a high-heeled shoe would have been more than enough to do the job if it had connected with my cranium.

Groggy as I was, I managed to catch sight of the murderer as she fished a tobacco pouch out of Billy Bastogne's jacket. I heard the contents of that pouch rattle as she pushed through the curtain.

She was gone in an instant—but not before I got a good look at her.

I heard a shot coming from outside the Lilac Garden. A woman screamed. Then the purple curtain was ripped aside, and a tuxedo-clad waiter dropped to his knee beside me—no, not a waiter. It was—

"Jack," I gasped. "Where did you come from?"

"I was watching you the whole time, doll. I even tried to get your attention when Billy ducked through that secret door behind the bandshell, but no dice."

"You were double-crossed, Jack—"

"I know, honey. I saw her for myself. Phyllis Harmon killed Billy Bastogne. Then she took a shot at me."

I tried to sit up, but everything spun. Was it the champagne or the blow to the head? Probably both.

"You better go catch her," I said, forcing a smile.

"I'll be back as soon as I can."

When Jack was gone, I managed to push myself into a sitting position, even as the room faded into a purple mist. Soon the haze was too thick to see my hands in front of my face, and my heart began to pound.

"Jack!" I called. "Jack, where are you? Come back!"

But he didn't. I was alone and suddenly cold, so cold that I started to shiver.

I tried to stand but the floor dissolved and melted away, dropping me into a bottomless void. Kicking and thrashing, I fought to stay but the pull was too powerful. Descending through space and time, I shouted my objections, arms flailing, until the yawning darkness cut off my cries and swallowed me whole.

CHAPTER 34

To the Principal's Office

Chase after the truth like all hell and you'll free yourself, even though you never touch its coat tails.

—Clarence Darrow, "The Sign" May 1938

I WOKE UP a few minutes before my alarm rang. Once
again, I was on the floor, my legs tangled in my sheets, my
pillows piled up around me.

"What a night," I muttered. "I wake up more tired than
when I go to sleep."

Of course Jack didn't reply. He would likely be AWOL
for a few hours—and on a day when I needed his spirit the
most. I had to go to Spencer's school, apologize, and explain
what happened. I needed to defend my son like an ace attor-
ney, and I couldn't wait around for my ghost to reappear.

Before I could channel Clarence Darrow, however, I made
a quick call to Eddie Franzetti, hoping he'd share any developments concerning the mysterious Enzo Santoro (if that was
even his real name). But the police dispatcher informed me
that the deputy chief took the morning off—Mrs. Franzetti
was getting a medical test in Providence. When I heard that, I
expressed my concern. The dispatcher confided it wasn't anything serious and I sighed with relief—and a little frustration.

The Santoro update would have to wait.

Consequently, I turned my attention to my own situation. Last night, Jack tried to prove to me that I could handle myself in any situation. Okay, lesson learned. Now it was time to put my PI spirit's tutorial to the test.

With my car still impounded and my adrenaline high, I made a snap decision. Instead of sending my son off to catch the school bus, I left Spencer snoozing in his bed while I grabbed my son's bicycle and pumped the pedals like a Peloton princess. Breathing hard, I raced straight for Quindicott Elementary School and managed to reach the administration office before the homeroom bell sounded. My heart rate was up, my mind wide awake, and I was ready for a fight!

The young secretary looked up when I entered the reception area.

"May I help you?"

"I'm here to see Mrs. McConnell. My name is Penelope McClure. Spencer McClure is my son and—"

She literally jumped to her feet when I mentioned Spencer's name. Apparently his reputation for juvenile delinquency preceded him. The secretary scurried around an open filing cabinet and into an interior office. Before I could draw breath, the young woman was back.

"Please come with me, Mrs. McClure."

As soon as I was ushered into the principal's office, Eleanor McConnell rose to greet me.

"So nice to see you, Mrs. McClure."

With my nerves steeled for a fight, I gaped at the woman. Younger than any principal I remembered, and a new mother to boot, Eleanor McConnell usually displayed a sunny disposition, but her cheerful greeting and warm smile were far from what I expected, considering the grave charges the school had leveled against my son.

"Please, sit down, Mrs. McClure. I thank you for saving me a trip. I was about to visit you at your store."

"Really? Has the school board reached its decision so soon?"

She shook her head. "The school board wasn't informed about this situation."

"I'm puzzled," I replied. "Why?"

"Because this has all been a terrible misunderstanding."

I nearly fell off my chair. "But didn't the school nurse accuse my son of poisoning her? Didn't Officer McCoy suggest criminal charges were pending?"

Principal McConnell replied in a calm, reasonable tone, which my own voice seemed to lack. "Mrs. McClure, let me explain."

"Please do."

"After I sent Spencer home with Officer McCoy, Mr. Burke approached me. Do you know Mr. Burke?"

"We met once. Spencer speaks highly of him."

"Mr. Burke was in the school lab with your son and two other students when the nurse was . . . *branded* is the word, I guess, with purple food coloring. Spencer immediately confessed to doctoring the juice, assuring everyone that the mixture was harmless. Of course, harmless or not, with our policy of zero tolerance, I had no choice but to suspend him pending further action."

"I sense a 'but' coming."

"Mr. Burke and the other two students, who were getting ready for the science fair, knew about your son's interest in forensics, in fingerprinting, in law enforcement, and they deduced that Spencer was simply trying to catch a thief."

Principal McConnell placed both hands flat on her desk and leaned forward.

"Spencer caught more than Miss Merrimac's juice thief, Mrs. McClure. He helped to capture a major felon and recover thousands of dollars in stolen goods."

"I . . . I don't understand."

"Since the beginning of the school year this place has suffered some serious thefts," the principal continued. "Supplies have consistently gone missing. A computer was stolen from the supply closet. A video camera vanished from the audiovisual room. And just last week I consoled a sobbing substitute teacher who had her engagement ring and mobile phone stolen out of her locker while she was conducting gym class."

"I'm sure Spencer didn't know about any of that."

"No one knew," the principal replied. "I kept the truth under wraps for good reason. I didn't know if the guilty party was a student, or someone on the support staff, or heaven forbid another teacher. But thanks to your son, we now know who the culprit is."

"I really don't understand."

"Because Mrs. Falstaff fell for Spencer's trap, I became suspicious and had her personal locker opened. Trust me, it's all legal, her locker is on school property, so we had every right to find out what was inside. Sure enough, we found the missing computer, the stolen engagement ring, mobile phone, and several other items that had gone missing."

"I'm happy Spencer helped, but can't Nurse Falstaff still press charges against my son?"

The principal shook her head. "She was playing the victim. Spencer was correct, she was in no danger. And he didn't serve her the drink. She was the one who took another teacher's juice bottle from the fridge and drank it. Nevertheless, there won't be any charges filed by Nurse Falstaff simply because Chief Ciders has already arrested her on charges of grand theft."

"There's a lot of that going around," I muttered.

"Needless to say, I don't condone Spencer's methods, but I can't deny they were effective."

Mrs. McConnell rose. "Spencer can come back to school in the morning. And worry not, I will strike today's absence from the record, because it was our fault he missed school."

I felt a rush of relief and pride. I didn't condone Spencer's stunt either, but his heart was certainly in the right place.

"Thank you, Mrs. McConnell," I said, shaking her hand. "Before I go, I'd like to thank Mr. Burke, too."

Mrs. McConnell's sunny smile brightened.

"Of course. He'll be thrilled to hear Spencer is returning. Right now, Mr. Burke is in the lab with the other science fair entrants. Come on, I'll take you."

CHAPTER 35

Unblinded by Science

I got a crazy teacher, he wears dark glasses.

—Timbuk 3, "The Future's So Bright I Gotta Wear Shades," 1986

WHEN MRS. McCONNELL and I entered the school lab, we were immediately startled by an explosive spark that lit the entire room in a stark white flash.

In that quick, bright spark, I saw Mr. Burke. The elementary school teacher was down on one knee, using an arc welder to connect a steel triangle onto what looked like a long, tapered metal pipe.

A safe distance away, a boy and girl watched with awe. Even though they sagged under the weight of oversized safety vests, their eyes were wide behind their welders' masks.

While he worked, Mr. Burke explained what a "stabilizer" was and how it was essential for aerodynamic flight. Inside that metal mask, he sounded like a chipper Darth Vader.

"That should do it, Tim," Burke said when he finished, wiping his brow with the sleeve of his safety jacket.

"Thanks, Mr. Burke," the boy cried, admiring the teacher's work.

That's when Alan Burke realized he had company. After our greetings, Principal McConnell excused herself, and I turned to the students to say—

"I want to thank you all for helping to get Spencer out of trouble. Because you were such good friends, he'll be back in school tomorrow."

The boy and girl cheered.

"No problem, Mrs. McClure," Mr. Burke replied. "Susan, Tim, and I . . . we all understood what Spencer was trying to do. We knew about Spencer's interest in law enforcement, too. That's because we all learn together. It broadens the science fair experience."

He nudged the arc welder. "I'm sorry Spence missed this demonstration. I hope he'll be here tomorrow for act two."

"He will be," I promised. "Though after getting into so much trouble with food coloring, I can only wonder what mischief an arc welder will inspire."

I noticed a standing board covered with dozens of photographs, all of them taken in the wild, all of them numbered.

"And what's this?"

"Susan Trencher's project," Mr. Burke said proudly. "She's concerned about our local ecology. Susan has been mapping illegal dumping sites in our area."

Susan's green eyes sparkled behind fiery red bangs and wild curls. I'd gone to high school with her father, Ethan, who now ran a local campground with his wife, and the resemblance to her dad was uncanny. Susan also shared his love of nature.

"I found twenty-seven different sites where garbage has been dumped," Susan proclaimed. "All of these places are within a one-mile radius of Quindicott or Millstone."

Susan had beautifully photographed ugly things— shorelines littered with old tires half-buried in the sand. A smashed-up car lying on its side and slowly rusting. Another car—just a chassis, really—half-buried in tall brown weeds within sight of the railroad bridge.

She had a photo of the all-but-abandoned fire-prevention tower on the junction to Millstone and another of plastic bags entangled in tree branches near the wild bird sanctuary. Many shots were taken in sections of the creek filled with rusty beer cans, plastic cups, food wrappers, liquor bottles, and broken glass.

I was about to turn away when an image seized my attention, and I focused on that single photograph.

It wasn't the purple blossoms of the New England asters that caught my eye, though they were plentiful in the picture. Nor was it the lovely sunset in the background. The tiny hairs on the back of my neck prickled when I saw a distinctive teardrop trailer parked on a sandbar. Its wheels were half-buried in the muck, and the trailer itself was splattered with mud and surrounded by water—it was easy to see why Susan thought the vehicle had been abandoned. But I was pretty sure it wasn't, at least not intentionally.

It's Norma's teardrop trailer! I silently screamed.

It sure looks like it, doll, Jack Shepard replied, surprising me with his sudden appearance. *That's A-number-one quality detective work. I see you've been busy while I was away.*

Don't compliment me yet, Jack. We haven't found the trailer, only a picture of it.

I whirled to face Susan Trencher. "That picture, was it taken near Michaelmas Pond?"

Susan shook her curls. "No, the trailer is on the other side of Millstone, the part of the creek that isn't reclaimed yet. I found the place because the state made a dirt road to use for their cleanup project."

"Do you remember when you took this picture?"

"Sure, two days ago. The day after the big storm. There was mud everywhere. I almost lost my boot," Susan pointed to the picture. "That's why there are so many purple flowers in the photo. It's as close as I could get because of the mud."

Susan manipulated the map on her notebook screen. "Let me sync this with Mr. Burke's printer and I can print out directions for you."

Alan Burke glanced at the map over Susan's shoulder. "If I may ask, Mrs. McClure, why are you so interested in this trailer?"

"It belongs to a friend of mine. It was . . . involved in a theft," I replied, fudging the truth without actually lying.

"Here you go, Mrs. McClure," Susan said, handing me a printout of her map. The spot where she found the trailer was clearly marked.

"Thanks, Susan, you really helped me out."

"And this is for Spencer," Mr. Burke said, handing over a folder. "It's his homework. Warn him there's a quiz tomorrow."

Classes were in session as I walked along the halls toward the exit, and pleasant memories of my own schooldays flashed through my mind.

Jack, however, had no patience for my trip down memory lane.

We've got to get to that trailer as soon as possible, Penny.

"It's been sitting there for days, Jack. I'm sure it will be there when we arrive."

Outside, I hopped back on Spencer's bike—and that's when Jack really started to ride me (excuse the pun).

No wonder we can't go to Norma's trailer right away. By the look of things, you've fallen off the curb.

"What is that supposed to mean?"

"Lemme guess . . . The book joint closed and now you're delivering newspapers?

"Not at all funny, Jack. I borrowed Spencer's bike, that's all. You know my car was impounded."

What are you using for wheels next? A little red scooter?

"Seymour and Brainert are meeting me in an hour—"

Those schmoes!

"Seymour has the wheels, Jack. And we're going to do exactly what you suggested. We're going to find Norma's trailer. And if we're really lucky, we'll find Norma, too."

CHAPTER 36

Off the Beaten Path

The toils and dangers of the wilderness were to be encountered before the adverse hosts could meet.

—James Fenimore Cooper, *The Last of the Mohicans*

WHEN I RETURNED to Buy the Book, Seymour and Brainert were waiting for me. Aunt Sadie was waiting, too. After I shared the good news about Spencer's school situation, she shared some news with me.

"Fiona called and mentioned that Peyton Pemberton's boyfriend returned to the inn this morning."

"Hollis West?" I said and Sadie nodded. "Does Fiona know where Hollis has been all this time?"

"No, she didn't talk to him. He parked his fancy car and went directly to the Lighthouse. She said Mr. West and Miss Pemberton haven't budged since."

Sounds like Mr. Beefcake and Miss Cheesecake are getting reacquainted, Jack cracked.

"Maybe they'll check out today," I said. "Unless their waiting for the state police to arrest Norma."

Sadie sighed. "I'm sure that's exactly what they're doing, Pen. And Fiona's still quite upset."

"Speaking of Norma, we'd better hit the trail," Seymour

advised me and Brainert. "I hope you both brought your hiking boots. We have a lot of ground to cover."

"Not as much as we first thought," I said and told them about Susan Trencher's science project.

I pulled out the map she'd made for me. The girl had thoughtfully attached a copy of the photo that gave me a clue. Seymour studied the image and nodded.

"Yep, it's Norma's trailer. I recognize that crack in the side window."

While Seymour and Brainert studied Susan's map, I ran upstairs, changed into sturdier clothes (jeans and a thick sweatshirt), and donned my hiking boots. After giving my son a hug and a kiss—along with a heartfelt talk, which included the very good news from Mr. Burke and Principal McConnell—I went back downstairs.

I told Sadie I'd delivered homework to Spencer, and I thanked her profusely for looking after him and covering the shop today. "Call me if you need anything or Spencer gives you trouble."

She waved her hand. "Stop worrying. You know this shop's a joy for me to run—especially after all your hard work turning it around. As for Spencer, he's a great kid. When he's through with his homework, I'll put him to work stocking shelves. You know he enjoys working in the shop, too."

"Come on, Pen, daylight's burning!" Seymour pressed impatiently.

"Go on now, get out of here," Sadie commanded as I gave her a tight hug. "And find our Norma."

"We'll do our best," I promised.

"Forsooth, this quest should tax us not," Seymour announced as I grabbed my coat. "Come, knights and lady, let us be off. The Volkswagen bus awaits."

"Huzzah, Sir Gawain!" Brainert replied. "I only hope that antiquated combustion-engine coach-and-four doesn't conk out on us."

Their banter continued until we hit the junction, most of it in an improvised, faux-medieval dialect.

Needless to say, Jack was not amused.

If I hear one more thee, thou, or forsooth, I'm going to find a shiv and cutteth their throats.

As we turned toward Millstone, Brainert and Seymour finally got serious.

"There's the spot where Brainpan got sideswiped," Seymour said, slowing down so I could get a good look. "You can see where his car scraped the oak tree."

"That's an ash tree, you dolt," Brainert insisted.

"Okay, I was wrong," Seymour said. "You don't have to be an *ash* about it. Get it? An *ash* about it."

The rural route ended at Millstone, and we got on the highway to go that last mile or so. According to Susan's map, the dirt road was just outside of town proper, but within the city limits.

"Little Susie should work for the US Geological Survey," Seymour said moments later. "There's the service road, right where she said it would be."

Seymour rolled his bus onto the shoulder of the lightly trafficked two-lane highway. He made a sharp right turn onto the dirt road, but we didn't get far. Two metal poles sunk in concrete were connected by a stout metal chain, blocking any vehicle from entering.

"I guess the engineers didn't want teens using this spot as a lovers' lane," Seymour said. "Looks like we're walking from here."

The bright promise of the morning had given way to an overcast and chilly afternoon. The dirt road was rough and as pitted as the surface of the moon—the storm had churned up the earth and transformed it into a field of mud. Though it was mostly dry now, there were still puddles of brown water to avoid, and lots of soft spots that sunk our boots.

The road seemed to narrow as trees and bushes on both sides began crowding us. Traffic sounds receded, replaced by urgent bird calls and the plaintive cooing of mourning doves huddled around the fallen trunk of a dead tree. When the strident caw of a lone crow echoed down from the cloudy sky above, Brainert declared—

"This place gives me the creeps. How far until we reach Millstone Creek?"

"Not far, according to Susie the Surveyor," Seymour replied.

Minutes later, we heard the sound of water and sniffed the dampness in the autumn air. Purple asters blossomed all around us, but something far more ominous grabbed my attention.

Large footprints had been made in the mud, and the ground had hardened enough to preserve their imprints.

I stopped dead, my mind racing. *Do you see this?*

Yeah, honey, I see it.

"Someone came here ahead of us, Jack," I said.

"Who's Jack?" Seymour asked, puzzled.

"Er . . . I meant to say *jack*boots." I pointed to the tracks. "Look at the size of those footprints. Someone was here before us."

"Young Susan came here, certainly," Brainert said. "When she took the photograph, I mean."

"Sorry, Brainpan," Seymour said. "These tracks belong to a size-thirteen human, extra wide—or maybe Bigfoot."

"Don't be absurd," Brainert sniffed.

"An undiscovered primate species in North America is a very real scientific possibility," Seymour insisted. "I wouldn't dismiss Bigfoot tracks or Sasquatch sightings out of hand."

"Why not Mothman?" Brainert cried. "Or the Yeti? Or maybe Godzilla? He's King of the Monsters, isn't he?"

"There are more things in heaven and earth," a smirking Seymour stated.

Personally, I was far less concerned about Bigfoot than I was about a certain foreign visitor to Quindicott named Enzo Santoro. The muddy boots in the back seat of the car were surely size twelves if not larger, and so were the footprints left by the man who murdered Dottie Willard.

Is Santoro some sort of hit man, Jack?

Somebody pushed old Dottie's button, Jack replied. *But I'm not sure the killer was imported. Anyway, you don't have to worry. Whoever made these tracks is long gone.*

You're sure?

These tracks are headed away from the creek, doll.

Oh God. If it was Santoro, he already found Norma's trailer.

If it was Signore Santoro, he might have already found Norma, too.

"Hurry!" I cried, picking up my pace.

Jack's suggestion got my heart racing, and I followed those tracks backward with a feeling of mounting dread. Seymour's long strides kept pace with me. Poor Brainert lagged behind.

Seconds later I rounded a thick clump of trees and found the brown waters of Millstone Creek spread out before me. And right there, in the middle of a muddy island surrounded by water, sat Norma Stanton's teardrop trailer.

CHAPTER 37

The Little Trailer on the Creek

The marsh did not confine them . . . and, like any sacred ground, kept their secrets deep.

—Delia Owens, *Where the Crawdads Sing*

THE MAN-SIZE TRACKS led right up to the shores of the formerly swollen creek. Those prints vanished in the shallow water, then reappeared on the muddy island. I could see footprints leading all the way up to the teardrop-shaped mobile home.

"Norma," I called as I stumbled into the murky water. "Norma, are you there?"

Fortunately, my hiking boots were just high enough to keep my feet dry. Again, Seymour stuck close, his own well-worn galoshes veterans at protecting the mailman from snow, rain, sleet, and gloom of night.

As soon as I reached the dirt-splattered trailer I knew it was deserted. A folding lounge chair lay on its side, half-embedded in the drying mud. Beside it the soggy remains of a campfire. The mobile home's tires had sunk into the mire all the way to the hubcaps. That mud had since hardened around them like concrete.

Breathless and cursing his soaking-wet feet, Brainert finally caught up to us.

"It looks like Norma used the service road to roll her trailer back here," Seymour speculated.

"Why didn't that chain blocking the road stop her? It stopped us," Brainert replied.

"I'll bet Norma unscrewed the bolts holding the chain to the poles," Seymour offered. "That's what the work crews do when they have to use this road. Norma has the know-how, for sure, and the tools, too, in that white van of hers."

"But why did she leave the trailer behind when she fled to Millstone?" Brainert asked. "Was she planning to come back for it later? What if someone found it? We just did."

"And someone else did, too," I said, gesturing toward the strange footprints.

"My point exactly," Brainert declared.

"I don't think she meant to leave her trailer behind," I said. "In fact, I believe that when Norma sideswiped your car, she was coming here to retrieve her trailer. We only assumed Norma was heading to Dottie Willard's place. I think we were wrong in that assumption."

"I'll bet the storm caught up with her," Seymour added with a snap of his fingers. "She parked her camper too close to the water. When the storm broke, the creek rose so quickly it surrounded the trailer and she could not pull it out."

"The mailman is correct, for once," Brainert conceded. "The waters have already receded. By tomorrow this island will be reunited with the shoreline again."

The huge footprints I'd followed circled the trailer once and multiplied around the sole door on the side. Seymour and I exchanged glances before he reached for the doorknob.

Amazingly, the trailer was unlocked.

I braced myself for a sight similar to the one on poor, dead Dorothy Willard's sunporch. But we found no one (living or dead) inside.

The weak sunlight, peeking through the overcast sky, illuminated a tiny combination sitting room, work area, and bedroom. A thin futon set in a wooden frame occupied one corner. A vintage standard typewriter sat on a DIY hinged shelf beside a thick wad of paper bundled by rubber bands.

I spied several Coleman lanterns, all heavily used, along with a portable propane hotplate. Canned foods lined a shelf; pots and pans hung from the ceiling; cube containers held everything from silverware and tea bags to tools and typewriter ribbons.

And there were books. Many, many books, lined up neatly on DIY shelves mounted on all four walls. Each shelf came complete with a metal locking rod to hold the books in place while the trailer was on the move.

Inside the cramped space, I smelled kerosene from the lanterns, and old charcoal from an iron hibachi tucked under the raised futon. Those fumes, along with the stale air, were quickly dispelled by the fresh, cool breeze pouring through the open door.

"I don't think anyone has lived here for a while," I said.

Seymour agreed. "But look at this. The lock has been broken." He pointed to knife marks on the doorjamb. "I think someone was here before us, and they got inside the trailer by jimmying the lock."

Brainert frowned. "Were they trying to rob the place?"

"They could have been looking for something of value," I said, "maybe even the jewels. But if Norma actually took them, I doubt she would have left them here."

"Maybe she had no choice," Seymour offered. "Maybe she couldn't even get close to the trailer with all that flood-water."

As I pulled back, I bumped my elbow on a small shelf bolted to the wall just inside the door. It had been used as a cutting board, and that pitted surface held a thermal cup, a paring knife, and an envelope with a letter folded on top of it. This letter had not been mailed, as the front of the envelope was blank.

Seymour saw the letter, too. "Allow me," he insisted. "I am a professional mail handler."

Though the envelope was blank, the letter inside was addressed to Norma. Seymour displayed the handwritten note before he read it aloud:

Norma,

If you don't already know, it was I who recorded your talks at the church and put them on social media.
You know who I am, though you never acknowledged me in any of the meetings, so you know why I posted your talks.
Something had to be done. This injustice has gone on too long. I am certain those involved will see the recordings and if they do, and if they act, then maybe The Truth will be revealed at long last, and damn the consequences.

The letter was signed "Louis Kritzer."

"Hey, I recognize that name," Seymour cried. "Louis Kritzer is on my mail route. He lives in an apartment on Broad Street."

"Have you ever spoken with him?" I asked. "What does he look like? Maybe I've seen him in the bookstore."

Seymour shrugged. "I don't think I ever saw or talked to him. But who can forget a name like Kritzer?"

Brainert spoke up. "On Broad Street, you say? That's not a very nice neighborhood. Not at all."

But Seymour, lost in thought, wasn't listening. "I wonder how Kritzer delivered this obviously private letter to Norma without actually addressing it?" he mused. "I doubt he came all the way out here to slip it under the door."

"That letter is not so private as you think," Brainert said. "Look closely at the envelope."

Seymour did, and I gasped at what he found: A swipe of brown mud made by a dirty hand laid a swath across the virgin white velum.

"Bigfoot obviously read that letter," Brainert concluded. "Unless, of course, it was Sasquatch, Mothman, or Godzilla."

"Ouch. Good one," Seymour conceded.

But I wasn't laughing, and neither was Jack.

If Mr. Muddy Boots read that letter, he might be planning to visit this Kritzer fellow.

Yes, Jack. Or the visit is over and so is Louis Kritzer, because I'm pretty sure the last person Bigfoot visited ended up dead.

CHAPTER 38

We're Going to Kritzerland!

Better three hours too soon than a minute too late.

—William Shakespeare, *The Merry Wives of Windsor*

"WE HAVE TO go there now!"

Seymour blinked. "Go where, Pen?"

"To Louis Kritzer's apartment on Broad Street. You have to take me there, Seymour. It may already be too late."

The mailman was obviously perplexed by my urgent plea.

"Why? Because Kritzer signed this letter? We don't even know what this note means, Pen."

"But I do know what it means. Some of it, anyway."

I told Brainert and Seymour about my visit to Reverend and Mrs. Waterman. About how Norma began attending the alcohol and drug abuse group at the church, how she began to give inspiring talks, and how someone had secretly recorded those talks and put them on social media.

"Which Louis Kritzer confessed to doing," I concluded.

"Yeah," Seymour replied. "And he hinted that the recordings would open a whole can of whup-ass, too."

"No, Mr. Kritzer said that they might lead to the truth," Brainert countered. "Whatever that truth might be."

Yeah, said Jack. *And damn the consequences, which tells me Mr. Kritzer believes there will be some.*

"We'll have to ask Louis Kritzer to explain things," I said. "But we have to find him to do it, before someone else does."

"Whom are you referring to, Pen?" Brainert asked.

I reminded them about the muddy footprints at Dorothy Willard's house. Then I told them what it might mean if the man who made those prints made the ones around the trailer, concluding with a question.

"What if that man decided to visit Kritzer on Broad Street?"

Brainert nodded. "Pen is right. Let's go."

"Whoa, hold on," I replied. "Someone has to stay here in case Norma returns."

Brainert moaned. "I don't like the sound of that."

"You guessed correctly, Brainiac, so you win the prize."

"Prize?"

"Sure. You get to camp out here while I drive the only set of wheels among us to a place only I know. And Pen is coming along because she's the only one who knows the whole story and can ask the right questions."

Maybe not the only one—

Quiet, Jack.

"That makes you the third wheel," Seymour concluded. "And because we don't need a spare tire on this trip, you're going to make yourself useful by waiting for Norma the Nomad to return home."

"Don't worry," I assured him. "You've got a phone. The signal is decent—"

"But, Pen," Brainert shot back, his tone verging on the hysterical. "What if the man with the big feet returns?"

"He won't," Seymour assured him. "He obviously got what he came for, whatever that was. And if he came for Norma, she's clearly long gone. But here's a plan, just in case. If he shows up again, run into the woods."

"That sounds suspiciously like no plan at all," Brainert groused.

"I think Seymour's right," I said. "Bigfoot is unlikely to return here. To pass the time, I suggest you check out the stuff in Norma's trailer. There's a stack of bundled-up paper beside the typewriter. Take a look."

Brainert folded his arms and stared accusingly at me. "That would be snooping, Pen."

Mother Machree! Jack cried.

"Yes, Brainert," I replied. "It *would* be snooping. Why do you think we're here?"

FIFTEEN MINUTES LATER, Seymour and I were back on the highway. We turned around at the next exit and after that the mailman kept his foot on the gas pedal all the way back to Quindicott.

While Seymour drove, I used my phone to call up Norma's YouTube videos. Together, Seymour and I listened to them, starting with an insightful one about how we see ourselves . . .

"So who are you?" Norma began. "Are you who the world says you are? And by world, I mean *your* world. Your crowd, your group, your friends, your co-workers, your family members. And that bigger bunch. Those cultural judges whose ways of measuring human value and community status change with the times and the fashions.

"Let me put it another way . . .

"When I was a little girl, I went to a carnival. I saw clowns, jugglers, games of chance—and a fun house filled with frights and gags and mirrors.

"One mirror stretched me skinny as a stick. Another blew my body into a fat balloon. There were mirrors that made me feel tall and others that made me look small. One distorted my head; another split me in two.

"I stayed in that room of reflections so long that when I came out, I felt almost dizzy, and a little lost, forgetting who I actually was.

"That, in a nutshell, is what today's world is doing to many of us. Seeing ourselves only in the fun-house mirrors of our jobs, our relationships, our social media, can sometimes be so distorted—even toxic and twisted—it can make us unwell. That's why we need to close our eyes, stop searching for ourselves in these misleading reflections, and learn how to look within . . ."

We listened to more videos, and I could see why Norma's talks had gone viral. She was wise and caring, with sharp, uplifting insights, and her love of literature showed. She often quoted favorite poets and writers.

"'Finish each day and be done with it,'" Norma proclaimed with gusto. She clapped her hands, wrung them together, pretending to wash them, then flung her arms wide and grinned.

"So wrote Ralph Waldo Emerson in a letter to his daughter in 1854. 'You have done what you could,' he said, 'some blunders & absurdities no doubt crept in. Forget them. As fast as you can! Tomorrow is a *new* day. You shall begin it well and serenely, with too high a spirit to be cumbered with your old nonsense.'

"I'll put it another way . . . the way I see things *now*—

"Your life is a book and every day a page is written. At the end of every day, I read my page and ask myself: Am I happy with this page? Is it truly mine? Or am I letting my fears write my book for me? Have the wailing worries of the world silenced the sound of my own voice?

"How about you? Are the wishes or criticisms of *others* writing your daily page for you? Because if they are, before long, it will be their book. Not yours.

"'This day,'" Emerson wrote, "'is too dear with its hopes & invitations to waste a moment on the rotten yesterdays.'

"Close your eyes now and turn the page. Look at that beautiful blank page of tomorrow, just waiting for you to write your story. Smile as you consider the possibilities! What will you write tomorrow? What will your page be?"

As Seymour and I continued listening to Norma's video speeches, it was clear that something had happened in her past. She often referenced the difficult journey of life and admitted in one of the videos of sinking into such a dark place

that she became a substance abuser herself before fighting her
way back to the light of recovery. But there was nothing to
indicate that these talks were incendiary in any way.

What was this "Truth" that had obviously upset Mr.
Kritzer? The videos didn't tell us, other than affirming
Norma had gone through a dark time in her past. I would
have to ask Kritzer himself to explain the meaning of his
letter when we found him.

Forty minutes after we "deserted" Brainert—his word—
Seymour swung the rattly Volkswagen bus onto Broad
Street. Located on the far edge of Quindicott, this boulevard
lacked the charm of some of the nicer neighborhoods.

Formerly the home of several garages and a tire company,
those automotive centers were empty shells now, though the
semi-industrial ambiance remained. There were few trees,
the houses were mostly Victorian, and not all of them were
well-kept. I saw litter on the street and spied more than one
car jacked up on bricks, along with old appliances and just
plain junk—all of it cluttering narrow driveways between the
houses.

"This is the place," Seymour announced.

*That's an apartment house? Looks more like a funeral
home*, Jack cracked.

Jack wasn't wrong. The building was an old gray Victorian, larger than most of the houses around it. Once a single
residence, it had since been broken up into six different
apartments—this according to Seymour, who stuffed mail
every day into the burnished-steel lockboxes on the front
porch. Seymour rang Kritzer's bell several times, but there
was no response.

I tried the front door. It was locked tight. I turned to the
mailman for help. Seymour confessed he had never been
inside.

"Sorry, Pen, I have keys to the postboxes, not the—"

He was interrupted by a teenage girl struggling to get her
bike out the door and onto the street. She worked silently,
earphones firmly in place. Seymour politely held the door
open until she pedaled off—without even a thank-you.

"Kids today." Seymour sighed.

"Get in there," I commanded, giving him a gentle nudge.

The entranceway was as gray as the exterior. The wood-plank floor had been painted black. The place smelled of stale tobacco smoke and bad cooking. The dingy wallpaper was probably once white but had morphed into a putrid yellow that would have horrified Charlotte Perkins Gilman. But the worst part was the echoing racket coming from somewhere up the gray-green carpeted stairs.

"Somebody is watching television," I said over the noise.

"Somebody ought to adjust their hearing aid," Seymour snapped back.

"Why doesn't anyone complain?"

Seymour shrugged. "I don't know how many of these apartments are vacant. Half the mail I deliver here is addressed to 'occupant' or 'current resident.'"

"Where is Kritzer's room?"

"Apartment 4, Pen. It says so on the postbox."

"I see 1 and 2," I said, pointing to the doors on either side.

Seymour shrugged. "Up we go."

I honestly couldn't tell you if the stairs were creaky or not. The television was blaring so loudly it was impossible to hear anything else. Inside my head, however, things were different.

Brace yourself, the ghost suddenly warned.

I get that same feeling, Jack. Like we're already too late.

Apartment 4's door was half-open. And the noise was coming from inside that room.

I hesitated.

Not Seymour.

"Hey!" he bellowed, pounding on the door. "Anyone home? Like Ludwig van Beethoven, maybe?"

The door opened wider under Seymour's onslaught. I peeked in and saw a worn green couch, a torchiere, and an old-fashioned tube television. The broadcast was an old episode of *Barney Miller*.

Seymour and I exchanged glances. This time I led the

way, stepping slowly over the threshold and making darn sure someone wasn't lurking behind that door.

A couple of more steps and I saw a pair of slippers lying beside the couch, then a pair of pajama-clad legs.

"Mr. Kritzer?" I called, approaching the faded green couch. I stepped around to face the man, but there was no face to face.

I stifled a scream. Seymour peered over my shoulder, then squealed like a little girl.

There would be no talking to Mr. Louis Kritzer. His face and the back of his head were gone, the gun that did the damage clutched in his dead white hand.

CHAPTER 39

Mashed Couch Potato

There is nothing more deceptive than an obvious fact.

—Arthur Conan Doyle, "The Boscombe Valley Mystery"

I KNOW WHAT it looks like, doll, but this guy didn't off himself.

How can you be sure, Jack?

I'd check for a suicide note first.

"Seymour, do you see a note anywhere?"

Seymour, staring at the corpse on the couch, grunted a nonsensical reply.

"Do you see a note?" I repeated.

He shook off his shock and joined me in searching the immediate vicinity.

"Nothing," I concluded a few moments later. "And I don't even see a computer or a phone—unless his phone is tucked into his robe or something."

Seymour made a face. "Should I check, do you think?"

Doll, this stinks like a bad Broadway production, Jack insisted. *I could smell this setup a mile away.*

It seems wrong to me, too, Jack. And the lack of a phone or a computer—well, how did Mr. Kritzer post anything to social media without one or the other?

What's that tell you?

I didn't even have to think about an answer. *A missing phone or computer is the strongest evidence of foul play.*

Bingo, Jack cracked. *You win the booby prize.*

"So, Pen, should I frisk the dead man?" Seymour asked.

And there's your boob.

Get off Seymour's case, Jack.

Then get him off our case before he does something stupid.

"No, Seymour," I said aloud. "I don't think we should touch the body. Let's call the police."

Seymour made the call, telling the emergency dispatcher that he was the mailman and found his addressee dead. He was told to wait outside the apartment, and not to touch anything.

Phooey on that, sweetlips! Shake this joint down before the bulls get here and muck it all up.

I figured the dispatcher had given Seymour instructions, not me, so I didn't follow either of her rules.

First I unplugged the TV from the wall. It was the only way to silence the blaring noise, as I was fairly certain the volume had been turned up to mask the sound of the gunshot. If this was murder instead of suicide, I didn't want to smear any fingerprints that might be left on the dial.

Next I went to the tiny bedroom, where I found a phone charger cord but no phone—more proof it had been stolen. On the dresser I saw the dead man's wallet, a flyer from the Reverend Waterman's First Presbyterian Church, a paperback of Amanda Pilgrim's last novel (which he might very well have bought at my store), and a set of keys to this apartment and presumably a car.

I was about to slide open a few drawers when Seymour called a warning from the hall. "The QPD has arrived."

I slipped through the apartment door just as a pair of heavy boots hit the bottom step. It was only then that I remembered Eddie Franzetti was in Providence with his wife, and that this call would probably be answered by one of Eddie's officers—or worse, Eddie's boss.

My heart sank when a bearlike shadow appeared on the steps—and not the cuddly teddy kind. Chief Ciders was the very definition of curmudgeon, and he loathed Seymour Tarnish. Their animosity had begun over a youthful indiscretion (involving illegal fireworks), and the passing years hadn't improved their relationship, which is why the man's perpetual frown morphed into a bitter scowl when he spied Seymour. The chief of the Quindicott Police Department wasn't too happy to see me, either.

"You two?" He shook his massive head. "I think I would have been happier if Bonnie and Clyde called this in."

"Come on, Chief, you know that isn't possible," a goading Seymour replied. "Weren't you a member of the posse that ambushed that pair of desperados?"

Ciders crested the stairs and placed his hands on his ample hips.

"Just what is going on here?"

I opened my mouth to speak, but Seymour beat me to it.

"I came here to see Mr. Louis Kritzer. His TV was blaring, and he didn't answer his bell, so I came upstairs and found him deader than disco."

"Where is this dead man?"

Seymour jerked his thumb over his shoulder. Ciders brushed past us and into the room. Seymour and I both followed. Chief Ciders made a beeline to the couch and stared at the dead man long and hard.

"Is this the way you found him?"

We both nodded.

"Any note?"

"No," I answered. "But he might have left some kind of message on his phone, only I don't see it anywhere."

"We'll find it," Ciders replied. He got down on one knee and studied the head wound—Ciders had a strong stomach; I'll give him that. After a moment, he studied the gun.

"Obviously a suicide," he concluded, rising. "From the way the blood has congealed I'd say this happened last night."

"Are you sure it was suicide?" I asked.

Ciders nodded. "That wound is the right size for the caliber of the slugs in his gun, and it appears the fatal shot was self-inflicted."

"Surely the state police crime scene unit will determine what happened."

"We won't be needing them," Ciders replied. "I'm going to call Dr. Rubino to pronounce the victim dead and conduct an autopsy, then I'm going to send the corpse to Scully Funeral Home, where they have a facility to hold his remains until the next of kin is notified."

"But surely a suspicious death has to be handled by the proper authorities," I countered.

"A suspicious death, yes," the chief said, nodding. "But this is a cut-and-dried suicide—"

"But, Chief Ciders—"

He cut me off, to focus on Seymour. "The only suspicious thing here is why you came to see Mr. Krinkle—"

"Kritzer," Seymour corrected. "I came to see him on official business. It involved undeliverable mail."

Ciders' grunt indicated dissatisfaction with Seymour's reply. His beady eyes focused on me next. "And why were you here, Mrs. McClure?"

"Well, my car was impounded in Millstone, so Seymour was giving me a ride."

Those unblinking eyes narrowed suspiciously. "I think you're both taking me for a ride."

"I'm just trying to tell you that things might not be what they seem," I insisted. "This could be a setup to cover a murder."

Ciders scowled. "How so?"

"Well, Seymour told you the television was on really loud. Who turned up the volume and why?"

"Probably Mr. Kriskringle did it himself," Ciders answered.

"Why?"

"In order to mask the sound of the gunshot."

I shot the chief a doubtful look.

"Is that handgun the property of the deceased?" Seymour asked. "Does Louis Kritzer have a permit for that weapon?"

"I'll determine all that in due course," Ciders replied. "Now, if you two would clear out, I'd like to get this ball rolling."

Ciders gave us his broad back and called Dr. Rubino. As their conversation began Seymour turned to leave. I turned him around again.

"You heard Ciders," I whispered. "He's not going to investigate."

Seymour frowned. "Yeah, and you're right—who did turn the sound up? Not Kritzer. Why would *he* care who heard him pull the trigger?"

"The real killer's fingerprints might be on that volume knob," I murmured.

In a second Seymour dropped to his knees and pulled a handkerchief out of his shirt pocket. Without touching the volume dial with his hands, Seymour used his Swiss Army knife to pry it loose. In less than ten seconds the knob was off the television and in Seymour's pocket.

"What are you doing down there on the floor?" Ciders roared. "I thought I ordered you both to leave."

"Sorry, Chief," Seymour said, suddenly squinting while feeling around the worn carpet with both hands. "I seem to have lost my contact lens. They're very expensive, you know, and—ah, here it is."

Seymour picked up an imaginary contact lens.

"Listen up, both of you. You're done here. I'll see you in my office first thing in the morning to file a statement. Now, get out!"

For once I agreed with Ciders. We couldn't leave fast enough, and I knew just where to go with that TV dial.

CHAPTER 40

Hanging On

The telephone's such a convenient thing; it just sits there and demands you call someone who doesn't want to be called.

—Ray Bradbury, "The Murderer"

I WAITED UNTIL we were on the street before I spoke.

"Good job, Seymour. You grabbed it."

"Yeah," he replied. "But what did I grab? Sure, the volume knob might have fingerprints on it, but unless you've got a forensics expert—"

"Spencer's no expert, but he can lift a fingerprint off of anything. He proved that to me and his school principal."

Seymour shrugged. "Okay, but without a database, what is a fingerprint really worth?"

"We'll cross that bridge when we come to it."

"And I don't get why you didn't tell Ciders everything."

"Everything?"

"You know. About the possible connection to Dorothy Willard's murder, about the man with the big feet, about the letter to Kritzer . . . Everything."

"Seymour, you and I both know Ciders is a man of limited capacity—"

"To put it kindly," the mailman deadpanned.

"Meanwhile, you heard Deputy Chief Franzetti at the Quibblers meeting. He's been on top of this case from the beginning. I'll tell Eddie everything when he gets back from Providence."

Seymour glanced at his watch. "Speaking of getting back, we better pick up Brainert. It will be dark in an hour or so. He'll have a meltdown out there in the woods all alone if we don't make it before sunset."

"We have two quick stops to make."

"We do?"

"I want Spencer to get to work on those fingerprints, and I want to pick up your bugout kit."

Seymour's jaw dropped. "You know about my bug-out kit?"

"*You* told me. Don't you remember? Two years ago, on your birthday. When Harlan Gilman tricked you into eating those hash brownies."

"It's all a blur, Pen. For like a week after that."

"Well, you told me how you had a ready-made way to escape, to bug out, if you had to. You told me you had a tent, flashlights, supplies—and we're going to need them to camp out at Norma's trailer. With the storm over and the muddy ground firming up, I'm betting she'll return soon to get her things. We'll be waiting for her when she does."

"Fine, I'll grab the kit. But we'd better tell Brainert we're going to be a little late."

Seymour hit speed dial. After a moment, he ended the call. "That's funny. Brainert didn't pick up. My call went to voice mail, I guess he's . . . you know."

"No, I don't."

"Well, what's a bear do in the woods?"

"Ew! Seymour!"

"Maybe he doesn't want to be interrupted while he plays the bear and bares all in the woods. I'll call Brainert back while you slip Spencer the evidence."

But two more calls—one from Seymour at my bookstore, the other from me while I waited for Seymour to dig out his kit—went unanswered. By the time we were on the road again, I was starting to worry.

"Ah, you know Brainert," Seymour said. "That beautiful mind of his wanders and gets distracted fast. Mr. ADHD probably forgot he turned his phone off, and he's fallen asleep from boredom while poking around Norma's trailer."

Or the man with the big feet returned and ruined his day, Jack added.

I refused to go down that road and told him so.

You and I both know that sheepskin is useless in an investigation, Jack countered.

You said that about Seymour, too, but he did grab a piece of evidence—

You mean that picture radio dial? That was your idea, doll. Clever, too. You might make some hay out of that.

Right before we reached Millstone, I called Brainert again—and again, I got his voice mail.

"Maybe the bookworm let his phone battery die," Seymour suggested.

Yeah, Jack said, jumping in. *Or maybe he did*.

"Step on it, Seymour. It's nearly sunset."

We arrived just as the sun was sinking below the trees. We left the kit in the Volkswagen—because I was worried and because Seymour wanted Brainert's help dragging it to the campsite.

We hurried along the pitted road to the creek. As we waded across the shallow water to the island, I spied movement inside the trailer.

"Come out, Brainert," I called. "We're back."

The teardrop trailer shook a little, and so did my knees. A moment later, Brainert stepped through the narrow door, into the open.

"We were calling and calling," Seymour cried. "Didn't you hear your phone?"

"I . . . ignored it. I was busy . . . reading."

My rush of relief was short-lived. My good friend was pale, and tears streamed down his face.

"Brainert! What's wrong?"

"I . . . I just finished Amanda Pilgrim's new novel. It was quite poignant."

Seymour chuckled. "Since when have you read anything on the *New York Times* bestseller list? Or anything published in this century, for that matter?"

"How is that possible, Brainert?" I countered. "The book isn't even out yet. Aunt Sadie has an advance reading copy. Did Norma get one, too?"

"No, no, not that novel," Brainert said. "I mean her next book . . . Well, I assume it's her next book. She titled it *The Crows Will Carry Your Soul*."

"What are you talking about, Brainert?"

He turned, reached into the trailer, and pulled out some of the pages that had been bundled and stacked beside Norma's typewriter. He waved them under my nose.

"Look!" he cried. "Don't you see?"

Seymour stepped up. "See what, Brainiac?"

"That Norma Stanton . . . the woman we know as Norma the Nomad . . . is really the world-renowned author Amanda Pilgrim!"

CHAPTER 41

A Novel Experience

A reader lives a thousand lives before he dies . . . The man who never reads lives only one.

—George R.R. Martin, *A Dance with Dragons*

"YOU'RE ABSOLUTELY CERTAIN Norma Stanton is Amanda Pilgrim?" I asked Brainert. "I mean *the* Amanda Pilgrim. The woman who was nominated for the Babbitt Award for Arts and Letters?"

"She lost that one, Pen," Seymour said. "She was beaten by lyricist Billie Eilish."

"She was robbed!" Brainert cried.

"Never mind that," I said. "You're telling us that Norma— our Norma—is a bestselling author?"

"There is no doubt."

Brainert pointed to a flowery wallpaper-covered cardboard box on the trailer floor. "Aside from this brilliant novel with her nom de plume at the top of every typewritten page, I found that box, which contains all the communication from her agent, her editor at Salient House, someone from that company's publicity department, and copies of her contracts."

"Yeesh!" Seymour cried. "For a guy who was morally squeamish about snooping, you sure uncovered an awful lot."

Brainert scowled. "I don't know if that's an insult or a compliment."

"Since when have I ever complimented you, Brainiac?"

After that crack, Seymour climbed inside the trailer and began rooting through the box himself.

"Norma gets all of her mail delivered to a PO box in Maine," Seymour noted. "Wait! Here's a bank statement."

"Her new novel is unbelievably good," Brainert said. "*The Crows Will Carry Your Soul* is in the vein of Jack Kerouac, but far more poetic, perhaps because it's told from a modern woman's perspective. It's quite wise, profound really."

"Holy Finger Lakes!" Seymour cried. "Amanda Pilgrim has over three million dollars in her checking account!"

That doesn't sound like someone who would steal vintage jewelry no matter how much it's worth, now, does it, Jack?

People do things for all sorts of reasons, Penny. Don't absolve Norma quite yet.

Wow! Are you ever stubborn!

I call it cautious, honey. When it comes to the Tears of Valentino . . . Well, let's just say I was fooled, and it could happen to you.

"Put that box away, Seymour," Brainert insisted as he gathered up the manuscript pages he'd scattered across the futon. "I think we've invaded this woman's privacy enough for one day."

After that, we all returned to the Volkswagen and unloaded the camping stuff. Back at the site, Seymour set down waterproof tarps and put the tent up over them.

Meanwhile, I sorted through the various freeze-dried foods, cans, and army surplus MREs (that's meals ready to eat) that Seymour had packed in his bugout kit. In the end I was glad I'd convinced him to raid his own refrigerator before we left Quindicott. The thought of eating out of pouches stockpiled in the event of World War III was unappealing to me. But thanks to Seymour's kitchen we had plenty of cold lemonade, buns, and fresh hot dogs to roast over a fire.

And speaking of fires. "It's getting dark fast. Colder, too. Shouldn't we start a campfire?"

"I've already gathered the wood," Brainert said.

Seymour and Brainert stacked up the twigs and sticks in a neat pile. Then Seymour dashed on a little charcoal lighter fluid to get the blaze started.

Suddenly, Seymour frowned; he checked his pockets, then the heavy backpack he'd brought.

"Son of a—"

"What's the matter now, Seymour?" Brainert demanded.

"I . . . I think I forgot to bring matches."

My jaw dropped. "Are you saying that your bugout kit, the safety net you rely on to get you through the zombie apocalypse, the next pandemic, or nuclear war, actually lacks a way to create fire?"

"Hah!" Brainert whooped. "What were you going to do? Rub two sticks together?"

"I regard this exercise as a good test," Seymour argued. "A sort of trial run. I'll smooth over the rough spots and be more prepared next time."

"So, what do we do about a fire *this* time?"

Seymour sighed. "Norma has a bunch of kerosene lanterns in her trailer. She probably has matches somewhere, too."

With that, Seymour climbed into the trailer and began his search. After five minutes, it was getting much, much darker and we still didn't even have a spark, let alone a fire.

"I saw a hibachi grill under the futon," Brainert called. "Check there."

"Found them," Seymour called—to our infinite relief.

Suddenly a crash came from inside the trailer. Brainert and I both ran to see what the racket was about.

"When I put the hibachi back, the shelf fell off. There's a space behind it with another manuscript."

Seymour pulled out a six-inch-thick stack, the pages single-spaced and double-sided—the totally wrong format for any publisher to accept. Obviously this writing was nothing Norma intended to publish.

"It doesn't even have a title," Seymour said. "Just a date. June the eleventh, eight years ago."

"It's probably a freshman effort," Brainert said. "What authors call a trunk book. Put it back. We've snooped enough for one day."

By nine P.M. we were sitting around the campfire, roasting hot dogs. As the mystery meat sizzled, we talked about Norma, aka Amanda Pilgrim's literary career.

"I confess I only read her early novel, *The Second Death of Mercy Brown*," Seymour said.

"That's a horror story, isn't it?" I asked.

"It figures," Brainert said. "Blood and gore and sensationalism, and Seymour's there."

"It wasn't like that at all," Seymour countered. "Amanda Pilgrim turned the true-life Exeter vampire incident into a story about a dysfunctional family and the daughter they scapegoated, even after her death."

Brainert, dubious, raised an eyebrow. "Real life, you say?"

"There's no actual vampire in the whole novel, Brainiac. Mercy Brown supposedly hunted for prey right here in Rhode Island, but in reality her victims died from acute illnesses. And Mercy Brown wasn't the first suspected New England vampire either. There were vampire panics all over the Northeast in the nineteenth century. The big ones occurred in Connecticut and Vermont."

"I've heard a lot of legends about werewolves, vampires, and ghosts stalking New England," I said—and immediately regretted it.

Oh, come off it, Penny, Jack cried. *Werewolves and vampires I can buy, but what kind of joker believes in ghosts?*

Very funny, Jack.

"Yes, there are plenty of spooky stories set around here and I've probably heard them all," Seymour replied. "Of course, I have my own, personal favorite."

"Do tell," Brainert deadpanned.

Seymour grinned. "Okay, but remember. You asked for it."

CHAPTER 42

Campfire Tales

Be afraid . . . Be very afraid.

—Tagline, *The Fly*, 1986

"THIS FOLKTALE IS known as 'The Rutland Railroad Mystery' to people in Vermont," Seymour began. "But I prefer my own title. 'The Snow Beast of Brattleboro.'"

Brainert sniffed. "Rather on the nose, isn't it?"

"It's a folktale," Seymour returned. "You know, like 'The Adventures of Robin Hood.' A title like 'A Story of Income Inequality and Redistribution' wouldn't be near as charming, now, would it?"

Brainert waved his hand. "Proceed."

"Back in the 1850s, the Rutland and Burlington Railroad began running through the hamlet where Elroy Denton lived with his two sisters and widowed mother. Now, Elroy's mother celebrated her birthday in early December, The day before, Elroy collected his salary at the local stable, borrowed a horse, and rode to the village of Brattleboro. The proprietor of the millinery there later testified that Elroy had indeed visited his shop and purchased an ornamental comb."

"Oh, the suspense," Brainert moaned.

"It was nightfall before Elroy left Brattleboro. Elroy

reckoned he would be in bed before midnight. But a freak storm struck, burying the countryside in mounds of drifting snow. Despite the weather, the horse returned. But the beast was riderless.

"The next day a search party found Elroy. He was dead, struck by the local train during the blizzard. The searchers deduced the train whistle had startled the horse and it threw poor Elroy into the path of the onrushing locomotive. But that wasn't the worst of it."

"Spit it out, Seymour. What horrible thing happened to the young lad?"

"His head was missing!" Seymour announced theatrically. "The search party looked and looked, but they couldn't find it. Finally poor Elroy's headless corpse was laid to rest beside his father in the family graveyard."

Seymour leaned close to the fire, until his face appeared demonic in the wavering light. "Now, you'd think that would be the end—"

"I'd say hope would be a better word," Brainert muttered.

"Well, it isn't," Seymour countered, "because, later that winter, during another heavy snow, a conductor was literally ripped from the train as it passed through the place where Elroy died. His partner said it was like an invisible hand reached into the cab and grabbed him. Linemen found the conductor's broken corpse the next day."

Seymour's voice lowered to a near whisper. "Folks in the vicinity began hearing sobs and cries whenever it snowed. And during another blizzard, a second conductor was snatched from his locomotive by an invisible hand, only to be found dead the following day. This happened two more times, until the trains stopped running to Brattleboro because no conductor would risk becoming the Snow Beast's next victim."

"Finally got that title in there, eh, Seymour?" Brainert cracked. "Does this story have a point, or maybe just an end?"

"Well," Seymour continued. "A grizzled old veteran was involved in all the searches and realized that all the dead conductors ended up at the same spot—at the foot of a century-old oak tree. The old man convinced the searchers to dig through the snow, and that's where they found a human head—Elroy Denton's missing noggin! They went back, opened the grave, placed the skull in coffin, and the Snow Beast of Brattleboro never struck again."

Finished with his tale, Seymour slapped his knees. "So, what do you think?"

"I think your sorry little folktale reminded me of another story involving a railroad fatality," Brainert replied. "This tale, however, is much more terrifying, and maybe even be connected to our hunt for Norma."

I leaned forward at that. "How so?"

"Remember the Quibblers meeting," Braiert said. "When we were going through Norma's reading list, do you recall the title that gave me pause?"

"I remember you looked intrigued, but I don't remember the title."

"*The Troll Garden*, a collection of stories by Willa Cather. The story I'm thinking of is called 'Paul's Case.'"

"Never heard of it," Seymour said.

"Well, let me enlighten you. Paul was an alienated young man living a shabby working-class life in Pittsburgh, PA. His only joy was his job as an usher at a concert hall where he could surround himself with art and culture and get lost in the music . . ."

As Brainert talked, I couldn't help thinking of Jack's past and that poor young woman named Cora, putting up with terrible people like Harry Amsterdam and Syble Zane, just to be near the art she loved. The theater.

"After Paul got himself into trouble," Brainert continued, "his father forced him to quit his job as an usher and take an office position. But the drudgery was too much and one day Paul stole a considerable sum of money from his employer and fled to New York City."

"*Now* the story is getting good," Seymour noted with relish.

"Paul checked into a fancy hotel, bought new clothes, and lived the life he always dreamed of. But within a week the money ran out, and Paul learned not only that his crime had been discovered, but also that his father was on his way to the city to take him back to Pittsburgh. Rather than return to a life he loathed, Paul went out to the railroad tracks and threw himself in front of an oncoming locomotive."

In the shocked silence that followed, I couldn't help but think of Norma and *her* case.

Was it remotely possible she stole, like Paul, as a shortcut to something she wanted and couldn't otherwise attain? And what would that something be?

Seymour was less reflective. "Actually, Brainiac, it sounds to me like your yarn is a lot like mine."

Brainert blinked. "How so?"

"Don't you see? Both stories are about characters who just want to get a head."

CHAPTER 43

Hot on the Trail

Dreams are today's answers to tomorrow's questions.

—Edgar Cayce (attributed)

IT WAS LONG past midnight when I crawled into the tent and zipped up my sleeping bag, exhausted enough to spend the night on a waterproof tarp spread out on the cold, muddy ground.

The night air was damp but fresh and as a I breathed it in, my thoughts returned to Willa Cather's tragic tale of "Paul's Case," and the fact that Norma special ordered a book with that story in it.

Was it actually possible Norma identified with Paul?

As a successful author, she obviously appreciated art and culture. But Norma was also involved in a substance abuse program. Could she have fallen off the wagon into some form of drug or alcohol abuse? Could Norma have stolen the heirloom jewels in a self-destructive moment? Perhaps to pay for drugs? Maybe, like Paul, she refused to consider the consequences of getting caught in order to indulge the pleasure of her obsession.

The very thought made me twist in my sleeping back. *No! It makes no sense. Not for the woman I've come to know . . .*

Outside the tent, around the still crackling fire, Seymour and Brainert weren't discussing Norma—or anything remotely related to grand theft and cold-blooded murder.

Instead, the pair were playing a version of the game they'd invented back in elementary school. In the fifth grade, the nameless game consisted of Brainert throwing out the title of a comic book or TV show and Seymour twisting said title into something rude, crude, or obscene.

The boys had grown up since then, and they'd cleaned up the game and made it a bit more challenging as well. Nowadays, Brainert threw out the name of a movie, a novel—or in tonight's case, a Broadway show—and Seymour's job was to rebrand and transform it.

"*Rent* by Jonathan David Larson," Brainert began. "A play that explores social issues like multiculturalism and drug addiction."

Seymour's reply came without a moment's hesitation.

"*Kent* by Jerry Siegel and Joe Shuster. A play that explores the alienated youth of Clark Kent, aka Superman."

"*Wicked,*" Brainert fired back. "A play about the life and times of the Wicked Witch of the West."

"*Cricket,*" Seymour replied. "A play about the life and times of Jiminy Cricket."

"Try *The Lion King,*" Brainert said. "A play about a young cub forced to accept the burden of adulthood and the kinship of the jungle."

"*The Lyin' Around King*, a play about a big fat Garfield of a cat too lazy to even chase mice."

"Bah, too easy, but I've got you this time," Brainert bragged. "*Dear Evan Hansen*, a play about a high school misunderstanding that changes an entire town."

"*Dear Charles Manson*. And that one is self-explanatory."

Both men roared with laughter. I covered my head with a pillow. Only then did I hear a familiar and very welcome voice inside my head.

Had enough of those twin boneheads yet, doll?

"You bet, Jack."

Do you want to get back to the case of the stolen Tears?

"We're on it, Jack. We found Norma's trailer. Sooner or later, she's bound to turn up. She left too many things behind to just abandon them."

Not your case of the stolen Tears, doll. Mine.

"I guess it's okay. I can't fall out of a sleeping bag like I've been falling out of bed, can I?"

Then close your eyes . . .

"UP AND AT 'em, Penny!" Jack cried, shaking my ermine-clad shoulder. "We've got to cheese it before the coppers arrive."

The echo of a gunshot had just died away. I opened my eyes and found myself on the floor in a purple room, a bottle of French champagne for a pillow. A second look revealed a corpse sprawled on the carpet beside me—Billy Bastogne, the ice pick that killed him still sticking out of the back of his neck.

"Don't look," Jack said as he hauled me to my feet.

"I don't feel so good," I replied, wobbly on my dancing shoes.

Jack pushed me through the purple curtains. "We don't have time for that. Let's scram."

Jack was practically carrying me now, my heels just touching the floor.

"What's the rush?"

"We have to stay one step ahead of the cops, and in hot pursuit of those jewels before the trail goes cold."

Outside the Lilac Garden, I saw that women and their faux-celebrity dance partners were fleeing the other flower-themed alcoves in various states of undress—the gunshot had frightened them into a panic, which was no doubt the intent of the woman who'd pulled the trigger. I knew it was a woman, because as Jack dragged me past the bubbling fountain, the memories came flooding back.

"Jack, Phyllis Harmon double-crossed you—"

"She thinks she did," Jack replied. "But I was on to her scheme as soon as she started feeding me information."

"Then you knew that her employer is—"

"Harry Amsterdam, the original owner of the Tears of Valentino. Old Harry sent Phyllis to retrieve those diamonds. She thought she was playing me for a sucker, but I was on to her trick."

"Phyllis still got away with the jewels."

The jagged scar on Jack's chin darkened. "I never figured she'd rub out Billy Bastogne the coldhearted way she did—or take pot shots at me with a heater when I tried to snag her. I've got to say, that dame is full of surprises."

"What did you think would happen," I asked.

"I figured Phyllis would play the femme fatale and try to con the Tears out of me once I got my hands on them. But I thought wrong. Phyllis didn't trust me to get the goods. She must have been here all along, spying on you. When she knew Billy had the jewels, she made her move with that ice pick."

Still huddled against Jack's firm body, I shuddered. "What a horrible way to die."

"I never saw a pleasant way yet," Jack cynically replied.

"Why didn't Phyllis approach Billy herself?"

"Because Billy would be wise to her. He knew Phyllis was friends with Thelma Dice, the woman Billy murdered. He also knew Phyllis worked for Harry Amsterdam, so Billy would naturally be suspicious of her, figuring Phyllis would want to retrieve those diamonds for her boss."

Jack shook his head. "Phyllis Harmon couldn't do it herself. She needed me—and you—as much as I needed her inside dope, maybe as much as I need her now."

"Why in the world do you need Phyllis Harmon now, after all she's done to double-cross you?"

"Because she is the only link I have to those jewels. And because Phyllis is going to lead me to Harry Amsterdam."

We'd already crossed the empty dance floor—the sound of gunshots had ended the party in a hurry. The bandshell had been abandoned, too, the musicians gone so fast they left their instruments behind.

I was a little steadier now, and Jack released me. From

the street I heard a frantic blast of a police whistle, and the howl of approaching sirens.

"In here," Jack said, pushing me through the waiters' door that led to the wine cellar. We descended a short flight of wooden stairs and crossed a murky basement with a rough concrete floor, its walls lined with racks of champagne.

Jack found the cellar's back door, and we emerged in an alley half a block away from the Moondance entrance.

A police car, its siren whining, zipped by on the main avenue. We emerged from the alley a moment later. Jack offered me his arm and we calmly walked by the commotion at the women's-only nightclub, just another fashionable couple on an evening stroll.

"Where to now, Jack?"

The detective adjusted his bow tie with his free hand. With the other he held me close.

"Phyllis figured gunshots would put me off. She was wrong. So many Nazis took shots at me I got used to it. I stuck on her tail and she didn't even know it. Before I came back for you, I followed Phyllis out the door. I didn't have time to grab her before she hopped into a taxi, but I got close enough to hear the address she gave the driver."

"Where is she going?"

"Seventy-eight Hester Street. It's in Little Italy. A place called Luca's, she said."

"Why there?"

"I'm pretty sure Phyllis is delivering the goods to her boss. And you know what that means, don't you?"

"No, I don't."

"It means that the rest is easy, doll, a downhill ride on a fast sled."

"Hmm," I grunted noncommittally.

"We're going to visit the elusive Harry Amsterdam, we're going to shake him down for those Tears, we're going to deliver the jewels to the Queen of the Nile, and then Syble Zane is going to pay up."

Jack grinned, and some of those hard edges on his face melted away.

"I'm feeling good about this, baby, and you should be all smiles, too."

"Why?"

"You're one step closer to that dinner at Sardi's."

CHAPTER 44

Phyllis on Ice

Things you own end up owning you.

—Chuck Palahniuk, *Fight Club*

IT WAS NEARLY three A.M. when our cab rolled up to 78 Hester Street. On the ride downtown Jack and I had speculated that Luca's would be either a cheap restaurant or a dive bar.

Wrong on both counts.

"A *salumeria*?" Jack said, scratching his head.

"It's a delicatessen that specializes in Italian food."

"Yeah," Jack said in a voice laced with sarcasm. "I never would have guessed that from the stuff in the window."

Cured meats dangled from a rope behind the picture window. Rounds of Italian cheeses were piled high, along with massive jars of green and black olives.

We didn't need to try the door to see the store was closed. And not just Luca's. There was nothing but empty streets and darkened windows all around us, the deserted sidewalks illuminated by pools of light under each streetlamp. There was not another storefront in sight.

A chill wind blew down Hester Street. I pulled the ermine tight around my shoulders. I pitied Jack, still in his waiter's tux, without a coat or even a fedora to cover his head. He didn't seem to be bothered by the weather, though he was really steamed about the trail to Phyllis Harmon going cold.

"Where did she go?" he muttered.

"Are you sure you heard the address right?"

"There's Luca's, right where Phyllis told the cab driver it would be."

"Okay, you're right. Then where is Phyllis?"

Jack looked around. "Life in these parts is pretty sparse."

"We *are* a tad overdressed for a ghost town—no offense, of course."

Jack ignored my attempt at humor. "Phyllis might have given the cabbie this store as a reference. It's the only business on this block. If that's the case, she could be anywhere. We'll— Hey, wait a minute!"

Jack rushed toward a lighted window that turned out to be a door with a glass window set in the middle. The narrow door was nestled in an alcove right beside Luca's Salumeria.

Through the window I spied a tile-covered hallway lit by a naked lightbulb. Beyond that, a flight of stairs with a cast-iron railing led up to the second floor.

Near the opposite wall I noticed a pair of high-heeled legs sprawled across a canvas-covered heap of what looked like big square boxes.

Jack cursed, then twisted the doorknob. With a click, it opened. If Jack was surprised to find it unlocked (I was!) he didn't show it. He just pushed through the door and into the hallway.

I was right behind him.

Immediately, a blast of damp, icy air struck me. The floor was wet, and I realized those big canvas-covered squares were blocks of ice, maybe delivered here for use by Luca's deli next door.

Phyllis Harmon was sprawled on top of those frozen blocks. Jack rushed to her side, checked the pulse in her throat.

"She's still breathing," he said.

A tiny splotch of blood stained the breast of Phyllis Harmon's pink velvet dress. Jack gently turned the woman on her side, and I choked back a scream. She'd been shot—and the exit wound on her back was anything but tiny.

Suddenly Phyllis gasped and opened her eyes. As Jack moved her off the ice, I spread the ermine cape on the damp floor, and he gently laid her down. Phyllis began to shiver, and Jack cradled the grievously injured woman in the warmth of his strong arms.

"It's you," Phyllis gasped, forcing a smile.

"Who did this, Phyllis?"

"Turns out I was being followed while I was following you . . . and her," she replied weakly "Pretty funny if you think about it . . ."

She was struggling to stay conscious, and losing.

"Come on, stay with me, Phyllis. Did you see who shot you?"

She laughed bitterly, then began to cough. Blood flecked her red lips.

"Went up to meet Harry—" She raised her arm weakly and pointed to the stairs. "No card game tonight. He was meeting me alone. Before I knocked on his door, I heard someone down here. I thought it was you, but when I came back down again . . . I didn't even see the person who shot me . . ."

Phyllis gasped. Then she laughed again. More blood touched her lips.

"They didn't get them, though . . . The Tears are right there . . . I hid them in the ice."

She coughed again. "Harry promised me I could have the Tears someday . . . I don't care if they're valuable or not. They belonged to Rudolph Valentino once and now I own them . . . for a minute or two."

"Where's Harry?" Jack asked.

"Upstairs . . ."

I didn't wait for any more answers. I ran up the stairs two at a time.

"Penny, wait!" Jack cried.

Phyllis shook her head. "Too late . . . Too late . . ."

At the top of the steps, I found a single door, wide open. Light from an overhead bulb illuminated a green velvet card table surrounded by chairs. A well-stocked bar stood on one side of the room; on the other a wall safe was open, and empty. A few small bills littered the floor, as if the safe had been hastily looted.

I stepped closer and bumped my foot on something soft.

I looked down, then jumped backward.

Beside the table, on the unfinished plank floor, a corpulent dead man in a wool pin-striped suit lay sprawled among a scattered deck of cards. A neat bullet hole punctured the middle of his forehead.

Someone touched my shoulder and I yelped.

"It's Harry Amsterdam," Jack said. "I've seen his picture in the trades."

I whirled to face the detective. "And Phyllis?"

"She's gone."

"What happened here, Jack?"

The detective frowned. "I know what it's supposed to look like. Old Harry disappeared from time to time, and no one knew where he went. It looks like he was running high-stakes card games for the entertainment of his show business friends, who had plenty of money to lose."

I scanned the room, the card table, the bar, the open safe.

"This looks like a robbery, Jack. Someone, maybe the Germantown mob, got wind of Harry's games and killed him for the money."

"Sure, that's what it *looks* like. Only we're in Little Italy, and the Italian mob likely took a cut of Harry's take, which meant Harry Amsterdam was almost certainly protected by the Italians. Nobody, not even Germantown gangsters, would dare rob Harry and shut down a business that profits the Italians. Nobody in the know, anyway."

"Then who did it?"

Jack's scowl was almost frightening. "I know who. But first things first. Let's go find those stolen Tears . . ."

I followed Jack back down the steps. He'd covered the dead woman's face with ermine. Now he stepped over her still form and dug under the wet canvas. After a few moments, he fished Billy Bastogne's tobacco pouch from among the ice blocks.

With freezing hands, Jack handed me the pouch. Opening it, I gaped at the stunning teardrop diamonds gleaming in the glare of the naked bulb. I closed the pouch and wrapped it tightly.

As I turned, I noticed something small and shiny on the wet concrete floor. I bent low and picked it up. That's when I knew.

"Jack," I whispered, offering him a look at the tiny golden object I'd found. Our eyes met.

"That tell you something, does it?"

"It sure does."

"Good."

"So what now, Jack? What do we do next?"

"I'm calling in the law on these homicides. Then we'll deliver the Tears of Valentino to my client, as promised. But just to be sure, you and I need to talk to someone first."

"And I know who."

CHAPTER 45

Delivering the Goods

It's bad business to let the killer get away with it. It's bad all around.

—Dashiell Hammett, *The Maltese Falcon*, 1930

"WHAT'S THAT?" BRAINERT cried, startling me out of my dream.

When my eyes opened, I was no longer in Manhattan's Little Italy. I was back in Rhode Island, inside a tent pitched in the woods.

Seymour and Brainert were still outside. By the light of the roaring campfire, I could see their silhouettes through the tent's wall.

"What's what?" Seymour asked.

"I . . . I thought I saw a light in the woods. Maybe a flashlight . . ."

"Maybe just the lights from the highway," Seymour countered.

"We've been sitting here all night," Brainert replied, his tone haughty. "Never once did I see lights from the highway. Why should I suddenly see them now? Anyway, the road is a quarter of a mile away, through a stretch of woods. You would need X-ray eyes to see headlights."

Seymour chuckled, "'X-Ray Eyes.' Sounds like one of the songs from the musical *Kent*."

"Ho, ho, very clever," Brainert groused. "But I still think I saw a glow in the woods."

"Okay, okay. Where did you see this mysterious light?"

"Over there, I think. Or maybe it was there—"

"Oh, rats!" Seymour cried. "See what you made me do? My perfectly toasted marshmallow just fell into the fire. Now it's burning like a heretic at the Spanish Inquisition."

"Haven't you had enough?" Brainert cried. "You've eaten ten of them—"

"Twelve, Brainiac, but who's counting?"

"We're supposed to be standing watch, Seymour."

"Fine. You watch the woods. I'll watch my marshmallow."

The bickering soon subsided, and I heard only the crackling of the fire and Seymour's tuneless humming.

My eyelids closed once again . . .

"STEP IT UP, Penny. We're here."

Jack climbed out of the taxicab and helped me to the curb. He flipped the driver a quarter and told him to keep the change. The brilliant lights of old Times Square gleamed around us, and crowds of suited men and white-gloved women with stylish hats strolled the sidewalks.

We'd arrived at the Martin Beck Theater. The marquee read ANTONY AND CLEOPATRA BY WILLIAM SHAKESPEARE.

"Shake a leg, doll," Jack urged. "We've got a delivery to make."

A moment later we were in a narrow alley approaching the backstage doors. The door manager spotted Jack and slid steel gates aside to admit us. He offered Jack a respectful nod as we went by.

Jack guided me through the labyrinthine halls until I spied Charlton Heston's dressing room, and right beside it, the door marked SYBLE ZANE.

Jack turned the knob and waltzed inside the cramped

room. As I followed him inside he slipped off his fedora and tossed it on a chair.

The detective seemed perfectly comfortable, but the lingering scent of Syble's perfume made me antsy. Jack checked the Bulova on his wrist.

"Show's almost over. Miss Zane will be here in a minute or so."

I shook my head and felt a surge of outrage. "After all the bloodshed, I wonder if Syble Zane really is the legitimate owner of those Tears. I mean, Harry gave them to Thelma Dice, and when she was killed, he sent his secretary, Phyllis Harmon, to get them back. Clearly, Harry Amsterdam was claiming ownership of those jewels."

"Yeah, maybe," Jack replied. "But Harry Amsterdam didn't hire me. Miss Syble Zane did, and she has expectations."

Then the knob turned, and Syble Zane was standing in the doorway in full Egyptian undress. When she spied us, she stopped dead, her chain-and-metal bikini clanking. She recovered her composure quickly.

"Oh, it's you, Mr. Shepard." Syble's tone was aloof—a bold attempt to hide her obvious surprise.

"I hope you brought me some good news," she continued, closing the door behind her.

"Better than that, Miss Zane," a smiling Jack Shepard replied. He patted the lapel pocket under his jacket. "I brought you the goods."

Under the Cleopatra eye makeup, Syble raised a brow in genuine surprise. Jack noted the reaction, and his smiled morphed into a smirk.

"Very impressive work, Mr. Shepard," the actress purred. "Just how did you manage to find the Tears?"

"The same way you almost did. Yet despite pulling the trigger on a helpless woman, you couldn't quite manage to grab the jewels. But I did."

"Excuse me?"

"I followed Phyllis Harmon, just like you."

Syble's brows knitted in faux confusion and she cocked

her head. Her act was strictly B movie and didn't fool Jack, or me.

"I don't think I understand your meaning, Mr. Shepard."

"Sure you do," Jack insisted. "I kept you apprised of my every move, for expenses' sake. But that also meant only two people knew Phyllis Harmon was feeding me information. One was Penny here, and the other was you."

"I hardly paid attention to your reports. I have a career to manage—"

Jack ran right over her words.

"You also knew Phyllis was Harry's secretary and that she knew where the Broadway producer was, even if you and everyone else didn't."

"My interest was in the Tears of Valentino, Mr. Shepard."

"But you also hired me to find Harry Amsterdam, if you'll recall. And I did find Harry, but only after you iced him and made it look like a robbery."

Syble Zane winced as if stung. "Well, I never—"

"Yeah, you did. You followed Phyllis Harmon all the way downtown to Luca's deli. You jimmied the lock to number 77½ with a hatpin, and when Phyllis came down the stairs you shot her through the left lung."

Jack's laugh was harsh, and there was no humor in it.

"You thought poor Phyllis had already delivered the goods when you plugged her. But you were wrong. You even forced Harry at gunpoint to open the safe and prove he didn't have the diamonds; then you had to kill him to protect your identity."

Jack made a victory sign. "That's two premeditated murders. Enough to send you to the state pen for life. And you didn't even get the jewels. Of course, that wasn't your motive for killing Harry Amsterdam, was it?"

"I was his mistress," Syble fired back, her eyes as wide as a cornered animal's. "Why would I want him dead?"

"Because he held you by the neck with a contract you couldn't break." Jack scowled. "Yeah, I spoke with Johnny Palermo from the Broadway Guild. He told me all about Amsterdam's lousy exclusive contracts, and about how you've been making noise for months about wanting to break free and rush off to Hollywood, where the real money is."

"Fascinating story, Mr. Shepard. But you forget, I was onstage last night—"

"You weren't," Jack cut in. "I spoke with Miss Ingham—"

"Who?" Syble's eyes flashed.

"Cora," Jack shot back. "That sweet young production assistant you call a freak. Cora told me you ducked last night's performance. An understudy took your role. And I have proof you were at the scene of the crime."

Jack held up the shiny object I'd found—a tiny gold scarab. That little Egyptian beetle Cora had delivered to Syble Zane's dressing room the night we met her, the one that kept falling out of her earring. The earring Cora had mentioned Syble liked to wear outside the theater.

Now Syble Zane clutched her ear, feeling the indentation where the little gold ornament went missing, and the color went out of her. For the first time since I'd met her, the actress was speechless.

"You shouldn't be surprised that I figured it all out, Miss Zane," Jack continued with a wink my way. "I have a lot of connections and pumped a good bit of information out of them. It was easy to fit all the little pieces together into a neat story that pins the guilt on you."

In the silent moment that followed, Syble reached for her powder blue robe and slipped it over her skimpy costume. When she faced us again, her expression was composed, her eyes cool and calculating.

"So, what's it going to be, Mr. Shepard? A little bit of blackmail?"

Jack's reply was icy. "More than a little bit."

She tossed her head. "You want it all, then?"

"I want what's coming . . ."

She smiled. "Why don't you keep the Tears of Valentino, then? They're worth far more than the money I was going to pay you. You keep the jewels, and you keep your mouth shut."

"About the murders?"

"Yes!" she cried. "About the murders. Harry had it coming, anyway. It felt good to kill him. If I lose the Tears, so be it. I consider getting rid of Harry Amsterdam worth the cost."

Jack's smile was cold. "I hope you feel that way two minutes from now."

With that, Jack balled his fist and pounded on the dressing room wall. The door burst open seconds later, and two uniformed police officers entered.

Without a word, and without Mirandizing her, one of the officers seized Syble Zane's arms and cuffed the struggling woman's wrists.

"What's . . . What's happening?" the arrogant actress cried.

"We're arresting you for murder," the grizzled older officer replied. Then a voice boomed from the hallway.

"Take her to the station, boys. I'll be right behind you."

A police lieutenant pushed past the arresting officers and entered the dressing room. Roughly the size of a heavyweight pugilist, the man clapped Jack on the back so hard I thought the detective was going to hit the floor.

"Three murders solved, and a con artist headed to the slammer. You're a fine upstanding citizen, Jack Shepard, that's what you are."

"Penny," Jack said. "I want you to meet Lieutenant Sean Patrick Flynn of New York's Finest."

"Pleased," he said with a short bow.

"Did you hear everything Miss Zane said?" Jack asked.

"Oh yes, Mr. Heston was most cooperative in lending us his dressing room—ah, and here he is now."

Young Charlton Heston stepped into the dressing room and looked around.

"Is it over?" he asked in a voice familiar to (future) fans of everything from the Old Testament to *Soylent Green*.

"It surely is over, Mr. Heston," the lieutenant replied. "And we thank you for your cooperation."

As I watched them go, I considered all the real tears that had been shed over the Tears of Valentino, along with the tragic fates of Thelma Dice, Billy Bastogne, Phyllis Harmon, Harry Amsterdam, and finally, Syble Zane herself.

If there was any silver lining to this terribly dark cloud, I couldn't see it, though (in the end) Jack did.

"That was a neat trap you set, Jack. I'm going to file that away for future reference. Shall we go? You do owe me a dinner at Sardi's."

"One thing first," Jack replied. He pulled the tobacco pouch out of his lapel pocket and shook it. I could hear the Tears rattling inside. He set the bag on the dressing table and added a neatly folded note addressed to Cora Ingham.

Take this pouch to Johnny Palermo at the Broadway Guild. Tell him I sent you, and he should line you up with a loan, using these rocks as collateral. With that, you can afford to start your own theater company, one that values a girl with a few scars and a lot of Broadway experience.

Break a leg, toots!
Jack Shepard

CHAPTER 46

As the Crow Flies

I lay there, knowing that I was asleep, yet awake,
dreaming a real dream but not caring at all, enjoying a
consciousness that was almost like being dead.

—Mickey Spillane, *My Gun Is Quick*

THE STRIDENT CRY of a crow woke me from a sound
sleep.

I sat up as well as I was able, considering I had a sleeping
bag zipped up around me like a nylon cocoon. The tent was
empty, Seymour's and Brainert's sleeping bags were still
rolled up in the corner, and I realized they'd pulled an all-
nighter.

The cobwebs fell away as I climbed to my feet, but not
the memory of my dream.

I was glad to know that my initial hunch about distrust-
ing Syble had been correct. And my first theory about Cora
had been right, too. She really was Peyton Pemberton's great
aunt. One day, that shy, damaged young woman would mature into an acclaimed actress and head of her own theater
company. It felt like something to celebrate.

"Too bad I missed out on that dinner at Sardi's," I muttered.

Of course, Jack was not there to reply. And though I'd helped him solve his case, mine was still wide open.

I adjusted my clothes, slipped on my boots and a hoodie, and exited the tent. The campfire was a smoky memory. The folding chairs were empty. The teardrop trailer was closed up tight, and there was no sign of Seymour or Brainert.

I longed for a hot cup of tea, but all Seymour had in his kit was instant coffee. I took a drink from the water cooler and scanned the area in search of my fellow campers.

Millstone Creek had finally receded to its customary banks, and the place we were camped was no longer an island, just part of the shore. But the ground was still soft and muddy, and I spotted two sets of footprints heading into the woods.

Either Seymour and Brainert had gone off to investigate something—or they were busy doing what bears do in the woods.

I decided to follow their trail.

It was easy at first, but down among the weeds things got tougher. I barely managed to keep on their tail until I saw them both, just inside a line of trees.

"Hey, Pen! Look what we found," Seymour cried. Brainert was beside him, but the professor's eyes were on the ground.

I pushed through some saplings and reached the two a moment later.

"What is this?"

Seymour shrugged. "Search me. Crazy, huh?"

The circle was maybe fifteen feet across, with carefully manicured ground in the middle. The cleared area was outlined by a long, thin rope tied around tree trunks to create an irregular circle, about waist-high. Hundreds of bits of aluminum foil dangled from the rope, each painstakingly connected by hand.

"Aha!" Brainert cried, pointing to the sky. No, not the sky. One section of rope had broken, and the loose foil-covered string had blown high among the tree branches and become entangled.

"I did see light in the woods," Brainert said. "That foil is high enough to reflect the headlights from the highway. That's what I saw. I knew I wasn't wrong."

"Brilliant deduction, Holmes. Simply sterling," Seymour replied.

I used the break in the rope to enter the circle. The ground had been swept clean of weeds. Only some dry grasses and a carpet of sunflower shells remained. Right in the middle of the circle I found a cheap plastic basin buried in the ground. It was partially filled with muddy water and dead leaves, but I got the feeling that wasn't always the case.

I found more proof of my theory at the other end of the circle, where I found two empty mason jars, their former contents written on masking tape with a magic marker and slapped on the side.

"What are Juneberries?" I muttered aloud.

Whatever they were, I knew their purpose.

"What is this place?" Brainert asked.

"It's a bird feeder," I replied. "A great big bird feeder."

"Actually, it's a crow trap," a new voice said, startling us. "Though I don't actually trap any. I just feed the crows and observe them."

The speaker was standing among the trees, her hair covered by an oversize baseball cap, a flannel jacket over her slim shoulders. She held a giant bag of bird seed in one strong hand. A red scarf wrapped around her neck and partially covered the woman's face and muffled her voice, but I recognized her instantly.

"Norma Stanton!"

"Hello, Mrs. McClure. Hey, Seymour," Norma the Nomad replied with a smile and a tiny wave.

CHAPTER 47

The Varnished Truth

The man began to run . . . his wife and children cried
out to him. "Come back! Come home!" The man put
his fingers in his ears and ran on.

—Paul Bunyan, *The Pilgrim's Progress*

WE IMMEDIATELY BOMBARDED Norma with ques-
tions, but she brushed them off, intent on getting the bag of
sunflower seeds open and spread on the ground.

"Most of the crows have gone south, but a few chose
these woods for a winter roost. I haven't fed them since before the storm. I hope they didn't get too hungry."

As she stepped out of the circle, the crows began to caw.
Norma looked skyward, smiling. "Yes, they're still here."

Norma quickly repaired the rope, then led us away from
the circle so the crows could feed. On the way back to the
trailer, Brainert introduced himself with a heartfelt apology.

"I . . . We're all terribly sorry to have invaded your
privacy—"

"Yes," I explained. "We were looking for some hint as to
where you might have gone. We feared that . . . Well, that
something bad had happened to you."

"And of course," Brainert continued, "until I read your

manuscript, I had no idea that you were—are!—one of America's literary lights."

Norma brushed off the compliment the way she initially brushed off our questions, offering only a pragmatic reply.

"Well, I'm glad it was you who found my trailer. The last time I was stuck, my home was looted. They stole my radio, my camera, even my typewriter—and I had just purchased the parts to fix it."

Back at the campsite, Norma unwound her scarf, took off her hat, and shook out her pixie cut.

"We don't understand why you ran," I said. "Me, Fiona, Sadie—even Deputy Chief Franzetti—we all knew you didn't steal those jewels. We're terribly sorry we invaded your private life. We were looking for answers, that's all."

For the first time since I'd known this jovial woman, I heard a note of heavy sadness in her voice.

"Answers? I've been looking for answers for nine years," Norma said, then the cloud lifted, and she smiled. "But you shouldn't have to wait that long, and it's about time I told someone."

FIFTEEN MINUTES LATER, while Brainert, Seymour, and I sat on folding chairs in a semicircle around her, Norma revealed her story.

"You ask me why I ran from the Finch Inn," Norma began. "I can only think that it was instinct. Animal instinct, a psychologist might call it. You see, I've been running for nearly a decade."

The morning sun rose in a near-cloudless sky, dappling the muddy waters of Millstone Creek with hues of yellow and orange. In the woods, the crows cawed, grateful for the bounty of sunflower seeds their loving caretaker had brought them.

Their provider sat in the teardrop trailer's open door, clearly relieved to be home at last. The disposable cup of instant coffee Norma sipped from steamed in the morning chill. The mysterious manuscript sat in her lap. As she spoke, she fiddled with its crinkled pages.

"Ten years ago, I had a different name and a temporary job working as a domestic at the Ballard family's Palm Beach mansion. The family made its fortune in pharmaceuticals, turning a chain of drugstores into a manufacturing empire. But when I joined the staff, the family was in turmoil. Julian Ballard Sr. had recently passed and the business he founded was in disarray."

Norma shrugged. "Of course, I didn't know any of this when I took the job. I have never been a part of that world. Never have, and never will. I was a housekeeper, that's all.

"I worked conscientiously for a few weeks and impressed the head butler when I cleaned and polished a neglected Victorian picture frame in the dining room. He set me to work restoring the picture frames in the library, as well. He had workmen take the paintings down and line them up along one wall—there were over a dozen. I was supplied with tools, paint remover, varnish, and a month to complete the work."

Norma smiled. "The library was lovely; you should have seen it. It held an astounding collection of books, some of them ancient. I could have spent my whole lifetime there, reading them all.

"Even better, it was the kind of work I adore. Alone with my hands and some wonderful object I can make beautiful, my mind was free to wander, and the troubles in this world vanished, like that."

She snapped her fingers. "But it wasn't long before my solitude was shattered, and that's where the trouble began."

"On my fourth day of work, a young man came into the library to study. He introduced himself as Julian and told me he was working toward his bachelor's degree. Though the academic year was over, he was taking summer courses to speed up the degree process. He was a young man in a hurry, and I soon found out why."

Norma told us that man was Julian Ballard Jr. the oldest son of the billionaire who'd founded Ballard Pharmaceuticals. Julian was destined to inherit the business when he came of age, and he wanted to be ready. He was twenty, just a year shy of his "coronation."

"Over the next few days, I cleaned and varnished, and Julian studied. We began to chat. He was fifteen years younger than me, smart and sensitive, but troubled, too. Julian had a demon he could not control—an addiction to alcohol, which began, he confessed to me, when he was just twelve years old and sneaking drinks from the family's bar.

"As the days progressed, he opened up more and more. Julian told me he never knew his real mother, and he had nothing but contempt for his 'trophy-wife stepmother,' as he put it. But Julian reserved most of his disgust for his half brother, Hal."

Norma explained that she did not know the stepmother but thought Julian a good judge of character, so she took him at his word. Hal was another story.

"My brushes with Hal were always unpleasant. The staff hated him as much as they feared his temper. He was arrogant, abusive, spiteful, and just plain mean. Unfortunately, Hal's mother—Julian's hated trophy wife—treated her child like a prince. And if you were to ask me, that was the problem," Norma said.

"Though Julian's half brother Hal was barely sixteen, he had already gotten into minor scrapes with the law. He even assaulted a teacher at his exclusive prep school—an incident that cost the family almost a million dollars to cover up."

Norma admitted Julian was no saint, either.

"When he drank—which was only on weekends because he kept a strict study schedule—Julian became angry and sullen. On several occasions he loudly vowed to cut his stepmother and half brother out of the family fortune as soon as he took control."

With a shake of her head, Norma paused to finish her coffee.

"Eventually my assignment in the library ended, but Julian and I didn't stop meeting there to talk. I was under the impression that he saw me as an older sister, or perhaps even a mother figure."

Norma spat a bitter laugh. "I was wrong on both counts."

"One Friday night in mid-August, after Julian quarreled

with his stepmother and followed it up with too many shots of bourbon, he met me in the library. Only that night, he didn't want to talk . . . Julian wanted something else."

Visibly distressed, Norma fell silent again, this time to compose herself. When she spoke, her voice was low, her tone sad.

"I suppose what happened next was technically a sexual assault, but the whole thing was pretty pathetic. I easily fended off his advances, and Julian ended up tearfully apologizing.

"He got sick and dizzy after that, and I cleaned up his mess and helped him stretch out on the library couch. I covered him with my sweater, then I left the mansion and returned to my van, which was parked a few miles away at a trailer camp.

"The next morning, on the radio, I heard the horrible news. Poor Julian Ballard, my Julian, had been murdered, bludgeoned to death in the library with a fireplace poker. The news reporter said evidence had been recovered at the scene which implicated a member of the domestic staff."

CHAPTER 48

Untitled Manuscript

Nothing can bring peace but yourself . . . [and] the triumph of principles.

—Ralph Waldo Emerson, "Self-Reliance"

NORMA SWIPED AT a tear that touched her cheek at the memory.

"When I heard about poor Julian . . . Well, that was the first time I ran. I didn't have a clue what really happened to that sweet young man after I left the mansion that night, but I had my suspicions."

"If you suspected someone of the crime, why did you run?" Brainert asked.

"Oh, I suppose I could have proclaimed my innocence and stayed to face the music. But I remembered Julian telling me how his family 'bought' justice for their son Hal, and I knew I didn't have a chance of proving my innocence—not if my suspicions were correct. And if I was right, the Ballard family needed a scapegoat to pin the murder on. I knew that scapegoat would be me."

"So, you've been living in your van, driving from place to place ever since?" Brainert asked incredulously.

"Oh no, you misunderstand," Norma countered. "I've

been living the van life since I turned eighteen. I left home on four wheels, and I've been on the road ever since. That was my choice. But I never wanted to be a fugitive or change my name to 'Norma Stanton.' For the past nine years, I've been running one step ahead of the law."

"What do you think happened to Julian that night?" I asked.

Norma patted the manuscript in her lap.

"It took me years to piece it all together, and I had a lot of help along the way. My nine-year search for the truth is chronicled right here, along with my theory about what really happened."

Seymour spoke up, amazement in his voice. "But it was an active murder investigation, and you could not get near the witnesses, the crime scene, the files, or even the investigating officers. How did you manage to learn anything at all?"

"Over the years I surreptitiously contacted members of the domestic staff," Norma explained. "From their various accounts about the events that night and the days and weeks that followed, I reconstructed what I believe occurred."

"Dorothy Willard in Millstone was one of those people you contacted, wasn't she?" I asked.

Norma nodded. "Dottie worked for the Ballard family until she was laid off. The family sold off the Palm Beach property after Ballard Pharmaceuticals got caught up in the opioid scandal. Last year the company was dissolved."

"Did you know Dorothy Willard was murdered the day before yesterday?"

Norma hung her head and nodded. "I should never have involved her. She didn't know much, as it turned out, but she knew I was innocent and wanted to help. Now she's paid the price. She wasn't the first, either. Two years ago I received a sworn affidavit from a fellow named Stanley Crisp, who worked as a custodian at the mansion. Stanley testified that he witnessed Hal Ballard burning clothes in the mansion's incinerator the morning after the murder."

"Incinerators are always incriminating," Seymour noted.

"I was hoping he would help me clear my name, but it was not to be," Norma said. "Stanley Crisp drowned last year in a boating accident—if it *was* an accident. There were no witnesses."

"Did you know about Louis Kritzer?" I asked.

"I picked up the *Quindicott Bulletin* in a feed store where I bought the birdseed this morning," Norma replied. "That's how I found out about Dottie, and Louis."

"We found the note from Louis Kritzer, confessing to recording your talks at the group therapy sessions and putting them online," Seymour said. "Kritzer claimed he wanted justice."

"He was good friends with Stanley Crisp. Louis also believed Stanley met with foul play."

"Do you think Mr. Kritzer really committed suicide?" I asked.

"I don't know." Norma frowned. "Louis did suffer from bouts of deep depression, and he was on his tenth month of sobriety, which is always a difficult struggle. That was why he attended the reverend's group sessions."

"Well, there is no question that Dottie Willard was murdered," I replied. "I was there. I know. But I also know you did everything you could."

Norma shook her head. "I did nothing."

"Not true," I proclaimed. "You tried to protect Dottie's identity when you stole the Post-it note from Fiona's check-in desk."

"Excuse me?" Norma said, blinking.

"You remember. Fiona had a Post-it note stuck on the side of her registration computer with Dorothy Willard's address written on it, so she could contact you when you were away, presumably visiting Dottie, who you claimed was your sister."

"I didn't know about that note," Norma said, stunned.

"Someone took it the day the jewels were stolen. Fiona thought it was you."

"I . . ." Norma blinked again and shook her head. "I didn't take that note, but I know who did. That's why I ran from the Finch Inn the other day, why I have to keep on running."

I leaned forward so far my folding chair nearly collapsed. "I still don't understand. Tell us why you ran, and why you have to run now."

"I ran because Hal Ballard checked into the Finch Inn—and tried to frame me as a jewel thief."

"Hal Ballard was at the Finch Inn?" I cried. "Fiona never mentioned anyone named Ballard."

"Because of the scandals around Ballard Pharmaceuticals, Hal is going by his mother's maiden name now. He calls himself Hollis West—"

"The man who checked in with Peyton Pemberton!"

Norma nodded. "If anyone stole that Post-it with Dottie's address, it was Hal. He was the only one who had a reason to steal it. If Hal had something to do with custodian Stanley Crisp's death, I'm sure he suspected Dottie was helping me, too—"

"Which meant he had a motive for killing that poor old lady," Seymour said.

Norma nodded again. "And he wants me out of the picture—if not arrested, then dead."

"Arrested . . ." I thought a moment. "I doubt Hal's arrival at the Finch Inn was a coincidence. He and his girlfriend are Internet influencers, they would likely be aware of who else was hot or trending online. Your inspirational videos have gone viral on several platforms—and a recent video told the public where to find you."

"Well, I know *in my gut* that Hal Ballard, aka Hollis West, murdered his half brother," Norma said. "And his family has been covering up the crime by deflecting the blame to me. Getting me arrested for a jewel theft would have revealed my identity to the authorities in an incriminating way—and shut the book on the murder of Julian."

Norma must be right, I decided. *If the killer is Hollis West, then everything makes sense . . .*

I considered how easily it would have been to frame Norma for stealing the Tears of Valentino, if Peyton Pemberton had been in on it. And she had to be. The pair checked into the Finch Inn on Sunday together—with the jewels—

then Hollis departed. He could have taken the necklace and one earing with him, leaving a single teardrop behind, which Peyton could have planted on the maid's cart while grabbing a towel for her morning run. I thought back to those security camera images showing Peyton exiting her room without a towel—yet bounding down the stairs with one around her neck.

That was it! The great Finch Inn jewel heist was solved!

That also meant the suave Mr. Santoro was likely just what he claimed to be—a man on a mission to recover the Tears of Valentino—and not a murderer as I'd feared (despite those muddy boots in his back seat, just like plenty of fishing-loving locals and tourists possessed around here).

"So, Norma, what are you going to do now?" Seymour asked.

"I'm going to dig out my trailer, hook it up to my van, and get the heck out of here," she replied.

I held up my hand. "Not so fast." I faced her. "There might be a way to end this now. I think we can clear your name, get justice for Julian Ballard, and solve Dottie Willard's murder at the same time. But only if we have a little help from some friends . . ."

CHAPTER 49

A Way Out

All he wanted was a sanctuary, to get in out of the open
for a while, where they couldn't find him.

—Cornell Woolrich, "The Heavy Sugar"

ON THE ROAD back to Quindicott, I called Eddie Franzetti's office at the QPD. The dispatcher informed me that
Eddie was still in Providence with his wife and they would
not return until tomorrow—which meant part of our plan
was already wrecked.

Seymour, Brainert, and I would have to implement our
scheme—and likely face an armed man—without Eddie to
back us up. There was no one else on the police force familiar enough with the case to even grasp what we had to tell
them. If I let Chief Ciders in on our scheme he would likely
have all of us arrested!

Soldiering on with our original plan, Seymour, Brainert,
and I stopped at the Finch Inn next. It was nearly two o'clock
when we arrived and I kept an eye out for Hollis West's
fancy sports car. But it was Seymour who spotted the vehicle, parked at the far end of the inn's lot, beside the path
that led to the Lighthouse, where Peyton was staying.

While Brainert watched the desk, Seymour and I pulled

Fiona into the library and told her how we found Norma, what we learned, and our scheme to clear Norma of false charges of theft and murder.

Fiona reluctantly agreed to our plan but insisted I make all the arrangements. I was fine with that, so our next stop was Spencer's elementary school. After getting permission from the principal—let's face it, Mrs. McConnell owed me—I was handed a hall pass to visit Mr. Alan Burke's classroom.

I did not let Mr. Burke in on what was really going on, or what we were planning. I simply suggested a new venue for his science prodigies to showcase their projects before the science fair.

"I think that is a wonderful idea, Mrs. McClure. I'm sure my students would love to show off their skills to the people in our community."

"I'm sorry it's such short notice," I said, "but it has to be set up by tonight at seven o'clock."

"No problem. These are smart kids. They can pull it together in time."

"And remember what I said about Susan Trencher's project."

Mr. Burke nodded. "Up front where everyone in the community can see the pollution right in our backyard."

Well, something like that, I thought.

The end-of-school bell rang a few minutes later, and I grabbed my son before he got on the bus.

"Get in," I said, pushing him into Seymour's vintage Volkswagen. As usual, Spencer failed to see the vehicle's charm.

"It smells in here," he said.

"Hey, you little brat!" Seymour cried. "I'll have you know—"

"We went camping," I interrupted. "You're smelling the campfire smoke. Now, listen. I need to know if you got any fingerprints off that television knob."

Spencer's eyes lit up. "Two solid prints, Mom. I don't know who those fingerprints belong to, but—"

"We're going to find out," I interrupted. "And by securing those prints you may have saved someone from prison."

"Wow! Mom, you've got to tell me—"

"I'll tell you everything, but you have to wait until tomorrow. In the meantime, I want you to keep that knob and a copy of those prints in a safe place. Okay? Deputy Chief Franzetti is out of town, but as soon as he gets back I will be handing them over to him. Got it?"

"I got it, Mom. I'll be sure to hide it somewhere safe just as soon as I get home."

"And remember, mum's the word."

Spencer mock-zipped his lips, them muttered incomprehensibly.

"What?"

"I said my lips are sealed, Mom. That's why I mumbled. Didn't you get the joke?"

I got it, Jack said with a laugh. The ghost had returned, at last. *Your little scrapper is a real George Burns.*

Thank goodness you're here, Jack. I have plenty to tell you—

Oh, I've been listening, and watching. And I have to admit I'm impressed.

With me?

With the lummox and the sheepskin—

You mean Seymour and Brainert?

Yeah, the two stooges almost seem . . . competent. I am truly amazed.

Well, just wait a little, Jack. I'm sure they'll find a way to lose your newfound respect for them real soon.

Next, Seymour drove us over to the First Presbyterian Church. While the others waited in the car, I paid a visit to Reverend Waterman.

"You once told the flock that you and Mrs. Waterman met when you were both playing summer stock."

"That's true, and I remember that time fondly," the reverend replied.

"Of course. You met your future wife."

Reverend Waterman nodded impatiently. "That, too. But I was more excited about headlining *Guys and Dolls*. I played Sky Masterson. That was Marlon Brando's role in the movie, you know? We played nine weeks!"

"Well, I need you and Mrs. Waterman to do a little acting tonight, for a much smaller audience. An audience of one, in fact."

I filled them in on all I'd learned, then gave them the "script." The Watermans agreed immediately.

"What now, Pen?" Seymour asked when I returned to the Volkswagen.

"We've got all the actors in place," I said. "Now we have to get our own act together . . ."

CHAPTER 50

Stumble Bums

Timing is everything in life and in golf.

—Cecil Leitch as quoted by Arnold Palmer

"COME ON, SEYMOUR," I pleaded. "It's almost seven o'clock."

Seymour weighed the heavy sledgehammer in his hand. "It's vandalism, Pen."

"Do it!" Brainert commanded.

"But this is a BMW M4 convertible in Tanzanite Blue. It's a thing of beauty. I can't bring myself to—"

"Seymour," I said, "this is a complex operation which depends on precise timing and coordination."

Hah! Jack Shepard scoffed. *Then you're doomed.*

"Remember, Seymour," Brainert warned in an ominous tone. "A great American writer's future may depend on what we do here today. Why, our actions may echo in eternity!"

"Well, if you put it that way, Maximus."

Seymour raised the hammer over his head with both hands. He closed his eyes and cried, "My name is Gladiator," before he swung the tool with all of his considerable might, effectively shattering the taillight and the metal around it.

Seymour opened his eyes, then moaned at the sight of the destruction.

"Get out of here, Brainert," I commanded. "If all goes according to plan, Seymour and I will join you at Millstone Creek in an hour or so."

As Brainert drove off in his newly repaired car, Seymour and I crossed the Finch Inn parking lot. We saw more people than usual for a weeknight, all of them clustered around the entrance.

The Quindicott Elementary School bus told me Mr. Burke and the science fair kids had done their jobs.

Inside, proud parents and interested guests clustered around the inn's library, where the science fair contestants—including my son, Spencer—were showing off their projects. Susan Trencher had placed her display front and center, and the photo of the teardrop trailer figured prominently.

I approached the front desk and gave Fiona the nod, leaning close so I could hear her phone call to the Lighthouse.

"Hollis West? This is Fiona Finch at the front desk. I'm afraid there's been an incident . . . Yes, *another* one."

I could hear angry shouts on the other end of the line. Fiona rolled her eyes and waited for the ranting to stop before she spoke again. "Apparently a delivery truck has damaged your car. If you would come to the main house, I'll—"

Fiona blinked and put the receiver down. "He hung up, but I'm pretty sure he's coming."

I was pleased to see Mr. and Mrs. Waterman had hit their marks and were ready for their cue. The reverend even wore his clerical collar to make his performance all the more convincing.

Five agonizing minutes later, Seymour nudged me. "There he is, I recognize Hollis West from his beefcake shots you showed me."

Heads turned as a tall, strikingly handsome young man came through the door—or rather, someone I once *thought* was strikingly handsome. But now, after all Norma had told us about the real man behind the façade, I could see the cruel glint in Hollis West's eyes beneath his salon-highlighted bangs, the arrogant curl of his lips.

"Geez," Seymour groused, "even that guy's hair is smug."

I let the Watermans know it was curtain time. The reverend nodded, recognizing our target. He and his wife deftly cut Hollis off, blocking the young man's way to the front desk even as they discussed Susie Trencher's display.

"Terrible," Mrs. Waterman said. "All this pollution in our own community."

Reverend Waterman's eyes locked on one photo, as he performed a theatrical double take.

"Why, that's Norma Stanton's trailer," the reverend cried, clearly relishing his return to acting. "I'd recognize it anywhere. It's one of a kind. And there's a map that shows exactly where it's located."

Mrs. Waterman pretended to read the map, effectively blocking Hollis West's path.

"Why, we drove past this spot not two hours ago," she faux-whispered. "We both saw smoke from a fire. Norma must be camping there right now."

Hollis West was no longer trying to dodge the couple. Instead, he stood behind them, listening intently.

I felt a rush of relief. The picture of the trailer was only meant to get Hollis' attention. He already knew the trailer was there—he'd seen Louis Kritzer's letter, that's how he likely found Kritzer himself, just like we did. What Hollis needed to hear was that that *Norma had returned*. I could tell by the young man's expression that the message was received, loud and clear.

"I heard Norma was in some kind of trouble," Mrs. Waterman continued. "Something about stealing jewelry. What should we do?"

"I'll tell Chief Ciders. He's coming to the church tomorrow morning. It can wait until then, I'm sure Norma is going to stick around. She would never abandon her home."

As the Watermans drifted away, Hollis West smirked, and we knew the fish had taken the bait.

Seymour and I had to grit our teeth to keep from whooping and slapping high fives. We just grinned like fools instead.

A moment later, Fiona waved to Hollis West. "I have the information about who struck your car, Mr. West," she called. "For your insurance company, because as you know the inn is not responsible—"

"Yes, yes, I know," Hollis replied. "Let's make this quick."

"Go!" I whispered, pushing Seymour through the front door. "We've got to beat Mr. West to the trailer."

THIRTY MINUTES LATER, we were gathered at the campsite.

"Good grief, man!" Brainert declared, gawking at Seymour's getup. "You look like a walking haystack."

"It's a ghillie suit," Seymour proudly informed him. "Hunters and military snipers use it for camo."

"Why in the world would a simple postman possess camouflage? Have all of your colleagues gone postal? Are you planning a coup against FedEx?"

"As a matter of fact, I use it for my postal unit's paintball team, the Splatters. We're three wins and no losses this year."

"And why the golf club?" Brainert went on.

"I'll tell you why." Rustling in his camouflage suit, Seymour aimed the golf club as if it were a shotgun. "This Hollis guy is probably coming to the party armed. My Arnold Palmer nine iron makes a pretty convincing rifle in the dark. I'll persuade him that he's outgunned and get him to drop his weapon."

Jack didn't think so.

More likely? He'll get plugged, the ghost warned.

"If there's a weak link in this plan, it's the mailman," Brainert insisted.

Seymour scowled. "And you think your little rope trick will work?"

"These sorts of snares were effective during the Vietnam conflict," Brainert replied while he covered a rope loop on the ground with loose grass. "This will trap Hollis, I'm sure of it."

Yeah, Jack said, *but will that dinky little snare rope the killer before or after he pulls the trigger?*

THREE LONG HOURS later, I was standing alone behind a tree in the dark woods, fighting off gnats while watching the figure in the folding chair beside the teardrop trailer. She was wrapped in a flannel jacket and reading by the light of the campfire.

"Seymour? Brainert? How are you guys holding up?" I whispered into my phone.

I heard someone break a snore, then grunt. "Ah, yeah," Seymour said. "It's all quiet here."

"I'm fine," Brainert replied from his relatively comfortable position inside the teardrop trailer.

"I guess we didn't have to hurry," Brainert complained after a pause.

"Look, I'm sorry I disrupted your academic schedule with this—"

"Forget it, Pen," he replied. "All I'm missing is another wine party disguised as a faculty meeting. The last thing I need is the dean of the arts shoving copious amounts of that evil juice of Dionysus down my throat. I almost perished the last time—"

"Hah!" Seymour cried. "So, you finally admit you were *drunk* when you wrecked your car. I knew—"

"Quiet!" I hissed. "Someone's coming. I see a flashlight beam on the dirt road."

We watched in silence as a black-clad figure faded in and out of the shadows. The newcomer spotted the campfire and immediately extinguished the flashlight. With only a half-moon glowing wanly in the clear night sky, the figure once again melted into the shadows.

"Can anyone see him?" I whispered into the phone.

Brainert's response was so faint I could hardly make out his words. "I hear him, I think."

Finally I could see the figure again, definitely a man. I watched in silent horror as he moved stealthily behind our target in the folding chair, who was still seemingly oblivious to the stranger's presence.

The man pulled a handgun from his pocket and aimed. Though I expected it, I jumped at the gunshot blast.

The mannequin we'd borrowed from Judy's Dress Shop flew out of the chair, its head exploding. Plastic fragments sailed in every direction. The mannequin tumbled forward, landing in the fire. Flames exploded and in the bright flash I spied the shocked face of Hollis West, a knit cap jammed over his smug hair.

"Now!" Brainert cried, springing his trap.

From somewhere in the woods, the bent sapling snapped back into shape, yanking the rope. But the loop failed to catch Hollis West's ankle. Instead, it grabbed the toe of his sneaker, ripping it from his foot. Hollis was flipped end over end, and I heard a splash as his gun landed in the creek.

Realizing he'd been fooled, Hollis scrambled to his feet and took off in a limping run, the lack of a shoe slowing him down. As he bolted for the road, the bush right in front of him came to life, as Seymour sprang to his feet and aimed his golf club at the oncoming killer.

"Halt!" Seymour commanded, "or I'll— Yikes!"

Hollis literally bowled him over. The camouflaged mailman looked like a tumbleweed as he rolled along the ground.

"Get him!" I shouted, bolting from the woods. "If Hollis gets to his car, he's gone!"

Brainert rushed out of the trailer. Seymour jumped to his feet and took off after the fleeing shooter, with me hot on his tail. As I ran down the dark, pitted dirt road, I heard Brainert cursing behind me.

I was panting by the time we reached the highway. We'd parked our vehicles a quarter mile away to keep them hidden from Hollis. Now we had no way to give chase, as he dived into the open cab of his BMW and gunned the engine.

As Hollis peeled out into the night, the three of us stood watching in helpless frustration.

Jack? What do we do? Any ideas?

The ghost didn't answer. Not with words. But as Hollis sped down that highway, a sudden icy gale whipped around us. The chill wind lifted dirt and dried leaves, shaking the trees all along the road. Suddenly, the heavy dead limb of an ancient oak dropped to the ground, right in front of Hollis!

The BMW turned sharply to miss it and spun across the road, bouncing off a guardrail. Just then we saw a red Nissan, in the *wrong* lane, racing toward the stopped BMW. The Nissan was speeding well over the posted limit and traveling too fast to stop in time.

The second crash was horrendous, with both vehicles spinning around like bumper cars. It took forever for the echo of that collision to fade.

Brainert had joined us in time to witness the accident, and now we all ran toward the smoking, twisted wrecks.

Seymour and I headed for the BMW. We found that the airbag pillowed the unresponsive driver like a giant marshmallow. Seymour touched his neck.

"Hollis is alive, but he's out cold. I think he might be trapped under his airbag, too. I'll call 911."

As Seymour dialed, I noticed the BMW's trunk had been damaged in the impact. That's when another icy blast came rushing down the deserted roadway with enough force to blow the trunk's lid wide open. To my shock, the interior light went on.

Take a peek, Penny, the ghost whispered.

Still shivering from the supernatural wind, I spotted a man's leather bag. Its contents were spilled, and among the monogrammed shirts and designer slacks, I saw something gleaming.

Bingo! Jack cried in my head. *You just won the kewpie doll.*

I'd hardly compare the legendary Tears of Valentino to a kewpie doll, Jack, I said as I happily lifted the necklace out of the trunk.

Meanwhile Brainert reached the red Nissan. The airbag had been deployed in this car, too, but the driver was conscious. Now she struggled out of the wreckage, her business suit in disarray.

Brainert froze when he saw her.

"My God!" he cried. "It's the dean of the arts!"

The woman's eyes were unfocused, but her confusion had nothing to do with the accident.

"Professor Parker?" she called, slurring her words. "Is that you?"

She pulled her glasses out of her long, tangled hair and placed them over her eyes.

"It *is* you, Professor!" She wagged her finger, grinning stupidly. "Shame on you for missing the faculty meeting tonight. The Beaujolais was splendid. I do adore young wines, they are so . . . Ugh, I . . . I think I'm going to be sick."

Brainert stared, unmoving, even as she began to heave.

"Don't just stand there like a lump, Dr. Parker," the dean gasped. "Hold my hair."

EPILOGUE

When all's said and done, all roads lead to the same
end. So it's not so much which road you take, as how
you take it.

—Charles de Lint, *Greenmantle*

Quindicott, Rhode Island
Nine months later

"OH, THAT'S A lovely cover," Aunt Sadie proclaimed, and
I agreed.

Together we stood over the box packed with Amanda Pilgrim's new novel, delivered to our shop fresh from Salient
House.

"That dust jacket is matte," I noted, "and the crow is embossed. Publishers seldom spend that kind of money on covers anymore."

Sadie nodded sagely. "They knew this book would be a
winner."

I stacked copies of *The Crows Will Carry Your Soul* in a
neat pile on the Staff Picks table. I carefully set aside four
copies—one for display in the window, and one each for
Seymour, Brainert, and Fiona Finch.

"Spencer's forensic science book came in with the special orders," Sadie said. "I'm surprised he's still obsessed with that subject."

So was I, especially after he lost the science fair prize to Susan Trencher's ecologic display. Seymour thought the choice was political, but I didn't. Susan won because her subject was local, so locals gave her the trophy. Anyway, Susan couldn't lose after Tim Morton's do-it-yourself rocket crashed through the roof of the school gym.

Your little tyke did a lot more with his skills than win some rinky-dink trophy.

Jack Shepard—who'd been teasing Bookmark by floating loose packing paper around the room on his ghostly breeze—suddenly spoke up.

It's true, Jack. Spencer's self-taught skill at fingerprinting helped save Norma from life as a fugitive and expose Hollis West as a murderer. And all from that tiny television knob that Seymour grabbed from Louis Kritzer's apartment . . .

Bookmark, losing her battle with the elusive paper, pawed the air as if trying to catch her invisible playmate.

One thing is strange, Jack.

Just one? And this from a gal with a dead PI living in her head.

When all this started, you warned me that death always surrounded the Tears of Valentino, and I guess you were right. But in the end, the murders had nothing to do with the jewels.

You're not making sense, Penny.

Of course I am. Hollis West, aka Hal Ballard, killed Dottie Willard after she was forced to reveal where Norma was—and he had to cover his tracks. Ditto Louis Kritzer since both of those victims were potential witnesses against him for the murder of his half brother. None of these things involved the Tears of Valentino.

Jack's reply was a revelation.

Maybe the murders didn't involve the Tears of Valentino because the real Tears were gone.

That's true.

In the end, Peyton Pemberton's priceless jewels were fake, just paste and paint. Most of the teardrop diamonds had been sold off. All that remained of the original legendary necklace was the gold setting and a single diamond embedded in the earring, which was planted on Norma's maid's cart to fool the insurance company.

Peyton had run out of the funds she needed to support her lavish lifestyle. So she sold off the teardrop diamonds, one at a time. When they ran out, she cooked up an insurance fraud scheme with the help of her boyfriend, Hollis.

After Hollis was arrested and the Tears recovered, the police confronted Peyton with a host of criminal charges, and she quickly turned informer. To reduce her own sentence, she confessed that her boyfriend had helped her carry out the scheme to defraud the insurance company.

According to Peyton, Hollis was the one who insisted they frame Norma Stanton for the theft. After Norma's church videos went viral, Hollis panicked. He confessed his past crime to Peyton, the killing of his own half brother, and she agreed that framing Norma for the theft of the Tears would not only solve her financial problems (with a huge insurance settlement) but also close the book on the unsolved murder of Julian Ballard Jr. They'd be killing two crows with one stone. Only, as it turned out, Quindicott's crows dropped the stone on them.

I have to admit, I told Jack, *I'm a little surprised Peyton turned on Hollis so completely.*

You shouldn't be, doll. There's no honor among thieves—or cheesecake grifters.

I guess not . . .

As I considered that sad truth, I noticed Bookmark suddenly sit on her haunches in the middle of the room, roll over, and expose her striped belly, the same way she would for Sadie or Spencer or me. Could our cat actually sense or even see Jack Shepard?

Getting back to those Tears, I said to the ghost. *It's nice to know Mr. Santoro turned out to be just who he said he was, a representative of a man who wanted to purchase the Tears of Valentino at any price—and he did.*

That I don't get. Why lay out all that lettuce when the hot rocks are gone?

The collector thought the setting was worth the price anyway. It was the connection to Rudolph Valentino he wanted. For him it was never about the jewels.

I don't follow, doll. Why not?

Do you remember the movie Spencer, Sadie, and I watched on the Intrigue Channel last week, The Maltese Falcon?

Sure. Just like the bird manual it was based on, the movie had nothing to do with real detective work.

Not my point. The statue in the movie turned out to be a worthless piece of lead, right?

Sure.

Well, that worthless piece of lead sold at auction for four million dollars.

The ghost whistled, incredulous.

It's true, I told him. *That falcon is now considered one of the most valuable movie props in the world.*

A crazy world, I say.

You're right, Jack, but as Norma showed us, there's a lot of good in the world, too.

Once again, I picked up a copy of *The Crows Will Carry Your Soul* and looked it over. There was no author photo to speak of, and the "biography" consisted of one sentence: *Amanda Pilgrim is the pseudonym for an author who travels like a bird, moving with the seasons and the whim of the wind.*

I wasn't surprised. I already knew Norma cherished her anonymity as much as she loved her freedom. A few weeks after the Tears of Valentino affair, she climbed into her van and left Quindicott. No one knew if she'd ever return to our little town. I hoped she would but suspected otherwise.

Norma was part of an American literary tradition that spanned the history of our nation. She was one of those wandering Americans—seekers like Herman Melville, who sailed the South Pacific and hunted whales decades before he wrote *Moby-Dick*. Or the author of *The Call of the Wild*. Jack London was just a teenager when he hunted in the Bering Sea and visited Japan—and he really did seek his fortune in the Alaska gold rush before writing books about it.

And then there was Jack Kerouac, perhaps the most famous literary traveler of all time.

So, Jack said, interrupting my thoughts about Norma. *Did you enjoy your dinner at Sardi's?*

Yes, I did. You brought me on the perfect night. Being just feet away from Dean Martin and Frank Sinatra—it was like a dream! Which, I guess, it was. But do you know what the best thing about that night was?

You tell me, Penny.

That wonderful gift you left Cora Ingham—and after you convinced me she couldn't possibly become the stage actress that Peyton Pemberton described as her great aunt.

The ghost laughed. *I think you convinced yourself of that.*

By the way, Jack, do you know what Cora did with the money the Tears brought her?

Wasn't around long enough to follow up.

Well, I did. She went to Ithaca, New York, and started a theater company. They just celebrated their seventy-fifth anniversary. And do you know what else? Every five years they perform Shakespeare's Antony and Cleopatra. *They say it's the wish of the group's founder, the late Cora Ingham.*

Don't that beat all, Jack said. *So, Penny, what's next?*

Well, I have to get the new releases on the shelves and get ready for a Quibblers meeting tonight. And tomorrow there's a PTA meeting, and then a bake sale, and—

Jack made a rude yawning noise in my head.

As I suspected, he groused. *This burg is settling back into its sleepy, small-town ways. Why, it's enough to bore a guy like me to death.*

A sudden draft made me shiver, despite the warmth of

the sunny day, and I swore I saw Jack Shepard's towering form appear before me to send a ghostly smile my way.

I'll see you in your dreams, he whispered, touching the tip of his fedora.

Then the ghost was gone, fading back into the fieldstone walls that had become his tomb.

There's nowhere to go but everywhere, [so just] keep rolling under the stars.

—Jack Kerouac, *On the Road: The Original Scroll*

Your life is a book and every day a page is written . . . Close your eyes now and turn the page. Look at that beautiful blank page of tomorrow, just waiting for you to write your story. Smile as you consider the possibilities! What will you write tomorrow? What will your page be?

—Amanda Pilgrim

ABOUT THE AUTHOR

Cleo Coyle is a pseudonym for Alice Alfonsi, writing in collaboration with her husband, Marc Cerasini. Both are *New York Times* bestselling authors of the long-running Coffeehouse Mysteries—now celebrating nineteen years in print. They are also authors of the national bestselling Haunted Bookshop Mysteries, previously written under the pseudonym ALICE KIMBERLY. Alice has worked as a journalist in Washington, D.C., and New York, and has written popular fiction for adults and children. A former magazine editor, Marc has authored espionage thrillers and nonfiction for adults and children. Alice and Marc are also both bestselling media tie-in writers who have penned properties for Lucasfilm, NBC, Fox, Disney, Imagine, Toho, and MGM. They live and work in New York City, where they write independently and together.

CONNECT ONLINE

CoffeehouseMystery.com
 CleoCoyleAuthor
🐦 CleoCoyle

Ready to find
your next great read?

Let us help.

Visit prh.com/nextread

Penguin
Random
House